THE CORNISH COAST
MURDER

THE CORNISH COAST MURDER

JOHN BUDE

———

With an Introduction by Martin Edwards

THE BRITISH LIBRARY

This edition published in 2014 by

The British Library
96 Euston Road
London NW1 2DB

Originally published in London in 1935 by Skeffington & Son

Introduction © Martin Edwards 2014
Cataloguing in Publication Data
A catalogue record for this book is available from The British Library

ISBN 978 0 7123 5715 9

Typeset by IDSUK (DataConnection) Ltd
Printed and bound by CPI Group (UK) Ltd, Croydon, CR0 4YY

CONTENTS

INTRODUCTION

MARTIN EDWARDS

The Cornish Coast Murder, originally published in 1935, marked the crime writing debut of Ernest Carpenter Elmore. Probably thinking that his real name was a bit of a mouthful, and perhaps also to differentiate his detective fiction from his other writing, he opted for the snappier pseudonym of John Bude.

Like many debut novels, *The Cornish Coast Murder* had a small print run. There was no paperback edition (paperbacks were in their infancy in those days) and the publisher, a small firm called Skeffington, sold mainly to libraries. As a result, copies in good condition are today almost impossible to find. Anyone lucky enough to chance upon a signed first edition in a fine dust jacket (does any such book exist? I wonder) would possess a rarity of great value. This is partly due to the sheer scarcity of the novel, but also to the fact that in recent years Bude's work has become increasingly admired, and correspondingly more sought after by collectors.

Why is this? *The Cornish Coast Murder* provides a number of clues that help to explain Bude's growing popularity, more than half a century after his death. His writing style is relaxed and rather more polished than one would expect from a first-time novelist, and he pays more attention to characterisation and setting than many of his contemporaries. This is because he was, if not an old hand, already a writer who had experienced some success with popular fiction. He had a taste for weird tales, and in 1928, under his real name, he published a book with the rather wonderful title *The Steel Grubs*. In this novel, a Dartmoor convict comes across some alien eggs which hatch into the eponymous grubs. They eat the iron bars of the convict's cell, and needless to say, that proves insufficient to sate their appetite.

Bude, born in Maidstone in 1901, was a young man when he wrote *The Steel Grubs*. A major publisher, William Collins, bought his next novel of the fantastic. *The Siren Song* appeared in 1930, and although Bude soon became more interested in detective stories, he returned successfully to writing strange fiction under his own name in 1954 with *The Lumpton Gobbelings*, a fantasy with allegorical elements, in which an English village is invaded by naked little people and splits into two camps, those who are charmed by the newcomers and those determined to eliminate them.

The choice of a Cornish place name for his crime-writing pseudonym was probably an attempt to emphasise his focus on the setting for his first novel. At the time *The Cornish Coast Murder* appeared, detective novels with a recognisable and well-evoked rural background were less common than they are today. Perhaps anxious to avoid unintentional libel, authors who wrote rural mysteries often resorted to setting their stories in 'Midshire' or 'Wessex', a habit that persisted until after the Second World War. Bude was ahead of his time in realising that detective fans would enjoy mysteries with attractive real-life settings other than London. Pleasingly, the fact that the crime scene is on the coast proves central to the murder mystery.

Rather than giving rise to a series of books set in the same area, the success of this book prompted Bude to try variations on the theme in his next two novels, *The Lake District Murder* and *The Sussex Downs Murder*. Readers who hoped for a major Cornish-based crime series had to wait until the late 1960s, when W. J. Burley began to write books featuring the cop Charles Wycliffe, which were eventually televised with Jack Shepherd in the lead role.

Bude turned to fictional crime at the height of the 'Golden Age' of the genre, between the wars. This book appeared in the same year as *Gaudy Night*, in which Dorothy L. Sayers sought to elevate the detective story into the 'novel of manners', an ambitious project that provoked a division of opinion as to the extent of her success between passionate admirers and fierce detractors which persists to this day.

Bude's aims were not as lofty as Sayers's; his focus was on producing light entertainment, and although his work does not rank with Sayers's for literary style or with Agatha Christie's for complexity of plot, it certainly does not deserve the neglect into which it has fallen. Here, the detective interest is split between a likeable pair of amateurs, a vicar and a doctor, and the professionals. From his second book onwards, Bude would concentrate on accounts of police work, but the balance he strikes in this story provides a good deal of quiet entertainment, as well as an agreeable sketch of life in pre-war rural England.

The Cornish Coast Murder launched a long career; in all, Bude wrote thirty books about murder before his tragically early death in 1957. He worked as a stage producer and director, and also played a small but important part in the history of the genre, being among the handful of writers who joined with John Creasey to found the Crime Writers' Association at a meeting at the National Liberal Club on Guy Fawkes Night, 1953. The CWA now boasts over six hundred members based not only in the UK but across the globe, and its Dagger Awards are renowned, but much is owed to the pioneering efforts of men like Creasey and Bude, who had the vision to see the need for such an organisation, and its long-term potential and value.

The appearance of this British Library edition of *The Cornish Coast Murder* will be welcomed not only by collectors who have despaired of ever possessing a copy of their own, but also by crime fiction readers generally. Few will be familiar with Bude's name and work, but the pleasure given by this lively and well-crafted story is likely to tempt many to explore his later work as well. They will not be disappointed.

THE CORNISH COAST MURDER

CHAPTER I

MURDER!

THE Reverend Dodd, Vicar of St. Michael's-on-the-Cliff, stood at the window of his comfortable bachelor study looking out into the night. It was raining fitfully, and gusts of wind from off the Atlantic rattled the window-frames and soughed dismally among the sprinkling of gaunt pines which surrounded the Vicarage. It was a threatening night. No moon. But a lowering bank of cloud rested far away on the horizon of the sea, dark against the departing daylight.

The Vicar, who was fond of bodily comfort, sighed with the profoundest satisfaction. Behind him a big log fire crackled in the open hearth. A reading-lamp cast an orange circle over the seat of his favourite chair and gleamed, diluted, on the multi-coloured book-backs which lined most of the room. In the centre of the hearth-rug, placed with exact precision between the two arm-chairs, was a small wooden crate.

The Vicar sighed again. All was exactly as it should be. Nothing out of place. All ambling along just as it had done for the last fifteen years. Peace, perfect peace.

He cast a final look out of the bow-window and searched the ink-dark road for some sign of the Doctor's car. He glanced back at the clock. Twenty minutes past seven. Oh, well . . . still ten minutes to go before dinner, and the old rascal was never late. Trust Pendrill to be on time when it came to their little Monday evening ceremony. Neither of them would have missed it for the world. In an isolated village like Boscawen, of some four hundred souls, these old-established customs were meat and drink to men of the professional type like Pendrill and the Vicar.

The Vicar pulled the heavy curtains, shut out the ominous spectacle of what looked like an approaching storm, and settled down with the *Spectator* to wait for his guest.

Five minutes later he heard the swish of a car on the drive, a merry tooting as the car passed the window, followed almost immediately by the jangling of the front-door bell.

The next minute Pendrill was shaking his oldest friend by the hand and complaining about the foulness of the weather.

"Just in time," said the Vicar jocularly. "I was just going to sample the sherry on my own account. Sit down, my dear fellow, and toast your toes till the gong sounds."

The Doctor subsided with a grunt of pleasure and began to sip his sherry.

"Anything new?" asked the Vicar.

It was always one of his favourite opening gambits in conversation. He found that it got people talking. Not that Pendrill ever needed priming in this direction. He could sit for hours and talk "shop" without ever displaying the slightest fatigue.

"Oh, nothing much. The usual round. A cut hand, two rheumatics, a whitlow and a case of measles."

"Measles?"

"Fred Rutherford—one of your cherubic choirboys, I believe. Incorrigible lad. Always causing trouble in the village."

The Vicar's chubby face broke into a benign smile.

"This is more likely to cause elation—at least among the younger generation. I remember we always hailed an epidemic as a godsend when I was a boy. They closed the school."

The Doctor nodded. He was always uncertain if he ought to allow levity where his job was concerned. He didn't mind poking fun at the Vicar's choir-boys and charity fêtes, but medical matters were a different pair of shoes.

The gong throbbed melodiously in the hall.

"Ah," said the Vicar, tumbling alert in a moment. "Dinner!"

He followed his guest's angular frame on his own short waddly legs into the dining-room.

Later the Doctor returned, as was inevitable, to his own little world of stethoscopes and clinical thermometers.

"By the way, I was forgetting. Good news for you this time. It looks as if you're booked for a double christening."

"Oh?"

"Mrs. Withers—twins."

"Dear me—when?"

"To-night. I've just come away. I left Mrs. Mullion in charge."

"Twins," mused the Vicar. "Very unusual. I don't seem to remember another set of twins in the village since Mrs. Drear surprised us——let's see? Six years ago."

"Seven," corrected the Doctor. "I attended."

The Vicar smiled a little wistfully across the heap of nut-shells which were accumulating on his plate.

"Still at it," he said quietly. "Fifteen years of it and it's all going on just the same. Births, marriages, deaths. Major events all of them. I suppose our more successful colleagues, Pendrill, would say we were wasting our lives in a backwater. Nothing ever happens here. Nothing! It all flows along at the same slow pace, though heaven forbid that I should ever see it changed! I love this spot, Pendrill. It's my home—my spiritual home. I wouldn't change my set of parishioners for any other in the whole of Cornwall."

"Not even Ned Salter?" asked the Doctor.

"No! No! Not even Ned. Confound it, my dear chap, I must have one soul left to save. Otherwise what's my job worth? I should grow fat in idleness."

"Work," commented the Doctor as they rose from the table, "seems to have left few ravages on your person. I should suspect a tendency to diabetes if I didn't know you better."

They returned to the warmth and cosiness of the study where the Vicar threw a few giant logs on to the fire. He proffered a cigar-box.

"Try one," he urged. "Henry Clays."

It was all part of the solemn Monday evening ritual. He always proffered Henry Clays and Pendrill always patted his pocket and said, that without disparaging the excellence of the cigars, he preferred his pipe.

Coffee came in. They sank into their arm-chairs, smoking with the replete comfort of two bachelors who have dined well and now bask in the mellow light of each other's friendship and esteem.

Presently with a negligent foot the Doctor kicked the little crate on the hearth-rug.

"I see they're here," he said, pretending to be quite casual about the matter.

"As usual."

"I think we've got a good lot this time. A very good selection. I took trouble. I always feel when it's my turn that I want to cap the brilliance of your selection the week before."

The Vicar made a deprecatory gesture with his hand.

"May I?" he said, diving into his pocket and taking out a large, serviceable penknife.

"Of course."

With a leisurely hand, as if wishing to prolong the pleasures of anticipation, the Vicar cut the string with which the crate was tied and prised up the lid. Nestling deep in a padding of brown paper were two neat piles of vividly coloured books. One by one the Vicar drew them out, inspected the titles, made a comment and placed the books on the table beside his chair.

"A very catholic choice," he concluded. "Let's see now—an Edgar Wallace—quite right, Pendrill, I hadn't read that one. What a memory, my dear chap! The new J. S. Fletcher. Excellent. A Farjeon, a Dorothy L. Sayers and a Freeman Wills-Croft. And my old friend, my very dear old friend, Mrs. Agatha Christie. New adventures of that illimitable chap Poirot, I hope. I must congratulate you, Pendrill. You've run the whole gamut of crime, mystery, thrills and detection in six volumes!"

The Doctor coughed and puffed earnestly at his pipe.

A division of the spoils was settled on and three of the volumes were passed over to Pendrill. These would be exchanged for the Vicar's loot on the following Thursday. On Saturday night the whole six would be replaced in the little crate and returned to the lending library at Greystoke; whilst on Friday the Vicar would send off the list for the following week, culling his choice from the various papers and periodicals which invariably littered his desk.

For years the Doctor and the Vicar had indulged this vicarious though perhaps perfectly common lust for crime stories. It was one of the minor jokes of the parish. They made no attempts to hide their common admiration for those authors who, with spider-like tenacity, weave a web and expect the poor, harassed reader to disentangle the pattern and follow the single thread back to its original source.

Meeting each other in Cove Street, say on Friday, their conversation would invariably go something like this.

From the Vicar: "Well, Pendrill, have you got it?"

"Which?"

"The Three Toads Mystery, of course. The others were mere child's play."

Here Pendrill would wink and look knowing.

"Did you spot it, Dodd?"

"I did."

"Who?"

"No—I'm asking you."

"I've a very strong suspicion," the Doctor would then say with the air of a man who hasn't a strong suspicion, but a certain knowledge, "that it was Lucy Garstein."

And then a little gusty cry of triumph from the Reverend Dodd.

"I thought you would. I *thought* so."

And with the look of a man who harbours an immense wisdom, a sort of esoteric knowledge, the Vicar would amble pleasantly on his way to take tea with Lady Greenow at Boscawen Grange. Fancy old Pendrill being caught out by a simple red herring like that! The man was cracking up. He wasn't up to the old form of the early twenties. These new, psychological twisters, full of technicalities, were proving a little too difficult for Pendrill. He'd have to be put back on a course of early Conan Doyle.

Perhaps the Vicar had actually assimilated the tricks of the crime trade a little more ably than his co-reader. He remembered odd twists from earlier books, tiny deviations in evidence, smart methods of detection, cross-examination traps, all the minute bits and pieces which go to make up the author's paraphernalia in the writing of mystery stories. His head, now alas racing rapidly towards balddom, was crammed with the stock-in-trade lore of the professional detective. Often by the exercise of his very acute observation he surprised, even annoyed his parishioners, by sudden references to their movements on a certain day. Dear, no!—he hadn't shadowed them. Nothing so crude. He had by the simplest methods of deduction put two and two together and made four.

But heaven forbid that the shadow of any crime should ever fall across the grey-stoned cottages, the gorse-dotted commons and cliff-girdled seas of his beloved parish. He preferred to get his excitements second-hand and follow the abstruse machinations of purely imaginary criminals.

The book ceremony over, the couple fell into desultory conversation. Most of it concerned the sayings and doings of the locality, for neither Pendrill nor the Vicar found much time for recreations and visits outside Boscawen.

"How about our local man of letters?" asked the Doctor, breaking a long silence. "I haven't seen him about lately. Is he busy?"

"Very," replied the Vicar. "Putting the polish on his war novel. Autobiographical, so Ronald confided in me when I met him last. Between ourselves, Pendrill, I don't think that boy looks well. He appears ... well, strained—distraught almost. I dare say it's overwork."

"Possible," was Pendrill's noncommittal reply. "He's a highly strung type of fellow. The war, of course, played havoc with his nerves. But what d'you expect?—he was only a youngster when they sent him to France. It may take him years to live down the stress and shock of the war. This book may help him."

"How?"

"Get rid of the poison in his system—to put it medically. Purge his mind of accumulated phantasms. There have been cases ..."

The Vicar nodded. He was thinking of his last meeting with Ronald Hardy on the cliff-path and how disturbed he had been by the boy's white face and jerky movements. Boy, he said. But then, even a man of thirty-four seems young when one is nearing the last rungs of life's ladder. A fine and sensitive type, thought the Vicar. A mind like steel which had bent and bent but never snapped. A typical product of those nightmare experiences which had hounded the life of the world's young manhood not so many years ago. A pity, perhaps, that the boy had never married. He was the type which would respond favourably to feminine ministrations. He wanted looking after. He had the peculiar lost air of a man who lived so much in his work that the humdrum factors of existence both perplexed and annoyed him. There were rumours, of course. There always were rumours in Boscawen, particularly about Ronald. He had been looked upon as a figure of mystery and romance ever since he had settled in Cove Cottage two years ago. An author was a new species in the village. But, wondered the Vicar, was the rumour which coupled Ronald with Ruth Tregarthan based on anything more than mere supposition? He himself had seen them walking and talking together on a few occasions. But bless one! that was natural enough. Ruth was a charming, intelligent girl—a bit lonely perhaps living the "small life" in that bleak, old house with her uncle. Ronald was a vivid, entertaining talker once his natural reserve had been pierced. Somehow it seemed inevitable that they should find a sort of consolation in each other's company. But beyond that ... well, well ... it *might* be something warmer than a mere intellectual interest—on the other hand it might not.

His ruminations were cut short by a sudden exclamation. Pendrill was pointing at the window.

"Phew. Did you see that? Through the cracks in the curtain ... lightning. We're in for a tidy storm by the look of it."

As if to confirm his words a low rumble of thunder muttered, first in the distance, then rolled up and burst with a crash, seemingly over the roof of the vicarage itself.

"I've been expecting it," said the Vicar, adding, after a contented puff at his cigar, "I've an unholy fear of storms, Pendrill. Not for myself, of course—but for my church. It's so isolated and open. I can't imagine what would happen if the tower collapsed and the Greenow clock with it. I always keep an eye on the 'grandfather' over there, my dear fellow, until the storm blows over."

"Why?"

"Oh, reassurance. I look out of the window and set that clock by the Greenow one in the tower every day. Never fail to. When my clock strikes and the church clock fails to respond ... don't you see?"

"There'd be such an almighty crash ..." put in the Doctor. "Clocks wouldn't matter."

"Listen," said the Vicar.

Faint and melodious the Greenow clock chimed the hour, and the nine strokes which followed came thinly down the wind. Before the church clock had completed its task the Vicar's "grandfather" purred like a kitten and broke into a jingling accompaniment.

The Doctor pulled out his watch and shook his head, censoriously.

"Two minutes slow, Dodd. It won't do. You'd better abandon your old-fashioned methods and set your blessed clocks by wireless."

"Ah, this spirit of modernity," sighed the Vicar. He countered his friend's criticism with a hoary one of his own. "I'll install a wireless set in the Vicarage, Pendrill, the day after I see you attending divine service. All these years and you've never yet had the decency to sit under me. There's a sermon I have there ..." He nodded toward the big, mahogany, knee-hole desk near the window. "A high-spirited and, I may say, controversial affair. I'm delivering it next Sunday. Now what about it? I have to sit here and listen to you talking medicine. Why don't you return the compliment and hear me on religion for a change?"

"When you visit my surgery, I'll visit yours," contested the Doctor. "When I feel spiritually out-of-sorts I'll come to you for repairs, Dodd. But until then I'll remain——"

"An atheist?" enquired the Vicar maliciously.

"An agnostic," commented the Doctor.

"But, my dear Pendrill, don't you see that there is infallible proof that God——"

And the next minute they were launched on one of their interminable metaphysical arguments. The Doctor dour and scientific—the Vicar bubbling over with professional enthusiasm and persuasion, throwing out his plump hands, shifting in his chair, pulling wildly at his unlighted cigar, even hammering on his knee when Pendrill refused, through pretended ignorance, to take up a point in the pro-Christian side of the argument.

Above their heads, as the argument progressed, the elements also seemed to be wrangling. Peal after peal of thunder rode in from the sea and broke high over the rain-swept coast.

"Oh, I grant you that! I grant you that!" The Vicar was getting shrill in his excitement. "But why base all truth on scientific proof? What about Faith, my dear chap? Yes, Faith with a capital F. Good old early Christian Faith. After all Faith is the one essential ..."

The Vicar stopped, as it were, in mid-air. His hand, half-way through an incomplete gesture, dropped on to his tubby thigh. The telephone on his desk was shrilling away with the maddening insistence of a trapped mosquito. Overhead another long peal of thunder rose in a furious crescendo and exploded with a cannon-crack.

"The tranquillity of our country Vicarages ..." laughed Pendrill, as the Rev. Dodd eased himself out of his chair and toddled across to the ringing instrument. "England's rural quiet remains one of the ..."

"Please!" sighed the Vicar, glowering at Pendrill in much the same way as he would have glared at an incorrigible child. "It may be the Bishop!"

He took up the receiver. "Hullo? Yes. Speaking. Who? Oh, yes, he's here. Urgent? Hold on—I'll tell him."

He turned with a worried look on his usually amiable and cherubic features and frowned at Pendrill.

"For you. It's Ruth Tregarthan. She sounds upset, Pendrill. It's urgent."

Pendrill snatched the proffered receiver as a further blaze of lightning stabbed into the room through the chinks of the curtains.

"I'm here," he said briskly. "What's the trouble?"

For the moment the Vicar stood in a furore of curiosity. What was it? What had happened? Ruth's voice had sounded queer and—what was the expression he wanted?—horror-struck. That was it.

Then after curious staccato noises had issued from the phone, Pendrill's voice: "Good God! I'll come at once. Don't do anything until I get there." He swung round on the Vicar. "Tregarthan's been shot," he said curtly. "You must get on to the police. Ring Grouch and tell him to bicycle up to Greylings as fast as he can."

"Tregarthan shot?"

The Reverend Dodd stood in the middle of his study utterly bewildered. His puzzled eyes glinted strangely through the lenses of his gold-rimmed spectacles. Shot? Tregarthan? Poor Ruth. What a tragedy!

Pendrill had already rushed into the hall, shuffled himself into his overcoat and crammed his hat over his head. The

Vicar called out to him as he flung out through the front-door to where his car was drawn up.

"Pendrill! It's an accident, of course?"

The Doctor's voice came back above the hum of the car's engine.

"Accident? No! From what I can make out from Ruth—of course, I don't know the details—her uncle's been *murdered!*"

CHAPTER II

THE UNDRAWN CURTAINS

GREYLINGS, the house toward which Doctor Pendrill was heading in his car, stood close to the sea. It was a square, unimaginative building of grey stone and green-grey slate, materials which were, of course, quarried in the locality. It was an isolated place, shrouded on the land side by a few weather-stunted beeches, with its western windows looking out directly on to the slow swell of the Atlantic. The ground which intervened between the road and the house shelved considerably, whilst linking one with the other was a steepish drive about a quarter of a mile in length.

On the sea side of the house was a little walled-in rectangle of lawn edged with untidy flower borders, beyond which ran the cliff-path. On the far side of the path, the cliff, some fifteen feet high at this point, dropped sheer into deep water. There was never any foreshore visible along this stretch of the coast, for the simple reason that the land curved out from the village and formed a broad ness, upon the most seaward tip of which old Tregarthan, Ruth's grandfather, had elected to build his house. The windows were in rough weather continually wetted by the spray, for the Atlantic breakers pounding against the cliff-face rushed up like sheets of glass, their ragged crests whipped by the wind. Ruth's grandfather had declared that if his bedroom had only been large enough to swing a lead sinker, he could have fished from his upper windows. A justifiable boast seeing that his little patch of lawn was barely the length of an average fisherman's cast.

From the moment the cliff-path passed to the bottom of the Greylings garden, it began to recede in a slow arc toward Boscawen itself. The village, in fact, clustered about a sandy, rock-strewn cove typical of that particular coastline. Greylings was, by the cliff-path, three-quarters of a mile from the cove, though somewhat more by road, since the drive and the road itself formed two sides of a triangle.

At the point where the Greylings drive debouched into the road, but on the other side of it, stood the Vicarage. From the window of Dodd's study Greylings appeared between the Vicarage and the Atlantic, though considerably below it owing to the steep drop of the land. Adjoining the Vicarage was the church, a Norman edifice with a stout, square keep, and, of course, the famous chiming clock presented by one of the present Lady Greenow's ancestors. Whether the original architects of the church had placed it a mile from the village as a test of their affirmed faith, it is impossible to say. In any case Sunday in Boscawen always saw a straggling cavalcade of faithful Christians plodding along the bleak, treeless highway, to be mildly harangued at the end of their journey by their extremely affable pastor, the Reverend Dodd.

The Doctor, therefore, had only a few hundred yards to cover before he drew up in front of the unlighted porch of Julius Tregarthan's house. The rain had ceased and a smoky moon appeared, fitfully, among the shredding clouds. Thunder still grumbled inland, but it was obvious that the storm had passed over and was now spending its energies elsewhere.

During those few minutes of transit, however, Pendrill's brain was active with speculation. Why had Julius Tregarthan been shot? Pendrill drew a blank. He certainly had no great personal regard for Ruth's uncle, a feeling that was generally rife in the village, but there was a wide gulf between disliking a man and murdering him. Tregarthan was reserved, secretive even, liable to fits of ill-temper, which alternated with moods of surly cynicism and a general disregard for other people's feelings. On the other hand, he was a man of judgment and, as far as Pendrill knew, of absolute integrity. He was a Parish Councillor, a church-goer, president of one or two local clubs and a J.P. on the Greystoke Bench. As a man of independent means he had given generously, though spasmodically, to the various charitable organisations of the district. There was no mystery about his past. He had lived in Greylings ever since the death of Ruth's father, fifteen years ago and since Ruth's mother had died in her early childhood, Julius had been left sole guardian of his niece's welfare—a rôle which he had apparently filled with good sense and a full measure of generosity. Ruth had been educated at a boarding-school, spent a couple of years travelling on the Continent and had returned to Boscawen perfectly satisfied to make Greylings her permanent home until such time as she should, if ever, marry.

And now, into the placid routine of this very ordinary household, tragedy had broken.

No sooner had Pendrill slammed the door of his saloon than Ruth flung open the front-door and came to meet him, Pendrill was shocked by her appearance. All the colour had drained from her cheeks. Her usual practicality and common sense seemed to be atrophied by an excess of strong emotion. When she grasped hold of his hand he noticed that she was trembling violently. Without a word, slipping her hand through his arm, he strode into the lighted hall, threw his hat on to the telephone table and went into the sitting-room.

Tregarthan was lying on his side by the uncurtained french windows. One arm lay curled beneath him. The other projected at right angles from his body like a signal-arm. His massive head lay in a spreading pool of blood which had already trickled some feet over the polished boards along the edge of the skirting. The heavy jowl was thrust forward like the prow of a ship, whilst his teeth, tightly clenched, were bared in a hideously unnatural grin. Slightly to the left of his high forehead was a neat, black-rimmed hole.

There was no doubt that Tregarthan was dead. Death must have been instantaneous. Pendrill knew that as far as medical aid was concerned this man had passed beyond the reach of it.

During his cursory examination of the body, Ruth collapsed on to the settee, hiding her face in her hands, whilst Mrs. Cowper, the housekeeper, who had been hovering wide-eyed in the background, kept up a ceaseless flow of verbal consolation.

Cowper, the gardener and odd-job man, came forward deferentially and proffered his help.

Pendrill shook his head.

"There's nothing to do, Cowper, until the police arrive. He's dead right enough." He turned to Mrs. Cowper and cut short her inane babbling with an incisive air of authority. "Now, Mrs. Cowper, I want you to take Miss Ruth to her room." He approached the girl and helped her to rise from the settee. "There's no point in your remaining here any longer, my dear. I'll deal with the police when they arrive.

They will want to see you later, but until then I should just lie quietly on your bed. Understand?"

Ruth, somewhat calmed by the Doctor's matter-of-fact voice, nodded, speechless, and dutifully did as she was told. As Mrs. Cowper was following her out of the room, the Doctor called her back.

"Hot milk and a good stiff dose of brandy in it," he said. "And see that she drinks it. No nonsense. It's been a big shock."

Alone with Cowper, the Doctor closed the door and made a rapid examination of the room. He turned his attention first to the windows. These were in three sections; two fixed and one in the form of a door which opened outward on to the little rectangle of lawn. Each panel was subdivided into six panes. Three shots had starred the glass—one high up in the right-hand fixed window; one about six feet from the base of the door; and the third midway in the left-hand fixed window. It was obvious that the shot which had struck Tregarthan in the head was the one which had drilled its way through the central panel.

The curtains, which divided in the middle, were drawn right back. Pendrill turned to Cowper, who had followed him in watchful silence about the room.

"These curtains, Cowper—is that usual? I mean was it Mr. Tregarthan's habit to sit here with the curtains undrawn?"

"No, sir. That's just what I didn't understand when I first come in here. My wife always draws the curtains most particular before she serves the coffee."

"And to-night?"

"Oh, they were drawn, sir. I came in with a trudge of logs just after Mr. Tregarthan had finished his coffee. They were drawn then—I'll swear to it, sir!"

"You can do that later ... to the police," said Pendrill. "That sounds like the Constable now," he added, as the front-door bell jangled in the silence of the house. "Let him in, Cowper."

But it was not the Constable. It was the Vicar.

"My dear Pendrill, I had to come down. I've rung Grouch. He's on his way. I had to come. I was thinking of Ruth. Perhaps I can ..." His eye encountered the body of Tregarthan slumping by the window. "So it's hopeless," he added quietly. "Poor fellow."

Cowper drifted up looking a trifle green about the gills.

"If there's nothing more, sir ... it's upset me ... this."

"No. Go and have a stiff whiskey. But mind you—the police will want to question you when they arrive."

With a grateful nod Cowper drew his fascinated stare away from the body and stumbled quickly out of the room.

Pendrill pulled out his pipe and lit it. The Vicar, on careful feet, was ambling slowly about the room, peering at things through his gold-rimmed glasses.

"You've noticed these?" he said, pointing to the windows.

"Yes—three shots. The middle one got Tregarthan. No doubt about *that*."

"None at all, provided he was standing. But why should he stand at an uncurtained window when there's nothing outside to look at?"

"There was the lightning," suggested Pendrill. "He may have drawn the curtains to watch the effect of the storm over the sea."

"He did not draw back the curtains, I suppose?"

The Doctor told him about Cowper's statement.

"Curious," said the Vicar as he drifted away from the window to the far side of the room.

He was experiencing a peculiarly mixed set of emotions. Horror and dismay at the tragedy which had come so swiftly out of the night and put an end to Julius Tregarthan's life. A compassionate pity for the girl who had been so unexpectedly bereaved. But beyond these perfectly natural reactions he was fired with an ardent glow of curiosity and interest. One side of him warred with the other. He felt that it was abhorrent to look upon crime, especially murder, as anything more than foul and unthinkable. At the same time this little devil of curiosity kept on tugging at his sleeve demanding attention. Yes—he must confess it. Apart from the tragic human aspect of the case he was deeply absorbed in an explanation of the mystery. The detective element in him was spurred to new energy now that he was in the midst, not of a mystery story, but a murder in real life. It was wrong of him, of course, sinful even, but that little devil was stronger than his conscience. He wanted to find out. He wanted to solve the problem of Julius Tregarthan's death, if indeed there proved to be a mystery attached to the crime. Of course the police would take things out of his hands. It was their job to apprehend criminals. It was his job to instil his fellow-men with a brotherly love which would make criminals impossible. The argument was good. But the little imp of curiosity was better.

"Pendrill," he said, sharply. "Come here. Look at that!"

He was pointing to an indifferent yet graphic oil-painting of a full-rigged windjammer diving head-long into a watery abyss. The canvas, a large one, was fixed high up on the wall, and puncturing the stormy sky about an inch from the gilt frame was the unmistakable mark of a bullet.

"Bullet No. 1," said Pendrill. "The left-hand window."

"And over here?" demanded the Vicar, indicating a splintered hole in an oak beam just under the ceiling.

"No. 2," said Pendrill. "The right-hand window."

"And the third?" asked the Vicar.

"Probably somewhere about the room. Spent, of course. The bullet went clean through the brain. I made sure of that."

"Possibly this has something to do with it," said the Vicar as he ran his fingers over a deep dent in the face of an oak sideboard. The bullet's on the ground somewhere. Perhaps we——"

He was cut short by a further clanging of the front-door bell, announcing the fact that P.C. Grouch, after a stiff ride up the hill, had arrived at Greylings. Cowper showed him in and, at a nod from Pendrill, returned to his whiskey in the kitchen.

The Boscawen constable was panting with exertion after pedalling his thirteen-odd stone up the long rise from the cove. He was not cut out for speed and the unaccustomed need for haste, coupled with the alarming news that Tregarthan had been shot, had left him somewhat out of breath. He removed his helmet, wiped round the inside of it with his handkerchief, dabbed his forehead and nodded to the two men.

"Evening, gentlemen. Nothing been moved, I take it?"

"Nothing, Constable," said the Doctor. "Not even the body."

"He was dead when you got here, I suppose, sir?"

"Yes."

The Constable crossed over and took a long look at the body. It was the first time in the whole of his career that he had been called in to investigate a possible murder and he was not inclined to underrate the importance of the occasion.

"Umph," he said. "Shot through the head. No chance of it being suicide, I suppose?"

The Vicar pointed to the bullet holes in the window.

"Exactly," said Grouch. "No man could shoot himself through a window. What about accident, gentlemen?"

"Hardly," interposed the Doctor. "One shot—yes—but not three. Three shots have entered the room."

"Who first found the body, sir?"

"Miss Tregarthan. She's lying down in her room. I sent her there until you arrived, Constable. I've warned her that she may have to answer a few questions."

"Quite right, sir. I'll need a statement. Anybody else in the house at the time?"

"The Cowpers. Mrs. Cowper is upstairs with Miss Tregarthan. Cowper is in the kitchen."

"I'll want a word with them, too," said Grouch. "I've phoned police headquarters at Greystoke. They're sending over an Inspector. In the mean-time …" He pulled out his note-book and flicked it open with a thumb. "Suppose we have a few words with Miss Tregarthan."

"Perhaps you would like me …" said the Vicar, edging a little toward the door.

"No, it's all right, sir. I dare say the Inspector would like to ask you a few questions. Besides, I'm sure the young lady will feel more at home with you gentlemen in the room."

Ruth came down, still obviously shaken, but now more in control of her feelings. Some of the colour had drained back into her cheeks. The Doctor was about to place a chair for her when the Constable shook his head.

"Perhaps there's another room available," he said, with a quick nod toward the body. "The dining-room, perhaps."

In the more ordinary atmosphere of the dining-room, where a fire was still flickering, the air was cleared of a good deal of its tension. Ruth sank at once into an arm-chair, whilst Pendrill and the Vicar drew up a couple of chairs at the table. Grouch placed his helmet on the sideboard and took up his position opposite Ruth on the hearth-rug.

"Now, Miss Tregarthan, I understand from the Doctor that you were the first to discover the deceased. Have you any idea as to what time that would be?"

"I know almost to the minute," replied Ruth, in a restrained voice. "When I came in I remember the hall clock striking the quarter."

"And you went directly into the sitting-room?"

"Yes."

"I take it you'd been out?"

"Yes."

"You discovered the body, then, at nine-fifteen."

"Exactly nine-fifteen by the hall clock."

"Which way did you come into the house, miss? Down the drive?"

Ruth hesitated for a moment, looked down into the fire and said quickly.

"No—along the cliff-path. I'd been out for a walk."

The Constable glanced up sharply.

"Ah!—the cliff-path. You didn't notice anybody suspicious hanging about?"

"No."

"I suppose you realise, miss, that Mr. Tregarthan was shot from the side of the house?"

"Yes, I realise that now," returned Ruth quietly.

"From which way did you approach the house?"

"From the village."

"And you met nobody on your way here?"

"Nobody."

"And you heard nothing out of the ordinary—shots, for example—no firing?"

"Nothing."

The Constable sighed and drummed his pencil on the mantelshelf. That particular line of enquiry seemed to have drawn a blank.

"You entered the house, miss——?"

"From the side door. There's a path——"

"I know," cut in Grouch. "The path runs at right-angles to the cliff path along the garden wall." He smiled benignly. "You see, miss, I knew this place long afore you were born."

There was a pause, during which the Constable seemed to be working out his next line of approach.

"When you passed the bottom of the garden by the cliff-path did you notice the curtains were undrawn?"

Ruth nodded.

"But you didn't know anything was amiss?"

"Why should I?" asked Ruth quietly.

"Exactly. You didn't. You were wearing a mackintosh?"

"Yes—it was raining as you know."

"I take it, miss, that you got pretty wet?"

"I was soaked," agreed Ruth, puzzled by these seemingly irrevelant questions.

"And yet," went on the Constable, "you came straight into the sitting-room, without taking off your wet things and *without* realising that there was anything amiss with Mr. Tregarthan?"

"Yes—no—that is ..."

"Well?"

Pendrill and the Vicar were startled by Ruth's sudden hesitation. So far she had answered the Constable's questions without pausing to consider her replies. But this apparently innocent question about a wet mackintosh, for some strange reason, seemed to disturb her.

"Well, miss?" reiterated Grouch.

"I don't think I was worried about my clothes at the time. I'm used to the wet. It wasn't unusual for me to go in to my uncle before taking off my outdoor things."

"I see. Now, Miss Tregarthan, will you describe what you saw when you entered the room?"

Ruth did so in a low voice, pausing every now and then to regain control of her emotions. She still seemed on the verge of an hysterical breakdown, though her evidence was clear and concise.

"And after finding your uncle apparently dead what did you do?"

Ruth went on to describe how she had summoned the Cowpers and then rushed to the phone and called up the Doctor at Rock House. Learning that he was dining at the Vicarage, she had phoned there and told him of the tragedy. She had then returned to the sitting-room and ascertained, as far as she was able, that her uncle was dead. At the sound of the Doctor's car on the drive she had rushed out to meet him.

At the conclusion of her story the Constable turned to Pendrill.

"Could you give me some idea, sir, as to the time you received the phone call?"

The Doctor thought for a moment.

"I'm afraid I can't. It was after nine. I know that, but the Vicar and I were talking——"

"Wait a moment," cut in the Reverend Dodd excitedly. "I think I can help you, Constable. The telephone bell rang about twenty minutes past nine. I happen to know because it's one of my—er—idiosyncrasies to listen to the church clock during a storm." He then went on to explain about his fears for the safety of the tower. "Subconsciously I suppose I was waiting for the quarter chimes while I was talking with Doctor Pendrill. I distinctly remember hearing them. The tower, as you know, is only a stone's throw from the Vicarage and when the wind is in the right direction . . ."

"Thank you, sir," said Grouch, with an appreciative nod in the Vicar's direction. "I think that more or less fits in with Miss Tregarthan's idea as to the time she found the body." He turned to Ruth, who was now lying back with closed eyes in the armchair, as if trying to shut out the abnormal spectacle of a policeman in the Greylings dining-room. "Thank you, miss. I don't think there's anything more I want to ask you. You've been very helpful, Miss Tregarthan, and in an unofficial capacity I should like to offer you my sincere sympathy for what has happened." As Ruth, escorted by the Vicar, crossed unsteadily to the door, the Constable added: "Now, sir, would you mind calling Mrs. Cowper. I'd like to hear what she has to say."

CHAPTER III

THE PUZZLE OF THE FOOTPRINTS

MRS. COWPER came into the room in much the same way as she would have entered a lion's cage. She looked both nervous and apprehensive. Her eyes, reddened with weeping, glanced from the Doctor to the Vicar and then came to rest, with a sort of fascinated glassiness, on the Constable. Grouch waved her unceremoniously into the arm-chair and without wasting time, put the housekeeper through a similar catechism to that which he had adopted in the case of Ruth Tregarthan.

"Now, Mrs. Cowper, I want you to be pretty sure about what you're going to tell me," he warned. "It's easy to imagine things at times like these. But I want the facts. That's all. The plain facts. Now—when did you last see Mr. Tregarthan alive?"

Mrs. Cowper, taking the Constable's warning to heart, considered this question deeply before essaying to answer it. She cast a wary eye at the other inmates of the room as if suspecting a trap and replied with a sort of defiant deliberation.

"It was when I took in his coffee as usual at a quarter to nine. He was a regular man, was Mr. Tregarthan, and he liked things done regular. Quarter to nine he liked his coffee taken in and a quarter to nine he had it."

"Were the curtains drawn to when you went in?"

"No. I drew them myself. That's usual."

"Right across the windows?"

"Right across, Mr. Grouch," said Mrs. Cowper decidedly. "No one can lay it up against me that I didn't perform my duties to-night the same as usual."

It was obvious that Mrs. Cowper's nervousness was taking the form of an indignant resentment that she was suspected to have been in any way responsible for her master's death. She knew Grouch, unofficially, as Grouch had married her sister-in-law, and this did nothing to ease the abnormality of the situation. Grouch in his official capacity was another being from Grouch sitting over a cup of tea in Annie's parlour down at Laburnam Cottage. A fact which put Mrs. Cowper off her balance.

"Now that's all right," said the Constable soothingly. "I'm not trying to incriminate you, Mrs. Cowper. I only want straight answers to straight questions. Understand?" He consulted his note-book. "So you last saw Mr. Tregarthan alive at a quarter to nine or thereabouts. Now, after that time, did you hear any unusual sounds—shots—any firing? Eh?"

"No—I heard nothing unusual except the storm, of course. All them crashes of thunder right over the chimneys. I remember remarking to Cowper that——"

"Exactly. Nothing unusual. Now this is a very important question, Mrs. Cowper, and I want you to think carefully. Did you see anybody, a stranger for example, pass any of the windows to-night?"

"Not that I noticed, Mr. Grouch, seeing it was dark and——"

"Or anybody hanging about round the house earlier in the evening?"

"No, I——" Mrs. Cowper broke off suddenly and gaped as if with astonishment at the excellence of her own memory. Pendrill and the Vicar sat up and exchanged a quick glance. The Constable took an eager step forward.

"Yes?"

"Now I come to think of it, you putting your question like that, I did see a man. He popped out of the bushes, sudden, like a rabbit and started arguing with Mr. Tregarthan. On the drive it was. I saw it all from the kitchen window when I was making ready to dish up the dinner."

"At what time was that?"

"Just after eight it would be. I mentioned it to Cowper at the time. It being queer seeing a man spring out like that."

"He appeared to have words with Mr. Tregarthan?"

"Yes—violent words. I thought at the time they were that fierce."

"You didn't hear what was said, I suppose?"

Mrs. Cowper shook her head with an air of disappointment, pondered for a moment, and then cheered up at a sudden recollection.

"Wait a minute, Mr. Grouch. I did catch the tail-end of it, as it were. Nothing much, mind you. Something about 'getting even' or words to that effect."

The Constable whistled softly through his teeth.

"Those were the man's words, not Mr. Tregarthan's?"

"Yes—he said—drat! It's on the tip of my tongue—he said—'I'll get even if I swing for it.' That's it! I didn't think anything much of it then."

"Naturally. You've done well to remember, Sarah," said Grouch, descending from his official Olympus, and granting

Mrs. Cowper a broad smile. "It may prove to be valuable information. Now as to this man. Can you describe him?"

"Well—he was shortish."

"Very short?"

"I suppose so. He looked a real titch beside Mr. Tregarthan, but then, he was a big man."

"Yes—can you describe his looks?"

Mrs. Cowper shook her head.

"He was standing back in the shadow of the bushes. There was only the light from the kitchen window."

"What was he wearing?"

"I can't rightly say."

"You noticed nothing particular about his clothes?"

"Only his gaiters. I noticed he was wearing gaiters when he went off up the drive."

"Gaiters! Well, that's something. You've done very well, Mrs. Cowper. I shan't have to bother you any more, unless the Inspector wants to ask you a few questions later on. Will you send your husband in to us now. I won't keep him a minute."

The moment Mrs. Cowper had closed the door the Constable swung round on Pendrill and the Vicar.

"Well, that's something, gentlemen! Very suspicious, eh? A quarrel. High words! Seems that we shan't have to look far for our man after all."

Pendrill nodded.

"You've done well, Grouch. The Inspector should be pleased when he arrives. Eh, Vicar?"

"Eh? Eh?" demanded the Reverend Dodd, coming out of a brown study. "Inspector—pleased? Very. Remarkable progress, Grouch."

And he lapsed forthwith into another deep rumination, wherein he turned the facts of the case over and over in his mind, a little disturbed, considerably bewildered. He wondered, somehow, if the case was going to be quite as simple as it was beginning to appear on the surface.

Cowper, now in a happier frame of mind, thanks to a stiff whiskey, soon proved to be an unimaginative and therefore reliable witness.

He corroborated his wife's story about the strange man on the drive, but was unable to give any further details as he had not gone to the kitchen window. He had been engaged in filling a coal-scuttle in the adjacent scullery when his wife had called him to come and look. But, as Cowper rightly said, Mr. Tregarthan's business was not his and he had other things to attend to. With regard to his actions after dinner, he had gone into the sitting-room with a trudge of logs just after his wife had taken in the coffee—that was to say, about a quarter to nine. He thought Mrs. Cowper might have been a little early with the coffee, because Miss Ruth had left the dinner-table half-way through the second course and Mr. Tregarthan had not lingered long over the sweet. He did not think that Mr. Tregarthan had any particular enemies, and as far as he, Cowper, was concerned, the whole thing was a "ruddy mystery." It had upset him and he felt very sorry for Miss Ruth, who, he reckoned, would take "a packet of days" to get over the shock.

His evidence concluded, Cowper excused himself to the Vicar for having said anything in the heat of the moment that wasn't right and proper, and shaking the Constable unexpectedly by the hand, saluted the Doctor and went out of the room.

"And that's that!" said Grouch with an air of conclusion, shoving his pencil back into the binding of his note-book. "I'll have to run over this little lot with the Inspector when he arrives." He turned to Pendrill. "By the way, sir, how long would you say Mr. Tregarthan had been dead when you made your examination?"

"I should say fifteen minutes at the outside. Perhaps half an hour, but I doubt it."

"And it took you how long to come from the Vicarage?"

"Oh, two or three minutes."

"And say another three minutes for Miss Tregarthan to have got through to the Vicarage via Rock House. That leaves about nine or ten minutes. So in all probability, seeing that Miss Tregarthan found her uncle at nine-fifteen, the chances are that he was shot a few minutes after nine."

"Probably."

"And Mrs. Cowper saw him alive at about fifteen minutes to nine. So we can fix within reasonable limits, sir, the period of time within which the murder must have been committed. Between eight-forty-five and say, nine-five."

Further discussion on this point was interrupted by the arrival of Inspector Bigswell and a uniformed chauffeur. He had started from Greystoke a few minutes after receiving Grouch's intimation of the tragedy, but a faulty carburettor had hung him up *en route*. Unfortunately the engine had petered out on a lonely road and he had been unable to board a private car. He offered this explanation not so much as an apology for his tardy arrival, but to vindicate the excellence of police routine in the eyes of the Doctor and the Vicar. Pendrill judged him to be a man of keen intelligence, quicker witted, though more reserved, than the Constable. A man, moreover, who inspired confidence. He brought to the proceedings a cut-and-dried manner which was both efficient and business-like. Grouch drew him aside in the hall and gave a résumé of his enquiries, outlined the main points of the case, showed him the body, the bullet holes in the window and reported the results of the Doctor's examination. When the Constable had posted his superior up to date, the two men joined Pendrill and the Vicar, who were chatting in the dining-room.

Mrs. Cowper reported that Miss Tregarthan was in her room and wanted to know if the Inspector wished to see her again that night. The Inspector shook his head.

"As far as I can see it will be quite unnecessary for me to trouble her any further. I quite understand how she must be feeling. No. Tell her to get as much rest as she can. She's a rather trying time in front of her, I'm afraid." Adding as Mrs. Cowper was on the point of leaving, "You and your husband had better do the same, Mrs. Cowper."

When the housekeeper had retired, Inspector Bigswell addressed himself to Pendrill and the Vicar.

"I've no reason to keep you any longer, gentlemen."

"We can be of no assistance, I suppose, Inspector?"

"Well, I won't say that, Doctor. If you and the Reverend care to stay, I daresay you can give me a little local information as we get on with our investigations. The lie of the land, as it were."

"In that case . . ." said Pendrill with an enquiring look at the Reverend Dodd.

The Vicar nodded.

"Anything we can do, Inspector."

"Good," concluded Bigswell. "Suppose we start by making a further examination of the sitting-room."

The four men returned once more to the scene of the crime, and after the Inspector had made a cursory examination of the body, he had it laid on the big Chesterfield and covered with a rug which Grouch had found in the hall.

The Inspector's next move was to cut out the two bullets from the wall where they had lodged, the one in the oak beam under the ceiling, the other behind the oil-painting. The third bullet, the one which had crashed through Tregarthan's skull obviously at short range, was found near the fender, where it had apparently ricocheted off the sideboard. The Inspector placed the three bullets in the palm of his hand and examined them with interest.

"Well," he said at length, looking up at his little audience. "What d'you make of it? Revolver bullets, eh? Army Service pattern I should say. The sort of revolver carried by officers of the B.E.F. in the war. That won't get us far. It *may* narrow things down a bit, but not much, I'm afraid."

He swung round and pointed at the french windows, the curtains of which were still undrawn.

"That door—where does it go?"

"Into a little walled garden," explained Pendrill, who knew the place well. "Just a small rectangle of lawn surrounded on three sides by a flower border."

"Suppose we look," suggested Bigswell.

"I have a torch—a pocket lamp," put in the Vicar helpfully.

The Inspector smiled.

"So have I, sir, and the Constable ought to have … of the regulation pattern. Eh, Grouch?"

Grouch grinned appreciatively, rather flattered in sharing this little joke with his superior, and unhooked his lamp off his belt.

The four of them went out into the garden.

The wind had died down and the air, though fresh and salty, was no longer damp-laden. It was obvious that the rain had spent itself with the storm, for the sky had cleared and a crescent moon shed a ghostly glitter over the dark swell of the Atlantic. Under the brief cliff the waves were chopping and slapping, but beyond that the night was profoundly still.

Bigswell was so far puzzled by the case. There was little enough to go on. Mrs. Cowper's story about the strange man on the drive might prove to be a successful line of investigation, but the description of this man was extremely scrappy. Gaiters. That was something. Shortish. That was something further. But if the gaitered individual *had* committed the murder there was nothing to prevent him from discarding his leg-wear as being too distinctive. And shortish men were not uncommon! At the moment he was more concerned with finding the spot where the murderer had stood when he had fired the fatal shot. There might be—indeed there *must* be—footprints, for the ground, softened by rain, would be amenable to impressions, and since the rain had stopped shortly after the supposed time of Tregarthan's death, these valuable imprints should not be blurred.

"Now," he said briskly, flicking on a powerful electric torch. "Suppose we work methodically over these flower-beds. If the murderer did enter the garden over the wall he couldn't have avoided the beds. You notice their width. It would have taken an extremely agile fellow to have cleared them in one leap."

"And even if he had," put in the Vicar with a serious air of consideration, "he would have landed so heavily on the border of the grass that the marks would be obvious."

"Precisely," exclaimed Bigswell.

He darted a keen glance at the rotund little figure and made a mental note that the Reverend Dodd was a cleric with the right sort of intelligence. His mind ran along the right rails. It had the proper analytical twist.

"Well, let's make sure," he said.

The three rings of light travelled carefully over the empty flower borders, empty, that was, save for a few thin clumps of early daffodils. But the result was negative. On the lawn, too, the searchers drew a blank. It was perfectly obvious that nobody had set foot inside the wall that night.

"Which means that we must try our luck on the other side of the wall," said Bigswell. "Careful," he added, as Grouch plodded across the border and flung himself astride the curved cement coping. "No trampling about, Grouch."

The three sides of the wall were bounded by three distinct paths. At the bottom of the garden ran the cliff-path. On the Boscawen side was a rough track which led round the side of Greylings and entered the front drive through a clump of laurel bushes. Against the cliff end of this wall were piled a few hurdles, obviously bearing some connection with the sheep which grazed on the common. On the side furthest from the cove, the south side, a more defined track ran from the cliff-path to a side door in the south face of the house.

The north track, a mere ribbon of muddied grass, proved unprofitable. Save for a few half-obliterated hoof-marks left by the sheep there were no other prints of any kind.

Avoiding the cliff-path for the time being, by the simple expedient of recrossing the garden, the party made an exhaustive examination of the side-door path. There the Inspector found exactly what he was looking for—two sets of tracks clearly defined in the soft, soggy soil. One set ran toward the side-door, the other away from it. The footprints were those of a feminine foot in a high-heeled shoe.

"This, at any rate, fits in with Miss Tregarthan's story," observed the Inspector as the concentrated light from the three torches flooded on to a patch of the path. "She went out for a walk by the side-door and returned the same way. There's nothing unusual here. I didn't expect there would be. If you wanted to shoot a man standing in the window, Grouch, where would you take up your position?"

"On the cliff-path, sir."

"Exactly. The angle from either of these side-paths would be too acute, too chancy, as I see it. The cliff-path runs directly parallel with the house."

The little group, led by the Inspector, moved off on to the cliff-path. At once they were drawn up short as the Inspector stopped dead and uttered a soft exclamation of pleasure.

"Ah!" he said, squatting close to the ground. "This looks more like it. There's a new set of tracks here, Grouch. See, gentlemen. These, of course, are Miss Tregarthan's—notice the small, round heel. But these—" and he pointed to a somewhat broader foot "—belong to somebody else." He peered closer. "Hullo! Hullo! What's this? A heel missing?"

"A heel!" exclaimed Pendrill. "Which way do the tracks run?"

"Toward the village."

All faces were turned toward the Doctor who, with the air of a man on the scent of something, was prying closely at the footprints. Suddenly he threw back his head and laughed without restraint.

"It's all right, Inspector. I don't think you need trouble with those."

"Not trouble with them, sir?"

The Inspector seemed aghast at the Doctor's levity.

"No. It's Mrs. Mullion or I'm a Dutchman!"

"Mrs. Mullion?"

"The local midwife. She had to attend a case to-night in a cottage over at Towan Cove. I drove her there myself in the car. It was an urgent case—twins as a matter of fact. And getting out of the car, and I suppose not being used to that sort of conveyance, she wrenched her heel on the running-board. I'll swear that's her foot right enough."

"It's certainly small for a man's," acknowledged the Inspector. "She would have returned this way to-night?"

"Yes. Towan Cove is about half a mile along the cliff— about a mile and a half from the village. A good bit further by the road. The cliff-path offers a short cut between the two coves. I would have run the good woman back, only she wanted to stay on for a bit to make sure everything was as it should be with Mrs. Withers. That was my patient's name. I couldn't stay longer myself as I had a dinner appointment with the Vicar here."

"What time did you leave the cottage?"

"About seven-fifteen, I imagine."

"And Mrs. Mullion?"

"Well, I can't say exactly. She may have stayed an hour, perhaps an hour and a half. I shouldn't think longer. Everything was going along quite satisfactorily."

"Suppose she stayed an hour," went on the Inspector quickly. "That means she would have left the cottage about eight-fifteen. Allowing her fifteen minutes to walk the half-mile along the cliff—we mustn't forget her damaged heel—that means she would have passed this spot about eight-thirty. You see where I am getting to, sir?"

"That she *may* have been somewhere in this locality when the murder was committed."

"Exactly. If she left at a later hour it is almost certain she must have passed within a few minutes of the fatal shot being fired. I think it might be advisable for us to get hold of Mrs. Mullion tomorrow, Grouch, and put a few questions to her."

"But you don't mean . . ." put in the Vicar, aghast.

"That she shot Tregarthan? Hardly. But she may be able to give us information which will help us to find out who did."

"There's a third alternative, sir," said Grouch respectfully. "Perhaps it's already occurred to you. Mrs. Mullion might have passed the house *after* the murder was committed."

"Yes—I thought of that. It's possible. Still, there's no harm in putting her through a little third degree, as the newspapers have it."

"Which gets us, you realise, Inspector, no further with the footprints."

The Inspector, who was by then on his hands and knees, peering again at the footprints, seemed at a complete loss.

"You're right there, sir. It sets us back half a mile. Take a close look at the path, gentlemen—you too, Grouch. How many recent sets of prints do you see?"

After a moment Grouch said:

"Three, sir. Two of Miss Tregarthan's. One belonging to Bessie Mullion."

"And over here?" asked the Inspector, moving a yard or so along the path.

"Still three."

"And here and here and here?" demanded Bigswell, advancing in jerks along the track under the wall.

The result was the same. Three tracks! For a stretch of twenty yards, which the Inspector considered a feasible angle from which Tregarthan could have been shot, an exhaustive inspection brought no further footprints to light. The little group extended its activities to the hoof-pocked and half-muddied turf which bordered the cliff-path beyond the wall. They found nothing! Three tracks and three tracks only were visible and those on the path itself. Two belonging to Ruth Tregarthan. One to Mrs. Mullion.

"Well, I'll be b—busted!" exclaimed the Inspector, realising the Vicar's presence in the nick of time. "What are we to make of that? Miss Tregarthan? Mrs. Mullion? Surely a woman——?"

"It's impossible, Inspector," remonstrated Pendrill. "Why, good heavens, I've known Ruth since she was a kid! She couldn't have done a thing like this. Her uncle? It's ridiculous! You might as well accuse my old friend the Vicar here, as accuse that girl!"

"And Mrs. Mullion?"

"A steady, respectable, unimaginative country-woman. Good at her job. A motherly old soul, if I know the meaning of the phrase. As to her handling a revolver—my imagination boggles at the thought. She'd miss the house at fifteen feet, let alone a man standing in that window. What do you say, Dodd?"

"Eh?" The Reverend Dodd during the Doctor's argument had moved off a little way, making a further inspection of the footprints on his own account.

"Ruth! Mrs. Mullion! Ridiculous, eh?" reiterated Pendrill.

"Oh, dear me—yes, of course. Unthinkable, Inspector. You must be on the wrong track there."

"Well, it beats me," concluded Inspector Bigswell as he cut off his torch. "I don't think we can do much more out here. It looks to me as if we're up against a first-class mystery." He pulled his cape a little tighter round his neck. "Brr! It's getting chilly, gentlemen. A Cornish cliff at the end of March is hardly a comfortable place for a conference. How about returning to the house?"

"If you care to come up to the Vicarage," said the Reverend Dodd. "Perhaps a little refreshment ..."

He tailed off vaguely. The Inspector accepted the invitation, and leaving Grouch and the chauffeur to keep watch on the house, the three men piled into the Doctor's saloon and drove off up the drive.

The Vicar, sitting alone on the back seat, was silent. He was disturbed and puzzled by the results of the evening's investigations. Those three tracks! Very curious. Ruth. Mrs. Mullion. Yet more curious were the two inferences he had drawn from a further inspection of Ruth Tregarthan's footprints. That little round heel—obviously a high-heeled shoe. The storm and the torrential rain. Would a sensible, country-bred girl like Ruth leave her house in the midst of a storm in flimsy, high-heeled shoes? She had always worn brogues, good, stout, walking shoes, when the Vicar had seen her out and about in the locality. *She normally wore brogues.* Then why, when it was raining, did she suddenly elect to tramp along the cliff edge in what appeared to be house-shoes?—or at the most, town-shoes?

And secondly—yes, indeed it *was* rather like setting out the points in a sermon—why was the track returning to the side-door different from the track leading from it? There was less heel in the first, more toe. Which meant? She was running. Why? To get in out of the rain? Hardly that, since she had apparently set off quite cheerfully in the middle of the storm. Besides, Ruth was used to the wet. She had not lived the major part of her life in Boscawen without learning to ignore the vagaries of the elements. She was a typical country girl. Yet she had run. The nature of the footprints had changed about mid-way along the garden wall. Yet Ruth had told Grouch that she did not know anything was amiss until she reached the sitting-room and found her uncle dead.

And further—that question about the wet mackintosh. Again it was unlike Ruth to avoid the exercise of common sense. That question seemed to have disturbed her. She had hesitated, appeared uneasy, stammered. What did it mean exactly? Was Ruth trying to hide something from the police?

Did she, despite her denial, know that her uncle had been shot before she entered the sitting-room? Say, for example, when she was on the cliff-path at the bottom of the garden?

The Vicar suddenly felt a great depression weighing on him. He stared uneasily at the spectral landscape which stretched out on either side of the drive. Behind his gold-rimmed glasses his eyes, devoid of their customary twinkle, were narrowed to two thin slits of perplexity and trepidation.

CHAPTER IV

STRANGE BEHAVIOUR OF RUTH TREGARTHAN

INSPECTOR BIGSWELL, despite the cosiness of the Vicar's study and the excellence of the refreshment provided, did not remain long at the Vicarage. Satisfied that he had obtained a good wad of local knowledge from Pendrill and the Reverend Dodd, he returned at once to Greylings. The Doctor, who after the excitements of the evening felt pretty exhausted, offered to drop the Inspector before returning along the road to Rock House. But Bigswell, who wanted a few moments to himself and found walking a stimulating brain tonic, politely refused the offer. So the two of them said "Good night" at the Vicarage gate and went their separate ways.

As Bigswell saw it, little more could be done that night. There might be a weapon hidden somewhere in the vicinity of the house or at any rate a further clue or clues, but it was useless to make an exhaustive search until daylight. The murderer, whoever he was, must have had a fair amount of time in which to make himself scarce after the fatal shot had been fired. In all probability he had an exact knowledge of the surrounding country, and although the police in the district had been warned before the Inspector left Greystoke to keep an extra vigilance on all roads and to take note of any suspicious character, Bigswell did not hope for much in this direction. It was a lonely bit of coast, criss-crossed with tracks, well wooded a little way inland and sparsely inhabited. Besides, so far, he had no description to broadcast of the man or woman they were looking for. The Man with the Gaiters *might* have something to do with the crime, and enquiries would have to be made; on the other hand it might have been mere coincidence. Unfortunate, of course, if it brought the man under suspicion, but there was always the chance that he could explain his presence on the drive.

The footprints definitely puzzled him. He had hoped by an examination of the cliff-path to settle on some definite clue, some means of identification. Of course, either Mrs. Mullion or Ruth Tregarthan might have committed the crime. Neither of them were above suspicion. Both had been on the cliff-path at a late hour, apparently unobserved, and both had had the opportunity to shoot Tregarthan through the window. These were two further lines of enquiry which would have to be followed up.

Beyond this—what did he know? Tregarthan had been shot at by a person or persons outside the house and that one of the bullets fired, seemingly from an Army Service revolver, had entered his skull and killed him instantaneously. So far no evidence had come to light that he had any special enemies; neither was it possible, at the moment, to fix any definite motive for the crime. It was probable on the other hand, considering the nature of the crime, that it was a premeditated affair—a matter, without much doubt, of malice aforethought. The criminal must have known that Tregarthan was in that particular room at that particular time, for, with the curtains drawn, it was impossible to see in through the window. In some way (and Bigswell made a note of this point) the murderer had attracted Tregarthan's attention so that he moved to the french windows, drew back the curtains and looked out into the night, offering a clear target against the brilliant light of the room. This fact seemed to rule out the idea of a homicidal maniac. Of course, there was the chance that Tregarthan might have been watching the storm over the sea, but from what he had learnt from Pendrill and the Vicar he was inclined to rule out this supposition. Tregarthan was a man of rigid habit, precise, not particularly imaginative and with little appreciation of nature and natural phenomena. Bigswell felt that it would take more than a storm effect over the sea to move Tregarthan from an easy-chair, where he had, by evidence supplied, been reading the newspaper, and take him to the window. Yet something had lured him to the window. What?

By this time the Inspector had reached the circular patch of gravel in front of the severe, stone façade of Greylings. But instead of entering the house, he dodged right, through the dark clump of laurels, and followed the tiny path which led over a broken stile and thus down the north side of the garden wall. Reaching the wall he climbed over it and, switching on his torch, he made a minute inspection of the narrow cement strip which ran under the french windows. From this the grass dipped in a brief bank to the level of the lawn, forming a small terrace. The cement was still damp, and on its smooth surface, thrown into relief by the slanting rays of the torch, were numbers of tiny pieces of gravel!

The Inspector gave a muffled grunt of satisfaction, and with the industry of a pecking hen his fingers darted here and there, until he had a collection of these small pieces in his hand. He returned again by the north track to the drive. In his left hand he scooped up a sample of the surface, and moving to the light shed from the hall windows, he made a careful comparison of the two specimens of gravel. To his amazement, for he had not expected this result, the two specimens coincided!

The gravel which had been thrown against the window to attract Tregarthan's attention was identical with the gravel on the other side of the house!

This he felt was important.

Drumming lightly on the front door, he was let into the hall by Grouch and proceeded to the sitting-room, where Grimmet, the chauffeur, was lounging in an arm-chair reading the paper. On seeing the Inspector he sprang up and stubbed out a half-smoked cigarette. Bigswell poured the two little heaps of gravel side by side on a table.

"What d'you make of those, Grouch?"

Grouch quizzed them for a moment.

"Same gravel, sir—in both heaps."

The Inspector explained how he had collected the right-hand pile under the window.

"Does it strike you as peculiar at all, Grouch? I mean that the two heaps should be the same. What's the general run of stone round these parts?"

"Crushed limestone—slate—granite. That's as far as my knowledge carries me, anyway."

"Then the gravel for the drive was imported stuff, eh?"

"That's right, sir," exclaimed Grouch, who was beginning to realise the trend of these questions. "Not done so long ago neither. About three months since, I should say. I remember the stuff being unloaded from a lorry up on the road."

"Nobody else in the place has used the same gravel to your knowledge, Grouch?"

"No, sir. Unless it's off my regular beat. Local stone—that's the cheapest road material and to my way of thinking ... the best!"

"Good," ejaculated the Inspector with a brisk air. "This gets us somewhere at last. I think we can say that whoever murdered Tregarthan first snatched up a handful of gravel from the drive to throw against his window." He paused for a moment, frowned, and went on. "But what puzzles me is why there are no footprints on that north track. The chap must have made a pretty wide detour, Grouch, to avoid leaving a clue. It argues a pretty keen intelligence. The whole business looks intelligent to my way of thinking—damn carefully thought out." He took up his hat which he had set aside during the conversation and moved toward the door. "Well, Grouch, there's nothing more to be done to-night I'm afraid. You'd better stay here until you're relieved. I'll be over early in the morning. Nothing to be touched. Nobody to leave the house. Understand? We'll have to broadcast a description of that man on the drive and give the papers some details. It may bring a few people forward. Can't get it in until the midday editions now. There'll be an inquest of course. Let's see, what's to-day?"

"Monday, sir."

"Probably on Wednesday or Thursday then. We must get hold of the midwife and anybody else who may have happened to be round about the house to-night. I'll see Miss Tregarthan and the Cowpers first thing in the morning. You've done well, Grouch. Good night."

"Night, sir."

The police chauffeur came forward and followed the Inspector out to the car. As they were about to step out on to the drive, however, there was the sound of rustling in the laurel bushes.

"Quiet!" hissed the Inspector, pulling the other man back into the shadow of a dumpy fir tree which grew beside the projecting wall of the stone porch. "Don't move, Grimmet."

With great care the Inspector, making a peephole with cautious hands, peered out between the thick foliage.

A figure muffled in a thick coat with a high, fur collar came swiftly out of the bushes, hesitated a moment and crept on light toes across the crunchy gravel and slipped into the porch. They heard the front door being opened with a latchkey—the minutest scrape of the key against the lock—then a pause, as if the prowling figure was making certain that nobody in the house had overheard. But before the door could be as silently closed, Inspector Bigswell sprang from his hiding-place and thrust his toe into the shutting door.

There was a stifled cry from the other side, the door swung open and Inspector Bigswell found himself face to face with a wide-eyed and speechless young lady.

At the sound of the girl's involuntary cry, Grouch lumbered out of the sitting-room, where he had been running over his notes.

"Good heavens!" he exclaimed. "Miss Tregarthan!"

It was the Inspector's turn to show astonishment.

"Ruth Tregarthan!"

"That's right, sir. I'd no idea——"

"All right, Grouch." He moved into the hall and shut the door. "Allow me to introduce myself, Miss Tregarthan—Inspector Bigswell of the Greystoke Division, County Constabulary."

Ruth inclined her head but made no effort to reply. She seemed bewildered and shaken by this sudden encounter. Her eyes, still reddened by recently shed tears, moved this way and that with the helpless anxiety of a trapped animal.

Taking her arm the Inspector, followed by Grouch, led the way into the dining-room. He indicated the arm-chair where Ruth had already sat when answering the Constable's catechism.

"Now, Miss Tregarthan," said the Inspector sternly. "Can you give me some explanation as to why you left the house to-night when you had been expressly warned by the Constable not to do so? You understand of course that I'm bound to take a serious view of your action?"

Ruth nodded.

"I quite understand."

"And you quite understood the Constable's order?"

"Yes."

"And yet you left the house?"

"Yes."

"Why?"

"I couldn't sleep. I tried. But the horrible vision of my uncle as I found him to-night kept on floating before my eyes. I tried to shut away the picture. But I couldn't. I turned on the light."

"When?"

"About ten minutes ago."

"You were in the sitting-room then, sir," interpolated Grouch.

The Inspector swung round smartly.

"All right, Grouch—I'll manage this." He turned back to the girl. "You turned on the light—what then?"

"I felt restless. I felt I couldn't stay in the house a moment longer. So I slipped on a coat over my night-things and crept down the stairs."

"Turning out the light?"

"Yes."

"And then?"

"I heard voices in the sitting-room, and knowing the Constable had orders not to let anybody leave the house, I crept across the hall and let myself out of the side-door."

"Why?"

"I've told you! Don't you understand? I couldn't bear to be in the house any longer. My uncle lying there ..."

For a moment Ruth, burying her face in her hands, was unable to go on. Exhausted and shocked by all she had been through that night, her nerves gave way, utterly, and she began to sob.

The Inspector waited in silence until the girl gained control of her hysteria.

"And then?" he asked—adding in kinder tones: "I'm sorry to have to question you like this—but you understand, miss?"

Ruth looked up and nodded. In a whisper she went on: "Outside I turned down to the cliff-path, intending to go for a walk. But somehow—out there!—in the moonlight my fears returned. I kept seeing people lurking in the shadows. For a time I stayed quite still—not daring to move—then I walked round to the end of the garden to see if you had moved from the sitting-room."

"And found we hadn't, eh?"

"Yes. So I returned along the other track and came on to the drive through the laurel bushes. And then——"

"And then we jumped out on you, Miss Tregarthan, and gave you the fright of your life."

"Yes."

"You realise," said the Inspector gravely, "that you were very wrong in disobeying the Constable's orders?"

"I do—now. Yes. It was foolish of me, I know, but I was overwrought. I still am. You don't understand, Inspector!"

"I think I do," said the Inspector quietly, taking the girl's hand. "And now I want you to go to your room and get some sleep." He smiled. "To please me, Miss Tregarthan." He helped the trembling girl to the door. "And mind," he concluded, "this time no escapades. Promise?"

Ruth summoned up the ghost of a smile.

"I promise," she said.

When her door had closed in the passage above, the Inspector turned on Grouch and shrugged his shoulders. Grouch tilted his helmet and scratched his head with the end of his pencil.

"Well I'll be blowed, sir!"

"You may well be, Grouch." He lowered his voice. "I don't like it. I don't like it at all. Granted she's overwrought. But that story—a bit thin, eh?—to say the least of it!"

Grouch delivered himself of an oracle.

"It's to my mind, sir, that there's more in this case than meets the eyes."

Inspector Bigswell nodded. It seemed as if he were about to speak, when he changed his mind, motioned to Grimmet and went out to the car.

CHAPTER V

THE INSPECTOR FORMS A THEORY

Before Bigswell motored over to Boscawen on the Tuesday morning he had managed to get in a fair amount of work at headquarters. The evening before, on his return, despite the lateness of the hour he had got in touch with Major Farnham, the Chief Constable, and put in a report of the affair at Greylings. The Chief Constable, who had been up late playing bridge, hurried over at once to headquarters and had a conference with the Inspector. They returned to their respective homes shortly after 2 a.m., having come to one or two conclusions in the meantime. For the moment, at any rate, the Chief Constable was against calling in the help of Scotland Yard. He knew the value of a well-oiled, delicately organised machine such as the Criminal Investigation Department of the Metropolitan Police, but he had an unswerving faith in the efficiency of his own men. His motto was—"Give 'em a chance and they'll take two"—and in this case he was quite ready to give Inspector Bigswell an opportunity to prove his intelligence.

Nor was he against the Inspector's suggestion that a guarded report of the crime should be sent to one or two of the big News Agencies. The Chief Constable did not underrate the value of the Press in bringing forward witnesses and he realised, anyway, that it would only be a matter of hours before the news leaked out and resulted in a grand trek of local reporters and special correspondents to the scene of the crime. As to the case itself, he expressed no opinion. It was, to his cautious way of looking at things, too early in the day to form even the vaguest theory as to how Julius Tregarthan had met his death. The Inspector knew better than to contradict his superior and left the conference rather pleased with himself and life in general, because the Major had decided against appealing for help at the Yard. It was a chance for him and the solving of the problem would be a feather in his cap.

Shortly after eight on the Tuesday morning, a fine, windless day full of the white sunlight of early spring, a police car swung out of Greystoke H.Q. and headed over the bleak, undulating uplands toward Boscawen. The Inspector sat in front with Grimmet, whilst a burly Constable occupied a considerable portion of the double-seat at the back. Bigswell, who abominated a moment's inaction, jotted down a few notes as a rough guide to his programme for the day.

First, a re-examination of Miss Tregarthan and the Cowpers. The instigation of a further search for clues round about the house. Another look (and this time he thanked heaven by daylight!) at the footprints on the cliff-path. The cross-examination of the village midwife, Mrs. Mullion. Then enquiries in any direction as to anybody who had been near Greylings on the previous night. Enquiries as to the identity of the Man with the Gaiters. An exhaustive search among Tregarthan's effects, in the hope of unearthing some documentary evidence which would point a finger toward the murderer.

These notes formed a rough plan of his intended activities, though he realised that any sudden twist in the case might send him hurrying off at a tangent, to pursue any unexpected line of enquiry which seemed profitable.

Grouch met him at the door of Greylings and reported that, so far, nothing further had transpired during the Inspector's absence.

"I took the liberty, sir, early this morning to shut off the cliff-path at the bottom of the garden with a couple of hurdles."

"Good, Grouch. Had breakfast?"

The Constable grinned.

"Mrs. Cowper, sir——"

"Very well. You can go off duty now if you like. Want some sleep, I dare say?"

"Well, sir——"

"All right, Grouch. Back here by twelve. Everybody up in the house?"

"Miss Tregarthan's having breakfast now, sir."

The Inspector went into the house and Grouch, mounting his bicycle, pedalled off slowly up the drive.

The sun was now well above the sea and the morning was full of that sweet tang which is, invariably, the aftermath of rain. A few sea-gulls, pivoting white against the sun, sped and circled over the grey rocks of the coast. Their mournful cries mingled with the tinkle of a sheep-bell, where a scattered flock was feeding on the rising common behind the church. Beyond the sombre, box-like contours of Greylings, the Atlantic ran out to a far horizon like a glinting sheet of lead, whilst nearer in the slow swell glittered with thousands of tiny diamonds and broke into long advancing lines of dazzling white foam.

Ruth Tregarthan stood by the window of the dining-room, staring across the green slope of the cliff-edge to where the village lay nestling in the unseen cove. At the Inspector's knock she started, turned sharply on her heel and braced herself for the coming ordeal.

Bigswell came in with an apologetic air and at once excused himself for breaking into Miss Tregarthan's privacy at so early an hour. Then without more ado he settled down to business.

The first part of his examination, save for a few additional questions, went over the ground which the Constable had already covered. Ruth described again her discovery of the body and her subsequent actions, giving her estimate of the time that she had found her uncle dead. Then, without appearing to set much store by his questions, the Inspector switched over to another line of cross-examination. He began to ask the girl about her actions *before* she discovered the crime at 9.20.

"You went out I take it, Miss Tregarthan, after dinner? Or rather——" He consulted his notes of the night before. "You went out half-way through dinner. You left your uncle at the table. Why did you do that?"

"We'd had a disagreement and as we were both getting rather heated I thought it would be better not to prolong the argument."

"You'd quarrelled with your uncle? Or perhaps he had quarrelled with you—is that it?"

"Yes—I suppose you could put it like that."

"What was the quarrel about?"

Ruth glanced at the Inspector and seeing him looking keenly at her dropped her gaze and remained silent.

"A private matter?" suggested the Inspector. "Something you would rather not talk about?" Ruth nodded. "Well that's all right, Miss Tregarthan. I'm only here to investigate the crime and collect such evidence as may enable me to lay hands on the criminal. You're not bound to answer my questions, you know. Now can you give me any idea as to what time you left the house?"

"I can't say exactly. But I should think somewhere about eight-thirty. Perhaps later. I know we didn't sit down to dinner till eight-fifteen. My uncle had been out and didn't return until after eight, which is out usual dinner-time."

"I see. And you went straight out?"

"Yes. I slipped on a mackintosh and a hat, and left the house by the side-door."

"It was raining at the time, of course?"

"Yes."

"You're apparently not frightened by storms, Miss Tregarthan."

"No—one gets used to being out in them, living in the country."

"Quite so. When you left the house where did you go?"

"Toward the village along the cliff-path."

"It's a short-cut, I take it?" Ruth agreed. "Did you by any chance visit anybody in the village? I mean were you taking an idle walk, or did you intend to visit a friend when you reached Boscawen?"

Ruth hesitated for a moment, bit her lip, pondered and finally decided on the form of her answer.

"Yes," she acknowledged in a low voice. "I did intend to see somebody."

"Can you let me have their name?"

"Is it necessary?"

"I'm afraid so, Miss Tregarthan. You see time is always an important factor in a case, and if you visited somebody last night they may know what time you left their house. Now this would be corroborative evidence as to the time you reached Greylings. We know how far away the village is by the cliff-path and can estimate, roughly, how long you took to walk the distance. You see, miss?"

"Yes," said Ruth. "I quite understand. I went to Cove Cottage—one of the first houses between here and Boscawen. It's owned by Mrs. Peewit, a widow. Since her husband's death she's been forced to let rooms for a living."

"And you went to see Mrs. Peewit?"

"No—not exactly. I went to see her present lodger—Mr. Hardy."

The Inspector scribbled a few hurried notes in his book and went on casually.

"I suppose Mr. Hardy is a single gentleman? I mean Mrs. Peewit attends to his wants and so forth?"

"That's right. He's an author—a novelist, as a matter of fact. He's been with Mrs. Peewit for about two years now."

"I see. And last night, Miss Tregarthan, you thought that since you were out for a walk you'd visit Mr. Hardy?"

"Yes. It was raining pretty heavily, and as I know him fairly well I thought I'd drop in for a chat."

"And you found him in?"

Again Ruth hesitated.

"No—as a matter of fact, I didn't," she said slowly. "I saw Mrs. Peewit, of course, but Mr. Hardy was out."

"Nothing unusual about that, I suppose? After all he didn't expect you?"

"Oh, no. He often goes down to the Men's Club at the Legion Hall and plays billiards in the evening. Knowing this I didn't trouble to wait. I left a message with Mrs. Peewit to say that I'd called on Mr. Hardy, and came straight home."

"By the cliff-path?"

"Yes."

"I see, Miss Tregarthan. Well, that's been a very helpful little talk." Inspector Bigswell rose. "I'm sorry that you should have been put to all this trouble. Let's hope the affair will soon be cleared up. There'll be an inquest on Wednesday or Thursday and I'm afraid you will be handed an official summons to attend. Probably at the local inn. We thought it would be more convenient than here. More room. Now d'you mind if I upset the routine of your house a little and have a chat with Mr. and Mrs. Cowper?"

"No, Inspector. You can have this room if you like. The Vicar rang through early this morning and asked me if I would care to stay at the Vicarage for the time being. His sister, whom I know quite well, is coming down to-day. If you've no objection I should like to accept."

"By all means. And the Cowpers?"

"They'll stay on here, of course."

"Well, Miss Tregarthan, if you take my advice you'll pack your things as soon as possible. Your uncle's solicitor has been informed of his death, I suppose?"

"Yes—Mr. Dodd phoned him and he's coming over from Greystoke this afternoon."

"Good." He held out his hand. "I'll let you know the moment there is anything to report."

"Thank you, Inspector. You can't realise how much this has upset me. I can't understand it! My uncle has no enemies. I can't see what anybody has to gain by this horrible crime."

And keeping back her tears with an effort Ruth crossed to the door and went out.

The Inspector then dealt with the Cowpers, having them into the dining-room one at a time. He did not trouble to verify the statements which the Cowpers had offered Grouch, but concentrated on questions which dealt with the relationship existing between Ruth Tregarthan and her uncle. Here, as Bigswell had expected, Mrs. Cowper was far more informative than her husband. It seemed in fact that where Cowper was content to accept the Tregarthans as his employers, Mrs. Cowper was devoured with an insatiable curiosity as to their private affairs and actions. She did not deliberately listen at closed doors or go out of her way to pry upon Ruth or her uncle, but she kept her ears and eyes abnormally wide open.

Stimulated to volubility by a few well-interposed questions, Mrs. Cowper declared that Miss Ruth and her uncle had never really got on since the girl had grown old enough to have a mind of her own. There had been frequent quarrels, of a verbal rather than a physical nature, often resulting in days of freezing silence between them. Of late these quarrels had grown more violent and Mrs. Cowper had entertained a fear that Mr. Tregarthan, a headstrong man when roused out of his normal reserve, would do his niece some physical injury. But as far as she knew this had never actually happened. Miss Ruth would often leave the house and go for long walks after one of these outbursts, which Mrs. Cowper considered was a sensible thing to do, as it gave them both time to cool down and get over their unreasonableness.

The Inspector then came to the quarrel at the dinner-table on the night of the murder. Did Mrs. Cowper know exactly what this quarrel was about? Mrs. Cowper didn't like to repeat the inner goings-on, as it were, of the family, but she did have a very shrewd idea as to what this particular row was about. The Inspector thereupon eased her somewhat elastic conscience and explained that all the information which he received was of a strictly confidential nature, and that Mrs. Cowper could speak up without fear of reprimand.

"Then," said Mrs. Cowper, taking a large breath, significant of a large and imminent flood of information, "it was about Mr. Ronald. Mr. Ronald Hardy, that is, what lives down at Cove Cottage with Mrs. Peewit. Very friendly he was with Miss Ruth, though never coming to the house when Mr. Tregarthan was there, as there didn't seem to be much love lost between them. The saying is, in the village, that Mr. Ronald is sweet on Miss Ruth and that she's biding her time like a sensible lass before saying 'Yes.' 'Course, I don't know if it had gone as far as that, mind you. But this much I do know." And here Mrs. Cowper grew emphatic. "Mr. Tregarthan would have objected to the marriage and make no mistake about it. Why he was so against Mr. Ronald, I don't know. He always seemed nice enough the few times I chanced to meet him in the village, though he was an author and a bit queer sometimes in the head because of him being shell-shocked in the war. But a nicer, better-spoken, well-set-up sort of lad you'd have to go a long way to find, to my way of thinking. Well, last night, just before I took in the joint, the door being open I couldn't help over-hearing a bit of the conversation. It was about Mr. Ronald— that much I'll swear to—though his name was never actually mentioned."

"What made you think it was to do with Mr. Hardy then, Mrs. Cowper?"

"Because of what was said. First I heard Mr. Tregarthan say something about 'It's got to stop once and for all! I forbid you to see him again!' I heard him thump the table as he said it enough to crack the glasses. He appeared half off his head with anger. I can tell you, it frightened me to hear him talking that roughly."

"And then?"

"And then I heard Miss Ruth say—'You've no right to interfere. I'm old enough to do as I please with my own life. It's a matter between him and me!'"

"And then?"

"And then I coughed behind the door and walked in with the joint. Later when I was out of the room I heard them start all over again. Then I heard Miss Ruth come out into the hall in a hurry, get into her outdoor things and go out by the side door."

This concluded, as far as the Inspector was concerned, the valuable part of Mrs. Cowper's evidence. What followed was mere gossip and hearsay, which the Inspector put an end to as soon as was tactfully possible. Cowper merely corroborated his wife's statement that Miss Ruth and her uncle were always "chewing their rag," as he put it.

Satisfied that he was at last getting somewhere in his investigations the Inspector ordered Grimmet and the burly Constable to make an exhaustive search in the grounds of the house and on the surrounding part of the common, in the hope that some further clue might come to light. Bigswell, himself, returned at once to the cliff-path and went over the ground which he had covered the night before. There was, as he saw at once, a new series of footprints which served to corroborate Ruth's story of the previous evening. These he dismissed for the time being as extraneous and concentrated his attentions on the earlier footprints made by Ruth before Tregarthan had been discovered dead. This time he was struck, as the Vicar had been struck, by those two curious and interesting facts—(1) That Ruth Tregarthan had walked to about midway along the cliff-path at the bottom of the garden, stopped, apparently, and, by the direction of the toes, stared into the uncurtained room, and then run at a high speed toward the side door. (2) That she was wearing at the time high-heeled shoes.

But why had she run? She, on her own statement, did not realise that anything was wrong with her uncle. Taking up his position mid-way along the wall the Inspector saw at once, by reason of the wide window-frames and the position of a small arm-chair, that Tregarthan's recumbent body would have been invisible from the cliff-path. And yet the girl had apparently taken one look at the window and bolted helter-skelter to the side door. And more than that—rushed without removing her wet attire, straight into the sitting-room. Why?

Inspector Bigswell hoisted himself up on to the low stone wall, filled his pipe, lit it fastidiously and began to evolve the first outlines of a theory, which would account for the manner in which Julius Tregarthan had been murdered.

His theory was something like this:

Ruth Tregarthan had quarrelled violently with her uncle over this love-affair between her and Ronald Hardy. For some reason (at present unapparent) Tregarthan had been dead against the match. Ruth had gone at once to Ronald, probably to let him know of this final *fracas* and to make plans for their future actions. She was in a violent temper. The continued opposition of her uncle to the man she loved had driven her, at this final stage, to desperation. Perhaps her uncle's consent to the marriage was, for some financial reason, essential. At any rate, Ruth, finding Ronald out, had returned along the cliff-path and seeing a light in the sitting-room, had snatched up a handful of gravel from the drive, returned to the cliff-path, thrown the gravel, and when her uncle drew aside the curtains she had shot him. Then, horrified by the results of her action, she had rushed, via the side door, into the sitting-room, to find, alas, that her uncle was already dead.

This was the Inspector's theory. Set out, step by step, in his mind he realised, at once, that though it explained away a good many of the facts of the case, it still left a great deal unexplained. Why, for example, had he found no footprints linking up the cliff-path with the drive, where the girl had gone to get the handful of gravel? It was reasonably certain that she would have used the little track which led through the laurel bushes. Where had the girl got the revolver? At Cove Cottage? She would hardly have had a revolver ready in the pocket of her mackintosh, and according to Mrs. Cowper she would have had no time to get one from elsewhere before she left the house. And what was her reason for that stealthy exit from Greylings on the previous night when she had been ordered by the Constable not to leave the premises?

The Inspector suddenly sat up straight and took the pipe out of his mouth.

What if the girl had managed to secrete the revolver in her bedroom during the general upset in the house, and later crept out to rid herself of such a damning piece of evidence? That was a reasonable explanation—far more reasonable than the somewhat halting explanation offered by the girl herself. She had slipped down to the cliff-path and flung the revolver into the sea. As the Vicar had told him the night before, it was deep water under that part of the cliff. Greylings was out on a broad ness and the cliff, though low, slid straight down into the sea.

The Inspector got off the wall and gazed down over the cliff-edge. He realised at once that it would be a hopeless task trying to recover anything which had been thrown into the water at that point. There was a strong swell round the ness and doubtless swift currents on the sea-bed, to say nothing of jagged rocks between which the revolver might have lodged. Dragging operations would be out of the question. Was it hopeless then to pursue this particular line of investigation? Wouldn't it be better perhaps to find out, not so much what Ruth Tregarthan had done with the revolver, but from where she had obtained it? Once prove that she had a revolver in her possession when she left Cove Cottage and the rest would be a mere matter of collecting further circumstantial evidence.

Two people might help him over this matter—Mrs. Mullion, the midwife, and Mrs. Peewit, Ronald's landlady at Cove Cottage. He decided without more ado to visit these two ladies.

CHAPTER VI

THE MISSING REVOLVER

RETURNING to the house, however, Inspector Bigswell found Pendrill and the Vicar waiting in the sitting-room, from which the body had been removed. Both of them were anxious to know if any progress had been made since their parting at the Vicarage. The Inspector shrugged his shoulders with a noncommittal air and proceeded to take down Mrs. Mullion's address from the Doctor. He was not yet prepared to state his views of the case. Time enough to do that when he had more pieces of the puzzle in his hand.

"By the way," said the Vicar, when the Inspector had finished with Pendrill. "You've heard about my proposal to Miss Tregarthan? The Doctor is taking her and her luggage up to the Vicarage now. Much more pleasant for her I feel. It will enable her, I hope, to regain a more normal outlook on things after this terrible *contretemps*. My sister will be there—a very understanding woman. It's a handicap for a girl not having a mother. A woman's sympathy is a very present help, I feel, in a time of trouble. Don't you agree, Inspector?"

The Inspector nodded absent-mindedly. He was only half listening to the Vicar's preamble. He realised that it might be expedient to get hold of Mr. Ronald Hardy and see what he had to say about his relationship with Ruth Tregarthan. He was surprised that the young man, who by now must have heard about Tregarthan's death, had not put in an appearance.

At that moment Ruth came down followed by Cowper with her suitcases, and joined by Pendrill, the little *cortège* went out to the car. The Inspector shot an enquiring glance at the Vicar, who remained standing in the middle of the room.

"Oh, I'm staying, Inspector. Miss Tregarthan has asked me to go through her uncle's papers in case there should be anything relevant to the solicitor's visit this afternoon. I have the keys of his bureau."

"I should be very much obliged then," put in the Inspector quickly, "if you would take a careful note of any correspondence which may throw light on the reason for Tregarthan's murder. It'll save me a lot of time and trouble. It means an official warrant, of course, and I haven't got one with me. Anything you may show me will be treated in strict confidence of course."

The Vicar agreed to this proposal and settled down forthwith to a methodical search of the big rolltop desk which stood, rather out of place in its ugly utility, in a corner of the sitting-room.

Out on the front drive the Inspector was met by Grimmet and the Constable who reported an unsuccessful morning's work. They had discovered nothing which might serve to elucidate the case in any way and the Inspector, who had rather anticipated this result, ordered Grimmet to start up the car and left the portly Constable in charge of Greylings. Just as the car swung round and headed up the rise of the drive, Grouch hove in sight and started to freewheel swiftly down the slope. The Inspector raised his hand and Grouch, applying his brakes with more fervour than discretion, skidded alarmingly and plunged sideways off his machine. Regaining the upright he saluted smartly.

"Are these acrobatics necessary, Grouch?" asked the Inspector with a faint smile. "I've got quite enough work in hand for the Coroner without asking him to hold an inquest on you. Anyway, leave your juggernaut here and hop in. You can direct us to Cove Cottage, and after that I want to see Mrs. Mullion."

As the car rose and dipped like a veering gull between the gorse dotted greenness of the open common, the Inspector arranged that Grouch should be dropped at Cove Cottage, so that the Constable could go down and interview the landlord of the Ship Inn. The Chief Constable had been in touch with the Coroner, a Greystoke solicitor, before the Inspector had left for Boscawen that morning and the inquest had been fixed for two o'clock on Thursday. As it was expected that a number of witnesses might have to be subpoenaed, Bigswell had suggested that a room in the local inn might prove more convenient and central than Greylings. He had little doubt in his own mind as to what the Coroner's verdict must be—murder, without a doubt, and in the view of the somewhat conflicting and puzzling evidence so far collected—"murder by person or persons unknown." For all that he felt distinctly sanguine as to his chances of driving home the crime, by force of carefully gathered circumstantial evidence, to one particular person.

Nearing the village the Inspector ordered Grimmet to slow up, whilst he took a good look at the general topography of the district. As the car topped the little rise at the end of the undulating road, Boscawen itself came suddenly into view—a scattered collection of grey-walled, green-tiled cottages clustering about a rocky cove, which was edged with a glorious carpet of smooth, silvery sand. Looking back, Greylings now appeared as an isolated little fort, standing well out on the broad ness, linked by the tiny thread of the cliff-path to the cove below.

The car came to a fork in the road—the metalled surface drove straight on down into the hollow, whilst a rough and slatey by-road dipped to the left and appeared to run directly into the sea. Grouch lent forward.

"If you drop me here, sir, I'll slip down and fix up with Charlie Fox about the room. You take the road here to the left and Cove Cottage lies on your right, about a hundred yards round the corner."

"Right! When you've seen the landlord, Grouch, put a call through to Greystoke if it's O.K. They'll be anxious to fix things up with the Coroner. Then meet me up at Cove Cottage."

Grouch saluted, got out of the car and trudged off down to the village. The car swung left and descended steeply toward the sea.

Cove Cottage proved to be a small, detached building, standing back, behind a tidy garden, from the road, surrounded by a few wind-swept crab-apple trees. Picturesque enough, but nothing out of the ordinary, obviously inhabited by a woman who believed in tidiness and utility.

Leaving Grimmet in the car, the Inspector went up the short path and finding no bell or knocker, tapped smartly on the well-weathered door. After a pause, footsteps approached within and the door was opened to reveal a straight, bright-eyed woman of about forty with slightly greying hair. On seeing a uniformed Inspector on her doorstep she started back.

"Good morning, ma'am," said the Inspector, with a quick salute. "Might I ask if you're Mrs. Peewit—the owner of the cottage?"

"That's right," said Mrs. Peewit with a puzzled air. "Is it me you're wishing to see?"

"Just a little matter I want to speak to you about," replied the Inspector reassuringly. "I won't take up much of your time."

"Then come in, please."

The Inspector followed Mrs. Peewit along the tiny hall and thus into a surprisingly large sitting-room, plainly but comfortably furnished, which Bigswell realised in a moment must belong to Ronald Hardy, the novelist. Under the window, which overlooked the Atlantic and part of Boscawen Cove, was a big desk littered with papers and all the usual paraphernalia of writing. A long row of reference books, dictionaries and other standard works stood on the desk between two book-ends fashioned in the shape of galleons. On a table under a smaller window stood a head and shoulder portrait of Ruth Tregarthan in a thin, silver frame.

"Now, Mrs. Peewit," said the Inspector, taking out his note-book. "I believe you're in a position to help me with a few enquiries I'm making."

Mrs. Peewit asked in a tremulous voice: "It's about poor Mr. Tregarthan, I've no doubt. I heard about it only an hour ago, sir. It's fairly upset me—me knowing Miss Ruth so well. It's all over the village about him being found murdered last night in his sitting-room. Shot through the head, they say."

The Inspector smiled. He knew how swiftly news travelled in small villages like Boscawen. Doubtless the milkman and the postman had been well primed with the facts of the crime by the Cowpers. Not that it mattered. The reverse in fact, since it might bring forward voluntary information from anybody who had seen or heard anything unusual the night before.

"They say right for once, Mrs. Peewit—and I'm down here investigating the case, see?"

Impressed by the somewhat lurid situation in which she found herself, Mrs. Peewit promised to do all she could to bring, as she said, the criminal to justice. She was emphatic in assuring the Inspector that such a thing had never, as far as she knew, happened in Boscawen before.

"Now, Mrs. Peewit, I want you to try and remember all that happened when Miss Tregarthan called on you last night." Mrs. Peewit looked surprised. "Oh, I know she did," added the Inspector. "She told me herself. You needn't fear to tell me the truth. I know a good deal as to what took place already."

"Well, sir," said Mrs. Peewit, "Miss Ruth called last night and asked if Mr. Hardy was in. Mr. Hardy, as perhaps I should explain, is——"

"Yes, I know all about that," cut in the Inspector. "He's lodging here. An author. What time was it when Miss Tregarthan called?"

"I can't say exactly, I'm afraid. It hadn't struck nine— I know that much. I should say it was about ten minutes to nine or thereabouts."

"I see. Yes—go on, Mrs. Peewit."

"Well, sir, I don't mind saying that I was a bit surprised seeing Miss Ruth at that time of the evening—particularly as there was a storm on, as you may remember. It's not been her custom to call on Mr. Hardy at such hours. She looked ill, too, downright ill, I thought—looked as if she had been upset over something. Of course I didn't make any mention of it, but I asked her to step into Mr. Hardy's room, seeing that she was so wet and that it was still raining cats and dogs. Mr. Hardy as it happened was out. He'd taken his car out a bit before Miss Ruth turned up and gone off somewhere in a hurry."

"Did Miss Tregarthan wait at all?"

"Yes, for a bit she did. I offered to dry her wet mac in front of the kitchen range, but she said she'd rather sit in here for a bit and just dry her feet at the fire."

"This I take it *is* Mr. Hardy's room?"

"That's right. This is where he writes. Wonderful books, so they say, though I'm not given to reading much myself—the newspapers being as much as I can manage in my spare time."

"How long did Miss Tregarthan stay in here alone?"

"Till just after nine. I remember the clock striking just before she called out that she wouldn't stay any longer, as she thought Mr. Hardy might be down at the Men's Club. So I opened the front door to her and promised to let Mr. Hardy know that she'd called."

"So she was alone in here," said the Inspector more to himself than to Mrs. Peewit, "for about ten minutes—perhaps a bit longer." He looked up suddenly.

"What time did Mr. Hardy come in last night, Mrs. Peewit?"

The woman's attitude changed immediately. She seemed to lose her growing self-confidence, whilst her features were illuminated with a mingled look of agitation and bewilderment.

"That's just it!" she blurted out. "That's just what worries me, sir! Mr. Hardy *didn't* come in last night!"

"What's that?" demanded the Inspector curtly.

"He didn't come in and what's more when I went up to take him his early cup of tea this morning his bed hadn't been slept in. He didn't turn up to breakfast neither! Since he left the house last night, about a quarter to nine, I haven't set eyes on him again, sir. I'm fair worried, I can tell you. He's a highly strung sort of young gentleman, due to shell-shock in the war, they say, and I'm wondering if anything's happened to him!"

"He left no message to say where he was going, I suppose?" Mrs. Peewit shook her head. "Did he take anything with him—I mean any luggage?"

"No, sir. He just put on his overcoat in the hall and called that he was going out. He seemed anxious not to waste time with a lot of explainings, if you see how I mean. I was worried about him then, sir, because he hadn't touched a morsel of his supper, which I took in to him the moment Mr. Tregarthan left the house."

"Tregarthan!" exclaimed the Inspector. "Was he here yesterday?"

"He called in to see Mr. Hardy about seven-thirty. I opened the door to him myself, but I never thought then that in a few hours the poor man would be lying dead in his own sitting-room with his head in a pool of blood."

It was evident that the Cowpers had broadcast a pretty sensational description of the crime at Greylings. The rush of yesterday's events when compared with the usual placid routine of Cove Cottage had, by their very strangeness, impressed themselves upon Mrs. Peewit's mind. The Inspector's few questions had served to stimulate the flow of these recollections.

"Yes—it would be about seven-thirty, perhaps later, when Mr. Tregarthan knocked at the door and enquired for

Mr. Hardy. Mr. Hardy was sitting in here writing at that very desk which you see over there, sir. He didn't like me to interrupt him when he was working. But I knew he and Miss Ruth were tidy close friends, and I thought that Mr. Tregarthan had brought him a message from her. So I plucked up courage enough to rap on his door and ask if he'd see Mr. Tregarthan. Mr. Hardy seemed surprised by the visit, but he asked me to show Mr. Tregarthan in. For a long time I heard the murmur of voices. I was sitting in the kitchen, and although the door of Mr. Hardy's room was closed, I couldn't help hearing a bit of what was going on inside. This isn't a big house as you can see. Well, later, sir, I heard Mr. Tregarthan raise his voice, sharp-like, as if he were dressing Mr. Hardy down. Mr. Hardy didn't seem to like the tone of Mr. Tregarthan's voice and he started argu-ing, too, at the top of his voice. There was a fair set-to—in fact, I don't mind telling you that I heard Miss Ruth's name mentioned more than once. It seemed that her uncle was objecting to the young man having anything more to do with his niece. Presently Mr. Tregarthan came out into the hall, looking a bit ruffled and red in the face. When I made as if to open the door for him, he waved me away. 'It's all right,' he said, 'I know my way out without your help!' And that was the last I saw of him. The last I shall ever see of him as it happens. He walked straight from this very door to his death! Poor man! Dreadful how sudden it comes, sir—just when you least expect it!"

But Inspector Bigswell had heard more than enough. Mrs. Peewit had loaded him with such a sackful of information that he wanted a moment's quiet in which to sort the wheat from the chaff. There was just one other thing he wanted to find out before he left Cove Cottage and he racked his brains for an intelligent means by which this information could be obtained without Mrs. Peewit's knowledge. Inspiration came to him. He removed his peaked cap, mopped his brow, coughed raspingly once or twice and remarked, casually, that it was thirsty work asking questions. Could Mrs. Peewit oblige him with such a thing as a cup of tea? He was sure Mrs. Peewit knew how to make a cup of tea for a thirsty man— strong, not too much milk and three lumps of sugar. Flattered by this unexpected request Mrs. Peewit subsided, at once, to a more normal frame of mind and bustled out to attend to the Inspector's needs.

Bigswell reckoned he had about three minutes in which to act. The moment Mrs. Peewit's footsteps had receded up the stone-floored passage, he went briskly to the desk and began to pull out the drawers. They were in two tiers each side of the spacious knee-hole—about eight drawers in all. The top ones were locked. With extreme deftness and alacrity he worked down the left-hand side, turning over papers, lifting files, groping here and there among a diversity of oddments. It was not until he came to the third drawer down in the right-hand bank that he found exactly what he was looking for. It had been a shot in the dark but the bullet had found its billet. Wedged between a double pile of blue exercise books was a leather holster. The flap was undone and if, as the Inspector reckoned, that holster had once held a revolver—well, *the revolver was no longer there!* Somebody, as he saw at a glance, had removed it recently, for the accumulated dust both on the holster and the exercise books had been disturbed by the brush of a hand or glove.

Closing the drawer, he was just in time to stroll away to the fire-place, when Mrs. Peewit entered with the tea. Gulping it down as quickly as politeness allowed, the Inspector thanked the woman and, warning her that she might be summoned as a witness at the inquest on Thursday, he hurried down the path to the car.

Grouch was waiting for him, sitting beside Grimmet on the front seat. On seeing his superior he sprang out and touched his helmet.

"I've seen Charlie Fox, sir. It's all right. There's a fair sized room at the back. He'll have everything ready by two o'clock Thursday. I phoned through to Greystoke as you said, sir."

"Good!"

Grouch drew himself up with pardonable pride, considering the importance of the news which he was bursting to deliver.

"And that's not all, sir. I took the liberty of asking Fox a few questions. He knows most everybody in the village and there's always plenty of talk running free in the bar at nights."

"Well, Grouch?"

"That chap with the gaiters, sir—I've got a line on him, I think."

"You know who it is?"

"As near as dammit, sir! Ned Salter, the black sheep of the Boscawen flock, as I've heard the Doctor call him. Poaching's his line. Been before the Bench on more than one occasion. Caught him red-handed myself working the burrows up near the Grange. A shifty sort of customer at the best of times.

Fox noticed his gaiters the other night in the pub. Some of the chaps was chipping Ned about it, saying he pinched 'em off a dossing keeper. That's as maybe, but there's something more to it than that, sir."

"Well?"

"Mr. Tregarthan was, as perhaps you know, chairman of the local Bench until a few months ago when he resigned. It seems that the last time Ned was hauled up before the magistrates, Mr. Tregarthan gave him three months without the option."

"And he probably deserved it," commented Inspector Bigswell, who was wondering impatiently where this rigmarole was leading.

Grouch agreed.

"But it seemed a bit hard on the poor devil when Mr. Tregarthan turned his wife and three kids out of their cottage, because they couldn't pay the rent. He owns the property and Ned being in no position to earn, him being over at Greystoke prison, there was nothing for the poor woman to do but to clear out. Well, Fox says that ever since Ned came out, sir, he's been swearing to get even with Mr. Tregarthan. Drinking like a fish, too, and saying things in his cups which he may well be sorry for."

"You mean he went so far as to threaten to——"

"Exactly," said Grouch. "Number of the regular customers down at the 'Ship' would be ready to swear to his words, so Charlie says." Grouch shook his head sagaciously. "It looks black, sir. Very black. That's my humble opinion anyhow."

The Inspector whistled. He couldn't see the wood for the trees. Ruth Tregarthan? Ronald Hardy? Ned Salter? Which?

They were all under suspicion. They all had a motive for the murder. They had all quarrelled with Tregarthan a few hours before his death. The puzzle was assuming gargantuan proportions. No sooner had the Inspector assembled a few bits to his satisfaction, when the puzzle altered shape, with all the startling inconsequence of a landscape in *Alice in Wonderland.*

CHAPTER VII

CONVERSATION AT THE VICARAGE

THE Reverend Dodd, after a fairly exhaustive search of Tregarthan's desk, set aside those papers which he felt were relevant to the visit of the family solicitor. Although he was, by nature of his profession, a man with a spiritual mission, the Vicar was by no means a fool in practical and business matters. By the exercise of a certain amount of justifiable low cunning and the milder forms of sharp practice the affairs of St. Michaels-on-the-Cliff had been placed on a sound business footing. It was said of him in Boscawen that he knew equally well how to save a soul or a sixpence, and more than one harassed villager in the throes of some domestic or economic nightmare had reason to bless the Reverend Dodd for his perspicacity. It came natural, therefore, for Ruth to hand over the material matters resulting from her uncle's death to her very old and very paternal friend, the Vicar. It was Dodd who had got in touch with Ramsey, the solicitor; Dodd who was making arrangements for the funeral; Dodd who had got in touch, at Ruth's suggestion, with Tregarthan's only brother in London and broken the tragic news to him with tact and understanding. With a grateful sigh Ruth abandoned herself to his care and allowed him free rein in the management of her financial affairs. It thus devolved upon the Vicar to go through the private papers and effects of the dead man.

There was not a great deal to cope with. Tregarthan had been a tidy man at his desk and nearly all his papers were neatly filed and labelled. The Inspector's hope that there might be some personal correspondence which might prove incriminating to the sender, was doomed to disappointment. Save for a few invitation cards and begging letters from charitable organisations there was nothing of a private nature in the desk. At least that was the Vicar's first impression. It was not until he had tidied the last drawer, when he noticed a small piece of common, ruled paper behind the drawer itself. It was more through instinct than curiosity that he turned the scrap of paper over and read the brief message written on the back of it. It ran, simply, in an uneducated hand:

> *I'm not wanting your money. I shall hold my*
> *tongue not for your sake but for his. I've no wish*
> *to hear further about this—M.L.*

Although the note puzzled the Vicar he attached little importance to it. The paper itself was already a bit yellowed with age and the very fact that it had slipped behind the drawer seemed to indicate that it had been written and sent to Tregarthan a considerable time back. Probably there had been some slight indiscretion on Tregarthan's part in the past and he had attempted, rather foolishly perhaps, to hush up the affair with a five pound note. Such momentary weaknesses of the flesh were not uncommon in middle-aged men and Tregarthan had doubtless been sorry for his actions the moment he had sat down to consider them. Certainly there was nothing in the note to suggest that it was in any way linked up with the crime. Although the Vicar was dubious of its value as evidence, he thought it would be as well for the Inspector to see it. He might have some ideas as to its purport and origin.

He thrust it, therefore, into his waistcoat pocket and, collecting the pile of papers which he had set aside for Ramsey's perusal, he set off for the Vicarage.

His sister, Ethel, had arrived and the three of them sat down to lunch. By common consent no mention was made of the subject which was uppermost in their minds. As the Reverend Dodd explained to his sister, Ruth must be nursed back to a more healthy outlook by the exercise of strict verbal discretion. She had suffered a great shock and was still faced with the Coroner's inquest on Thursday and her uncle's funeral.

Soon after lunch Ramsey arrived, looked over the papers supplied by the Vicar and after a few words of consolation with Ruth, returned to Greystoke. He had arranged for the will to be read after the funeral, which with the Coroner's consent was to take place at St. Michael's on Friday. Tregarthan's brother and only surviving relative had sent Ramsey a message to say that pressure of business prevented him from travelling down at once to Cornwall. He left the solicitor to wind up his brother's estate and to let him know when the funeral was to take place. To Ruth he sent a brief message of sympathy. But it was obvious from his somewhat casual acceptance of Julius' death that there had been no love lost between the brothers.

Hardly had Ramsey left the Vicarage and the Vicar settled at his desk in the study, when Inspector Bigswell drove up and asked for an interview. The Vicar was surprised by Bigswell's look of dejection. A great deal of the man's enthusiasm seemed to have deserted him and his forehead was wrinkled in a perpetual frown. No sooner was he seated at the cheerful fire, opposite the Vicar, when he plunged into the reason for his visit.

"Look here, sir—I don't mind telling you that the accumulating facts of this case fit one another about as neatly as the proverbial square peg into the proverbial round hole. Candidly I'm at a complete loss. First I'm inclined to veer one way and then another. I've collected a good deal of data since I saw you this morning, but it doesn't get us any further. The latest and most puzzling bit of information, which Mrs. Peewit was kind enough to hand out to me, is that Mr. Hardy left Boscawen last night in his car and has not returned since!"

"Mr. Hardy gone? You mean disappeared without leaving any address—without telling anybody where he was going?"

"Without telling anybody *that* he was going," corrected the Inspector. "In other words he's bolted. Mrs. Peewit naturally thought he was just going out for the evening. He often did, apparently. But it's more than that. He's left the district. I'm certain of it. Everybody knows him and his car in the village, and Grouch has made pretty exhaustive enquiries since lunch, and nobody's seen him since yesterday afternoon. I don't know what you think about it, but to my mind, the fact that he's bolted, looks pretty suspicious. He left Cove Cottage about an hour after he had had a violent quarrel with Tregarthan, but before the probable time that Tregarthan was shot. What I want to know is—where did Mr. Hardy go directly after he left Cove Cottage and what's happened to him since?"

"You're surely not suggesting that Ronald Hardy murdered poor Tregarthan and that his disappearance is connected with the crime?"

"That's exactly what I am suggesting. He had motive. A very strong motive. Mr. Tregarthan was opposed, strongly opposed to his friendship with his niece. They had, in fact, had violent words about this matter a few hours before Tregarthan was found shot."

"But the footprints," put in the Vicar with a mild air of censure. "Surely you haven't forgotten about those three tracks, Inspector?"

"No, I haven't! I wish I could. You see how I'm up against it? Conflicting evidence at every turn. If I am to believe the evidence of those footprints—and at the moment I see no reason why I shouldn't—Tregarthan must have been shot either by his niece or Mrs. Mullion."

"Impossible!" contested the Vicar. "Utterly impossible, Inspector. With your undoubted ability to judge human nature do you really believe, in your heart of hearts, that Ruth Tregarthan could have committed such a dreadful crime? Come, Inspector— frankly now! You can't suspect her!"

"And if I don't," said Bigswell sullenly, "we are left with Mrs. Mullion. And as much as I disbelieve Miss Tregarthan capable of murder, I see yet less reason to suspect Mrs. Mullion. Mind you, I haven't seen her yet. She's cycled over to Porth Harbour, so I was told at her cottage, and won't be back till late this evening. She may be able to help us clear up the mystery, but I doubt it. There's so much that's obscure. But this much I don't mind telling you—all the evidence to hand at the moment points to either Ruth Tregarthan or Ronald Hardy as the guilty party. It's not my job to rule out certain individuals because my heart tells me they're innocent. I *must* deal in facts and facts alone. You see my difficulty, Mr. Dodd? Sentiment's no good in a case like this."

"That's just where I must part company with you, Inspector," said the Vicar with a gentle smile. "I'm rather a voracious reader of mystery stories, and it's always struck me that the detective in fiction is inclined to underrate the value of intuition. Now if I had to solve a problem like this, I should first dismiss all those people who, like Cæsar's wife, were above suspicion, merely because my intuition refused to let me think otherwise. Then I should set to work on what remained and hope for the best!"

The Inspector laughed.

"It's certainly an original method of criminal investigation, Mr. Dodd. But I doubt if it would work out satisfactorily when you came to apply it to an actual case. This case, for instance."

"Oh, I daresay not," agreed the Vicar hastily. "I'm not trying to teach you your job, Inspector. I hope you realise that. Dear me, no! Far be it from me to disagree with your very excellent and efficient methods of investigation. You *know*. I don't."

"Exactly," said the Inspector. "Only in this case, to be brutally frank with you, I'm supposed to know and I don't. This Mr. Hardy, for example, how does your intuition react to him? Is he in the same class, sir, as Cæsar's wife?"

"At the top of the class!" said the Vicar emphatically. "I've met that young man on countless occasions and I flatter myself that I've translated his character fairly accurately. Moody, temperamental, perhaps headstrong—but not criminal, Inspector. After all, what had he to gain by Tregarthan's death?"

"The girl," put in the Inspector bluntly.

"Oh, nonsense! Nonsense! You surely don't think that Ruth is the sort of girl who would marry the man who had killed her uncle? A murderer?"

"But if she didn't know?"

"What are the criminal's chances of getting away with a murder?—if you'll excuse the Americanism!"

"Say about one in seven."

"And you think that a highly intelligent young man like Ronald would risk committing a crime with those odds against him? Surely not, Inspector? If he and Ruth were determined to get married at all costs why couldn't they adopt the obvious expedient of running away together? It's been done before, you know. My father did it. Tregarthan was not an insuperable obstacle in their way—merely a temporary irritant, shall we say. Don't you agree?"

"Well, there's something in that," acknowledged the Inspector grudgingly. "On the other hand, there's this young fellow's headstrong nature to take into account. Shell-shocked in the war, wasn't he? Probably kept some of his service equipment. His revolver, say. In an unbalanced moment there was no reason why he shouldn't throw logic to the winds and revert to instinct. Like elopement—it's happened before, you know." The Inspector's grey eyes twinkled. "You agree, sir?"

The Reverend Dodd sighed gustily and nodded.

"I suppose you've as much right to your theory as I have to mine. But I can't help feeling that you're groping up a blind alley in suspecting Ronald Hardy. There's probably a very simple explanation for his apparent disappearance."

The Inspector drew out his note-book and thumbed back a few of the pages.

"You may wonder, sir, why I'm taking you into my confidence like this. I'll tell you. Two heads are better than one. You know these two young people better than I do. But I want you to take a look at that."

And he leaned forward to hand the Vicar his note-book.

"Read it," he added.

The Vicar slid his glasses a little down his nose, and holding the note-book some little distance away, did as the Inspector asked.

The first paragraph was headed "Ruth Tregarthan," and below were appended the following points:

(1) *R.T. had quarrelled with the deceased about an hour before he was found shot. There were violent words. (Mrs. C.'s evidence.) "You've no right to interfere. I'm old enough to do as I please with my own life. It's a matter between him and me."*

(2) *R.T. has no alibi to prove that she was not on the cliff-path at the time when it was estimated (Dr. Pendrill's report) that the deceased was shot.*

(3) *R.T.'s footprints were found on the cliff-path and she does not deny she was there.*

(4) *R.T. on her own evidence says she did not realise anything was amiss when she reached the bottom of the garden. Then why did she* run *into the house after stopping midway along the wall and facing toward the french windows?* ("Ah!" thought the Vicar, "so he's noticed that point, too, has he?")

(5) *Three shots entered the room at widely scattered points. The garden is fifteen feet in length. This argues a poor shot. Probably a woman.*

(6) *Why did R.T. leave the house when she had been expressly ordered by Grouch not to do so? Surely it was to rid herself of incriminating evidence? Possibly the revolver.*

"Well," asked the Inspector, seeing that the Vicar had read to the bottom of the page. "What have you to say to that, sir?"

The Vicar placed the open note-book with deliberate care on the arm of his chair. He pushed his glasses slowly up on to the bridge of his nose with a forefinger. For a moment, so disturbed was he by the Inspector's marshalling of the facts, that he was unable to parry the indictment of Ruth's innocence with a counter-theory of his own. Viewed like that and set out with such damning clarity, he was forced to realise that Ruth was placed in a very precarious and unenviable position. Points 1 and 6 were new to him and he decided to question the Inspector further about these two happenings.

Bigswell, nothing loath, set out in a few concise sentences the evidence of Mrs. Cowper and her husband with regard to Ruth's quarrel at the dinner-table, concluding with his own version of what happened later that evening.

"May I take the first point first and deal with them one by one, Inspector?"

"That's exactly what I hoped you would do, Mr. Dodd. It's always been my principle to invite criticism. Truth doesn't always lie on the surface, eh? A good hammer-and-tongs argument is just what I need at this point in my investigations—so go ahead, sir, please."

"First then," said the Vicar, setting his finger-tips together and lying back in his arm-chair, "this quarrel. I set no store by that as evidence of Miss Tregarthan's guilt. Mind you, Inspector, I'm talking in your idiom now. I'm dealing with the facts of the case only. My intuition theory doesn't enter in—you understand? If Ruth had never before quarrelled with her uncle then, perhaps, this upset at the dinner-table might be more than a matter of coincidence—seeing that Tregarthan was shot an hour or so later. But she *had* quarrelled with her uncle before … frequently. We have the Cowpers' word for that. A verbal upset was quite in the natural order of things, and if Tregarthan had not been found dead that night, then nobody—the Cowpers included—would have considered this particular quarrel strange.

"The second point, of course, is unassailable. Unless any further witness comes forward, who actually heard the three shots fired and thus fixes the *exact* time of Tregarthan's death, and unless a further witness can prove that Ruth was elsewhere at that particular moment, then I grant you she has no cast-iron alibi.

"The third point—well frankly, Inspector, the third point puzzles me. I've no explanation to offer as to why only Ruth's and Mrs. Mullion's footsteps were found on the cliff-path. I can only suppose that the criminal by some ingenious arrangement obliterated his tracks as he went along. I've *read* of it being done. Whether it's practicable or not I can't say. Actually, considering the amount of rainfall, I'm rather wondering if we're not setting too much store by that particular line of investigation. A third set of prints *may* have been washed away. Weak, I admit—but a possible theory perhaps.

"The fourth point is interesting. I noticed the fact last night that Ruth had run into the house after looking in at the window."

"The devil you did!" thought the Inspector.

"But there's nothing really suspicious in her action," went on the Vicar blandly. "After all, it was a wet night. The sitting-room must have looked a veritable oasis of comfort from the cliff-path. Stimulated by the thought of a cheerful fire and a possible reconciliation with her uncle, the girl suddenly hurried on her way, by instinct, as it were.

"Then we come to your fifth point, Inspector—the scattered shots. You may remember that rather catchy ditty of W. S. Gilbert's about making the punishment fit the crime? You do? I thought you might! Well, here I feel I'd like to transpose the line—you're making the evidence fit the crime. You suspect Ruth Tregarthan. Ruth Tregarthan is a woman. The scattered shots suggest that a woman fired the revolver. You make your original suspicion stand on its head so that it *looks* like evidence against Miss Tregarthan. After all, Inspector, an unpractised male shot might be equally inaccurate—particularly if he was in the throes of a great emotional storm. No, really—I'm afraid that line of argument falls to the ground."

"And the last point," demanded the Inspector.

"Curious. Very curious. I'll admit Ruth's story does sound a little thin. On the other hand it does offer a feasible explanation for her action. She was distraught—in an unreasoning frame of mind—and therefore liable to indulge an utterly unreasonable whim. Women are often unreasonable, Inspector. Illogical, too. And here you're dealing with a woman under the stress of a violent shock." The Vicar paused, sat up and gazed at the Inspector with great earnestness through his gold-rimmed glasses. "Have I shaken your faith in the theory that Ruth had some hand in this dreadful event? Or do you still believe her to be the guilty party?"

The Inspector stretched out his legs, elbowed himself upright and stared into the fire.

"I don't know. I don't know what to think. You've fought me fair and square with my own weapons, Mr. Dodd, and I don't mind admitting that there's a great deal in what you say. Now, if it's not taking up too much of your valuable time, sir, would you mind turning over a page in that note-book and having a look at the next paragraph."

The Vicar did so, rather flattered and not a little astonished, that Inspector Bigswell had deigned to discuss the matter with him. Never, even in his most optimistic moments, had he visualised a scene of this nature—himself in one arm-chair, a police officer in another, and between them … a mystery.

If he had not been so appalled by the crime and its consequent effects on Ruth, he would have enjoyed the unprecedented situation.

He resettled his glasses on his nose and began to absorb the contents of the next paragraph. The page was headed "Ronald Hardy," and as before this bald announcement was followed by a number of clearly defined points.

> (1) *R.H. had quarrelled with deceased on the evening of his death. (Mrs. P.'s evidence.)*
>
> (2) *R.H. left Cove Cottage in a great hurry, having left his supper untouched, at about 8.45. (Mrs. P.'s evidence.) Did not say where he was going.*
>
> (3) *R.H. has not been seen since in the vicinity. Probably disappeared after the murder had been committed.*
>
> (4) *R.H. had a revolver. Webley pattern. .45 calibre. Bullets found prove to be of this type. Revolver, recently removed from holster now missing.*
>
> (5) *R.H. has, as far as is known at present, no alibi from 8.45 onward.*
>
> (6) *Known to be temperamental and liable to sudden emotional storms. Shell-shocked in the war.*

Finding that this apparently concluded Inspector Bigswell's indictment of Ronald, the Vicar handed back the note-book.

Seeing that the Inspector was quizzing him with a look of expectant enquiry, he shook his head.

"I'm sorry, Inspector. I'm not prepared to tackle *these* points one by one. For one thing I wasn't present when you cross-examined Mrs. Peewit, and for another, I don't pretend to know Ronald Hardy as intimately as I know Ruth. Points 4 and 6, coupled with point 1, do make the case against him appear rather black. His disappearance, as I said before, may be quite simply accounted for. I suppose you're making enquiries as to his whereabouts?"

"I've been through to headquarters from the 'Ship' where I lunched, and they're broadcasting a description of the young man. Also a description of his car. But by now he may be in the wilds of Scotland or abroad for all we know. Has he ever spoken to you, Mr. Dodd, of any relations or mentioned any particular friends?"

"Never. He always struck me as a somewhat lonely young fellow. Men of an independent and thoughtful nature often are. Beyond the fact that he had a Public-School-Varsity education and fought with the infantry in the war as a 2nd Lieutenant, I really know nothing about his past."

"Well, until we can lay our hands on Mr. Hardy and get a statement as to his movements last night, I don't think we can travel further along that line of enquiry. In the meantime, sir, what about this man, Ned Salter? You know him by reputation, I expect?"

The Vicar chuckled.

"Know him! Dear me—yes! He's one of Boscawen's public institutions. Much as I deplore his inability to discriminate between *meum* and *tuum*, I don't think he's really vicious. His misdeeds are of the minor order—poaching, petty pilfering and so on. But taken all in all I don't think Ned is the true criminal type. He's not subtle or intelligent enough."

The Inspector nodded dismally.

"Much as I imagined," he said. "I think we can dismiss his talk with Tregarthan on the drive as pure coincidence. Still I shall have to see him."

"By the way," went on Bigswell after a brief pause, "you went through Tregarthan's papers, I take it? Did you find anything useful?"

"Nothing, I'm afraid. Except this. I found it behind a drawer in his desk. It was thick with dust."

And he handed the Inspector the little slip of paper, which he had thrust into his waistcoat pocket. The Inspector looked at it in silence, then he folded it up and put it between the leaves of his note-book.

"Umph! Can't expect much from that, I'm afraid. Still if you've no objection I think I'll hang on to it for the present. No stone is too small to be left unturned, Mr. Dodd. We're up against a very tricky problem."

Before the Vicar could make suitable reply, there was the crackle of wheels on the drive and Grouch's helmeted head went by the window.

"Wants me, I expect," said the Inspector, rising. "I told him I should probably be up here." He held out his hand. "Well, very many thanks, Mr. Dodd, for your help and a very interesting chat. You'll attend the inquest, I suppose? I don't think we shall have to call on you as a witness, but it would be as well if you were in court."

"Oh, I'll be there," the Vicar assured him. "There's Ruth—poor child. It's going to be a great ordeal for her. I must do all I can to make things easy." He opened the door. "Good-bye, Inspector. You'll let me know the moment you have anything definite to report? I shan't rest easy in my mind until I know that you've placed both Ruth and Ronald entirely beyond suspicion."

The Inspector, saluted and met by Grouch, who had been shown into the hall, stepped out on to the drive.

"Well?"

"A message has just come through from divisional headquarters, sir. They've traced Mr. Hardy's car."

"Already! That's quick work!" It was only a matter of two hours since he had phoned through to Greystoke from the Constable's cottage, a description of the missing man and the car. "Where was it?"

Grouch grinned.

"A hundred yards from headquarters, sir, in Fenton's Quick Service Garage in Marston Street next to the main-line station. Mr. Hardy left his car there late last night and caught the Paddington express. Chap at the booking-office recognised Hardy from the description you sent. Looks as if he's bolted to London, sir."

The Inspector smiled grimly.

"Looks like it! He *has*! No doubt about it. If a man wants to stage a quick-vanishing trick he invariably heads for London. There's nothing much we can do about it from this end. It's a matter of routine for the Metropolitan crowd now. They may be able to trace his movements after he left Paddington. I think I'd better get on to the Superintendent again and see if he's done anything about it. You may as well shove that bone-shaker of yours in the back seat and come down with me to the village, Grouch."

"Bone-shaker, sir?"

"Yes—that suicidal contraption of yours there!" exclaimed the Inspector, pointing to where Grouch's bicycle was leaning against the wall of the Vicarage.

CHAPTER VIII

WAS IT RONALD HARDY?

AFTER the Inspector's visit the Reverend Dodd drew up his chair at the desk and restarted work on Sunday's sermon. He always roughed out the themes of his "talks," as he preferred to call them, on Tuesday afternoon, and to obviate any vital interruption, the maid always crept in with the tea-tray at four-thirty prompt and slid it silently on to his desk. But somehow, on that particular Tuesday, his inspiration proved stubborn. He courted it in vain. No sooner had he settled down to write a sentence or two, than his thoughts shot away at a tangent and he found himself running over the interview which had just terminated.

The Inspector's collection of data, and above all his perfectly logical suspicions, disturbed him. He had not realised until faced with Bigswell's notes how deeply Ruth was involved in the mystery surrounding her uncle's death. Now that he was alone and no longer forced by sympathy to contest the Inspector's opinions, he began to see that there was something cryptic and peculiar about the girl's behaviour. It was not that he mistrusted his intuition, which urged him that Ruth was innocent, but rather that he felt her actions were prompted by an unfortunate set of circumstances about which she intended to remain reticent. He hadn't the faintest idea what the circumstances were. He was not even certain that his diagnosis of her strange behaviour was correct. He only sensed that Ruth, forced by a difficult situation to adopt subterfuge, was hiding something both from Inspector Bigswell and himself.

That it was a necessary and praiseworthy concealment he did not doubt. Altruism was Ruth's strong point. She had always been the kind of girl to study other people's feelings in advance of her own. A champion of the weak. A shielder of the unwary and the headstrong. Time and again her own loyalty and practical common sense had averted trouble on local committees. Time and again she had shouldered somebody else's blunder and carried it without a murmur, accepting the resultant criticism as all in the day's work. Did this regard for others, or for another, explain away the oddity of her statements and her actions? The Vicar wondered.

He returned with a sigh to his sermon. For twenty minutes, blessed with great fluency, he wrote at breakneck speed and then, once again, his inspiration dried up and the facts of Tregarthan's murder began to revolve like a flock of blackbirds about his head.

The clock struck six. The St. Michael's chimes joined in, the vibrant strokes floating off down the wind. For a long time the Vicar stared at the half-completed sheet of writing before him then, unable to stomach his aridity of thought any longer, he went out into the hall, snatched up his tweed shooting-hat, selected a thick ash stick from the spray in the umbrella-stand and strode off down to the cliff. Dinner was not until seven-thirty. There was ample time for him to take a walk along the cliff-top as far as Towan Cove and return via the main road to the Vicarage.

Soon, leaving Greylings on his right, he struck on to the cliff-path and began to walk at a brisk pace toward the hidden cottages, which dotted the rocky foreshore of the inlet. The air was clear and keen, blowing in with a salt-tang from the leaden sea. A few silver, yellow clouds of incredible brightness stretched along the dark rim of the seaward horizon, splintered with a few misty rays of the lowering sun. A steamer was ploughing along about a couple of miles from the land, with a tattered smudge of smoke clinging about her funnel. Overhead the gulls cried mournfully or circled down to brush their breasts against the surface of the water, lifting and bobbing on the creamy swell like white corks. It was a scene, deep and tranquil, far removed from the ominous and ugly atmosphere which shrouded the grey house standing out on the blunt ness behind him.

Yet it was about Greylings that his thoughts, clarified by the brisk exercise, hovered. He could not rid himself of that insistent question—a question, no doubt, that the whole of Boscawen was asking itself—who had murdered Tregarthan?

Not Ruth. Oh most certainly not Ruth! Then who? Ronald Hardy? And if Ronald—why?

Here again the accumulated evidence collected by the indefatigable Digswell did indeed make the case against the young man look extremely black. Suppose Ronald, madly in love with Ruth and determined to marry her, had found in Tregarthan an unmovable opposition? Unmovable, that was, without resorting to the terrible expedient of murder. Was it possible that a man of Ronald's intelligence and character would descend to such inhuman means to gain his ends? And why should Tregarthan have such a vital say in their affairs? Ruth was twenty-five and Ronald at least seven years older. There was nothing to prevent them from taking matters into their own hands. As far as he knew Ronald had a small private income plus the money accruing from his writings, whilst Ruth, doubtless, had had an annuity settled upon her by her father. So it could not be money which stood in the way. And if not money, then what? Had Tregarthan some pull over Ronald Hardy? Had he possessed an unsavoury secret concerning the man's past and threatened to divulge it unless Ronald left his niece alone? Or perhaps Tregarthan knew of an hereditary taint in the Hardy family, of which Ruth herself was ignorant. From all accounts, whatever the reason, Tregarthan had seemed violently opposed to the match. It could not be through reasons of sentiment because it was well-known in Boscawen that Ruth and her uncle did not get on well together. Then why was Tregarthan so emphatic in his opposition?

Apart from that, suppose Ronald Hardy, in the throes of an emotional storm, *did* murder Tregarthan—surely when he returned to a more normal frame of mind he would recognise the hideousness of his action and brave the consequences? He was no coward. His war service was indicative of that. He had been twice mentioned in dispatches. Moreover his character was fine and sensitive, founded on an almost fanatical sense of honesty and forthrightness. He could not hope if he had murdered Tregarthan to continue his friendship with Ruth, and even if the crime was never levelled against him, was he the type to delude himself that marital happiness could be culled from a life of lies and concealment? It was fantastic. The young man was no fool. Ruth was no fool. Sooner or later that sort of spurious paradise would collapse like a house of cards about his head.

Yet he *had* disappeared. He had gone off suddenly, leaving no clue as to his present whereabouts, the very night that

Tregarthan had been found shot. Was it possible—the Vicar was horrified by the very suggestion of such a thought—that Ruth had killed her uncle and Ronald was trying to shield her by drawing suspicion on himself? Such things had happened before in the annals of crime. But Ruth? Ruth? That child?

The Vicar hated himself for advancing such an abominable theory. It was absurd. Unthinkable! For a long time he stood pondering, staring out over the darkening Atlantic.

Then what if the boot was on the other foot? What if Ronald had killed Tregarthan and Ruth, with full knowledge of the fact, was trying to shield Ronald? Terrible as the idea seemed it was certainly more acceptable than the other theory. Had Ruth by some means or other obliterated Ronald's tracks on the cliff-path and then, aware that her uncle might still be alive, rushed straight into the sitting-room, hoping against hope that it was not too late. She had snatched the revolver from Ronald, perhaps, hidden it in her mackintosh pocket, smuggled it up into her bedroom, and later that night slipped out of the house and thrown the revolver into the sea. That would account for her strange and apparently stealthy exit from the house. And the shots were scattered because Ronald, in the grip of a mental maelstrom, scarcely knew what he was doing. It would account for the revolver which, according to the Inspector, was missing from its holster in Ronald's desk. Yes—that theory would account for many things. But was it the truth? Was it really possible? Ronald-Ruth in collaboration?

Again the Vicar shied away from his explanation. It was, he realised, as full of holes as a cane-chair. Ruth had influence over Ronald. She was a level-headed, practical girl. She could not have connived with Ronald in planning such a dastardly crime, no matter how strong the motive which prompted the initial thought. Something was wrong somewhere. There was a link missing in the chain. There was some dark gulf which needed bridging. But could he, where so far the Inspector had failed, bridge it?

Let him adopt his intuition theory. Where was he then? His intuition forced him to believe that Ruth and Ronald were innocent. That left Ned Salter—the village Bad Man, the black sheep of his flock. He knew there had been trouble between Ned and Tregarthan over the Salters' evacuation of Rose Cottage. Tregarthan had imprisoned the man for poaching and then, because Salter's wife could not pay the rent, thrown the Salter family, at a moment's notice, out of the cottage. He himself had thought Tregarthan's action, to say the least of it, unpardonable. It was a cruel and unsportsmanlike trick—like kicking a man when he was already down and out. Salter, according to village gossip, had always sworn to get even with Tregarthan. Was this his way of doing so? But if Salter *had* murdered Tregarthan it argued a brilliantly planned and executed scheme, for as far as had come to light the man hadn't left a single clue behind him. Suspicion rested on Salter mainly because he *was* Salter. And because Salter *was* Salter, it seemed incredible that the man could have foreseen all the possible traps which might trip him up and commit, what might be called, the immaculate murder. The poacher had no subtlety—witness his numerous convictions before the Bench. For the most part he had found himself before the magistrates through the exercise of a profound and deep-rooted stupidity. The man was a fool, a born fool.

It was inconceivable that he had suddenly shed his fooldom, as a man sheds his overcoat, and emerged as a cool-headed and scientific criminal.

And Ned Salter was the last on the Inspector's "little list."

The Vicar, with a deep sigh of bewilderment, acknowledged himself defeated. There had been mysteries, more glamorous, more terrifying, more macabre than this in the stories which he had devoured so avidly, but none, he felt, so stubborn in yielding up its solution.

Darkness had fallen and it struck the Reverend Dodd, as he dipped down into the cove, that the mystery of Tregarthan's death was rather like the encroaching night. Here and there little gleams of light still shone out weakly, but even as one looked at them they slowly vanished, and the obscurity thickened until the landscape was of a uniform blackness.

A few lights showed as orange squares in the windows of the half-dozen cottages which dotted the lonely cove. Most of the property belonged, as the Vicar knew, to Tregarthan. Their obvious dilapidation did not speak well of the landlord—here and there stones were missing from chimney-stacks, garden walls were crumbling away and one or two broken windows were stuffed with sacking to keep out the winds. The Vicar wondered if he would call in on Mrs. Withers and see how the twins were getting along, but realising that his unheralded arrival at this hour of the day might cause a domestic panic, he passed her cottage on the left and descended by means of a rocky path to the foreshore.

A lantern was bobbing about on a natural slipway formed by a huge slab of granite, and the Vicar could make out the dim shadow of a man, crouching over a boat. As he approached the man, in rubber waders and a blue seaman's jersey, looked up. His hand went automatically to his forelock.

"Evening, Burdon," said the Vicar affably. "Baiting your lines?"

He noticed a tin full of clams which emitted a pale, phosphorescent radiance and a line barbed with a number of hooks, coiled in the bottom of the boat.

"Aye, sir," said Burdon. "Will you be coming out with me one evening? You've always said as you'd like to."

"Some time, Burdon—when I can spare the time. Fish been behaving themselves?"

The man, a gaunt, rather dour-faced fellow of abnormal height, lifted his shoulders.

"Weather's been against me," he grunted. "I've not been out for the past ten days. Lucky that I'm not like some of 'em, sir, depending on this for my living."

Burdon was a quarryman in the slate quarries on the far side of the cove. Towan Cove owed its existence, in fact, to the proximity of these quarries.

The Vicar nodded and wishing the man a good catch, he turned on his heel and started to climb the rough track which linked the cottages with the main road.

Once more alone his thoughts returned to the problem of Tregarthan's death. He dallied with the idea of questioning Ruth point-blank about her peculiar behaviour, in the hope that she might confide in him. Then, if the matter was one which could be put right by tactful explanation, he could see the Inspector and clear Ruth's name of suspicion. This, he finally decided, would be a sensible plan. He determined to have a few minutes alone with her after dinner that evening.

This, after explaining things to his sister, he managed to do without Ruth realising that this *tête-à-tête* had been deliberately engineered. Ethel, who was engaged in the sisterly occupation of darning the Vicar's socks, suddenly remembered that she had left her needles in the bedroom. Ruth and the Vicar were left alone in the study.

For a few moments the Vicar talked all round the subject of Tregarthan's death and then mentioned the Coroner's inquest.

"It will be an ordeal for you, I know, my dear child, but in a case like this an inquest is a mere formality. The Inspector intends to call a number of witnesses, but I doubt if the Coroner will wish to ask them many questions. The collected evidence is so conflicting. Curiously so."

"I know," said Ruth. "I can't begin to see the end of this dreadful affair. It's all so beastly! So sordid! I wish the mystery of uncle's death could be cleared up and done with—I want to forget it all. It's beginning to prey on my mind. I dream of it at night. I think about it all day. I can't help it!"

After a little pause, the Vicar said with great seriousness.

"You know, Ruth, I'm very worried about your reticence in this matter. I quite realise that you don't wish to talk about it, but I think I ought to tell you that Inspector Bigswell was up here this afternoon questioning me about Ronald."

Ruth glanced up quickly.

"Ronald! But what has Ronald to do with my uncle's death? He was down in the village at the time when my uncle must have been killed."

"No, my dear. I'm afraid he wasn't. That's just the trouble. The Inspector has found out that Ronald left Cove Cottage just before the estimated time of your uncle's death, and he's not been seen since. He's disappeared."

"Disappeared!"

"Nobody knows where he has gone to. He's just vanished into the blue, leaving no address. I'm afraid it's an unfortunate coincidence that he should disappear just at this moment, because it means that the police are naturally suspicious of his action."

"You mean they think he murdered uncle and then disappeared to avoid the consequences? But it's absurd! It's ridiculous! They can't think that of Ronald!"

"But they do." Suddenly the Vicar leaned forward and said with great earnestness. "My dear, do you know where he's gone? Do you know anything about his movements last night? Are you hiding anything from the police because you fear for Ronald's safety? You *must* tell me if this is so—concealment is out of the question. Truth and truth alone is the great essential at the moment. You may damage Ronald's case by holding back information. They're sure to trace his whereabouts in the end. It's only a matter of days, perhaps hours. So if you are hiding anything you must tell me, dear … for Ronald's sake."

"But I'm not! I'm not!" declared Ruth in a tortured voice. "It's impossible that Ronald has done this thing. The Inspector has no right, no reason to suspect him. Oh, I know he's got to make out a case against somebody, but it's absurd trying to incriminate Ronald!"

"But it's not only Ronald whom he suspects," went on the Vicar in a quiet voice. "As much as I hate to put such an idea into words, my dear, he suspects you." The Vicar, on seeing Ruth's look of mingled resentment and amazement, went on hurriedly. "Oh, I know it's nonsense! I told the Inspector so. We know, of course, that you had nothing to do with this terrible thing, but somehow we've got to persuade the Inspector to take the same view. Why did you leave Greylings last night when the Constable had given you strict orders not to do so? Don't you think, my dear, that it was a rather foolhardy action?"

"But I told the Inspector—I wanted to get clear of the house and breathe. I couldn't stand the atmosphere a moment longer. It was stifling me."

"And there was no other reason?"

Ruth glanced at the Vicar and looked down guiltily at the fire.

"What do you mean?"

"You weren't attempting to get in touch with Ronald, for instance? To warn him about something?"

"But I swear to you," cried Ruth, "that I did not see Ronald at all last night. I went along to his cottage, but he had gone out. I haven't seen him since. I'd no idea that he had disappeared until you told me a few minutes ago."

The Vicar sighed. He realised that Ruth could or would not help him to clarify the events of the previous night.

"Why did you suddenly stop on the path, look in at the sitting-room and then run into the house?" asked the Vicar. "You didn't know then that your uncle was dead."

"How do you know——?"

"Oh, I know, my dear. I used these eyes which God has been kind enough to grant me. But why did you do that?"

"I—I wanted to get in out of the rain," said Ruth glibly. "I saw the fire-light and the lamps burning and suddenly realised how wet I was. So I naturally ran the rest of the way. There was nothing odd about that, was there?"

"Nothing at all," agreed the Vicar with haste. "I merely asked you the question, my dear, because I wanted to know."

"It seems that everybody wants to ask me questions," said Ruth with a long sigh. "First Grouch, then the Inspector, now you. Shall I ever be able to forget this horrible nightmare?"

The Vicar rose, and, sitting on the arm of Ruth's chair, he took her hand.

"My dear child," he said. "You may be sure that I should not ask these questions unless I thought them essential. I want to find out things, analyse all the evidence, use my imagination, seek and find out. From now on I'm determined not to rest until I've persuaded the Inspector that you and Ronald have absolutely nothing to do with this dastardly crime. And having done that, I want to be in a position to tell him exactly who did have something to do with it."

"You've found out something?" asked Ruth with intense anxiety.

The Vicar shook his head.

"So far I've found out nothing. I know far less about the facts of this case than Inspector Bigswell. But you see, I have a method. I call it the intuition method of investigation— which may prove in the long run to be a very present help in a time of trouble. Shall we leave it at that, Ruth?"

CHAPTER IX

COLLABORATION?

INSPECTOR BIGSWELL after having put through his call to the Superintendent at Greystoke decided not to remain in Boscawen, as he had originally planned, to cross-examine Mrs. Mullion when she returned from Porth. In all probability the midwife had had an unadventurous journey back from Towan Cove, certainly an uncomfortable one. It was no easy matter to walk with one heel missing. If she had anything of importance to tell she would, thought the Inspector, have imparted it to Grouch before setting off for Porth that morning. It seemed certain, considering the swiftness with which the news of Tregarthan's murder had travelled, that she could not have left Boscawen ignorant of his death. Time enough to question her on the morrow, Wednesday, since the inquest was not until the day after. He left instructions, therefore, with Grouch, that he was to cycle up to her cottage later on and arrange for Mrs. Mullion to meet him at the Constable's office early next morning.

Grimmet then drove the Inspector back to Greylings, where a sprinkling of morbid sightseers was hanging about the drive entrance and the surrounding common. He found the burly Constable in charge, besieged by a couple of avid reporters, and after helping them out with a few guarded details of the affair, he arranged for the Constable to stay the night. He warned him not to let anybody into the house and to keep his mouth shut if questioned by any enterprising journalists. Then with a word to Grimmet to "step on it," he was speeded back, thinking hard, to Greystoke.

On arrival he learnt that the Superintendent wanted to see him without delay. He went through at once to the office. The Superintendent, a bullet-headed, grey-haired man of about fifty, was sitting at his desk writing. When the Inspector entered he looked up, nodded, pushed away his work and motioned Bigswell into a chair.

"Look here, Bigswell," he said without preliminary, "I'd better tell you straight that the Chief is getting a bit rattled over this business. I know you're not expected to get results in a day, but for heaven's sake, man, if you've got the first glimmerings of a theory, then trot it out. We don't want to bring the Yard into this. You know the Chief's motto—'Give 'em a chance and they'll take two.' And them, in this case, means you and me and the rest of the crowd here. You know as well as I do that if you've got no definite line of investigation to work on, it means letting in the experts."

Inspector Bigswell grinned.

"I like that, sir. The experts!"

"Well, that's what it amounts to. Criminal investigation is, in a manner of speaking, a sideline for the County Police. You know that. There's enough routine work to keep us busy, without sparing a man for any fancy business. See what I'm getting at?"

"You mean that the Chief will have to call in the Yard unless I can prove to him that I'm following up a definite line of enquiry?"

"Bluntly—that's what it amounts to. Well, what about it, Bigswell—any theory?"

For a moment the Inspector hesitated, then taking a deep breath he pulled out his note-book and flipped it open.

"Yes—I think I've got a really workable theory at last. You're acquainted with the main facts of the case, aren't you, sir?"

"I read your report of last night," said the Superintendent, slowly filling his pipe. "And I suppose your phone call this afternoon more or less posted me up to date with regard to to-day's investigations?"

"That's it, sir. Well, I've been doing some pretty stiff thinking on my way back from Boscawen and, as I see it now, the facts of the case are something like this. Ruth Tregarthan and Ronald Hardy were in collaboration. They had been planning this murder for some time, deliberately and efficiently. Tregarthan was violently opposed to their friendship. What hold he had over them, I can't as yet fathom. It may be that he knew something about Hardy's past life, something disreputable, and threatened to divulge this if they took matters into their own hands and ran away. As to the reason why he was so violent in his opposition to the girl's marriage—well that to me is pretty obvious. Money. Some arrangement, I dare say, in which the girl was to come into a packet of her father's money when she married, but which Tregarthan had a free hand with until she did. You see how I mean, sir? Now, as I see it, the murder was fixed for last night. Hardy was to creep along the cliff-path at the scheduled time and the girl was to absent herself while the business was being done. This would obviate any risk of her being tripped up if any awkward questions were asked. As luck would have it, Tregarthan quarrelled with her at dinner that evening—she seized the opportunity and dashed out, using the quarrel as her excuse. You see, sir, there was that storm. It would have looked a bit odd if she'd gone out in the middle of it. She may even have provoked her uncle to quarrel, to make her exit look more natural. That's as maybe. Well, now we come to the puzzle of the footprints. The three tracks. The girl's going both ways and Mrs. Mullion's going from Towan Cove to Boscawen. I confess I was puzzled at first. I didn't quite see how Hardy entered into the scheme of things, seeing that he couldn't have walked along the cliff-path without leaving some impression behind him. Yet as soon as I heard he'd disappeared, I felt certain that he'd had a hand in Tregarthan's murder." The Inspector paused and added with a deceiving air of nonchalance. "Well, sir, I think I've cleared that little difficulty away."

It was obvious that he really felt rather pleased with himself over the solving of what, at first sight, seemed an insoluble puzzle. The Superintendent puffed vigorously at his pipe.

"Well, go on, Bigswell," he said eagerly. "Let's have it!"

"It was Grouch—the local Constable, by the way—who first put the idea into my head. He'd railed off the cliff-path at the bottom of the garden with a couple of hurdles. Sensible chap, Grouch. I saw, at once, where he'd got them from—there was a pile of about half a dozen leaning against the garden wall. At the time I didn't think anything of it. But later, on my way back here in fact, I realised that in that innocent-looking pile of hurdles lay the solution to the mystery of the footprints! You take me, sir?"

The Superintendent refused to commit himself.

"Go ahead, Bigswell."

"Well, sir—it struck me that Ruth Tregarthan, on leaving the house by the side-door, went along the path at the bottom of the garden until she came to the pile of hurdles leaning against the north wall. That's the wall on the Boscawen side of the garden. All she had to do then was to place the hurdles on end to cover the soft patch of mud which borders the north track for a distance of about fifteen feet. These hurdles— wattled ones, by the way—are about six foot long. She had then formed a perfect track between the wall and the firmer, unspoiled grass of the common. She then goes back and picks up her track at the corner of the wall and starts off along the cliff-path to let Hardy know that the stage is set."

"You think it was her idea—those hurdles?" asked the Superintendent dubiously.

"No—his. He'd seen a few duck-boards in his time, I daresay. He probably arranged for the girl to have them planted by the wall for some reason or other and given her proper instructions as to what she was to do."

"I see. Go on."

"Well, now I come to something which I don't quite understand. Why did Hardy use his car? It looked as if he'd decided on his vanishing trick at the last moment, doesn't it? Actually he'd arranged to meet the girl on the cliff-path and get the O.K. from her about the hurdles. Then on account of last-minute wind-up he took out his car, so as to make a quick get-away, and approached Greylings by the road. That's how he missed the girl. Gave her a bit of a shock, I daresay, when she reached Cove Cottage and found he'd gone. Daresay she wondered if things had gone a trifle crooked at the critical moment. You'll notice she didn't wait long at his cottage. When, after a few minutes, he didn't turn up, she hurried off along the cliff-path to get those hurdles back into position. Natural, wasn't it?"

The Superintendent agreed.

"That's all very well, but from what I hear about the three shots, they must have been fired from the cliff-path. There were no hurdles on the path, remember."

"Tregarthan wasn't shot from the path," said the Inspector emphatically. "He was shot from the wall. Hardy got to the wall over the hurdles, probably in his stockinged feet, climbed along the wall, threw the gravel—supplied by the girl—against the window and fired the three shots. Simple, eh? He then went back the way he'd come, put on his boots, cut up over the common to the road, where his car was parked, hopped in and drove hell-for-leather to Fenton's garage."

"And the girl?"

"Returned along the cliff-path. Walked out along the hurdles. Picked 'em up one by one and stacked 'em against the wall. Found her returning track and continued along the cliff-path to the side-door. More than that, sir—you'll remember that I noticed she'd stopped, looked in at the window and then *run* to the side-door?"

"Yes."

"Well, if she knew nothing about the crime, why did she *suddenly* run like that? Answer—because she did know about the crime. She did know that the deed was a ... a ..."

"A *fait accompli*," suggested the Superintendent.

"That's the idea, sir. And the reason she knew it was a ... a ... what you've just said, sir, was because the curtains of the sitting-room were undrawn! She may even have noticed the shot-stars in the glass if she'd been expecting them." The Inspector stretched himself, picked up his notebook and stuck it back in his pocket. "Well, sir, that's my theory. It all seems to fit in pretty well, doesn't it? It doesn't leave much to be explained."

"No. It all sounds pretty conclusive, Bigswell. Looks like a smart piece of deduction," agreed the Superintendent. "There's just one thing—what about the girl's little escapade *after* the murder?"

"You mean why did she sneak out of the house, sir? Yes, I'm glad you've asked that. I couldn't quite fit that in at first. It puzzled me no end. Of course, the obvious explanation was that she had an incriminating bit of evidence that she wanted to get rid of. But what? The revolver? I couldn't quite see why Hardy should leave his revolver lying about, when he could have easily tossed it over the cliff into deep water. But then it struck me—he *didn't* intend to leave it lying about. It was an accident. Suppose it had slipped out of his hand and fallen on to the cliff-path? What then? He was in a fix, eh? He couldn't reach it from the wall. He daren't walk along the path to pick it up. He daren't stay there a second after the murder had been committed for fear that anybody had heard the shots. He knew the girl was scheduled to come back along the cliff-path to pick up the hurdles, so he left the revolver where it was. She came along. Saw it. Picked it up. Hid it in her mackintosh pocket, smuggled it into her bedroom and later threw it into the sea. You see how it all fits in, sir? I don't think we shall have to call in the experts this time. After all, it would look bad for us if we fetched the Yard men down here under false pretences. To my mind when we can lay our hands on Ronald Hardy we've got the murderer of Julius Tregarthan!"

"And the girl?"

"Well, sir, what do *you* think?" asked the Inspector tactfully. "I suppose we might say that I've made out a strong enough case against her sufficient to warrant her arrest on suspicion. But I've an idea that it would be better to hold back for a while."

The Superintendent agreed.

"Far better. Your hypothesis may be sound, but it's not cast-iron. We can't afford to make a mistake. Besides, if the girl is safe in Boscawen there's always the chance that Hardy may give us a line on his whereabouts by trying to get in touch with her. You never know. The intelligent type of criminal so often commits the most obvious and elementary blunders. The girl's at the Vicarage, you say?"

The Inspector nodded.

"What about the post? Still delivered at Greylings?"

"Probably. But I can find out."

"Do. Make a note if any suspicious-looking document turns up. The postmark may enable us to narrow the search. No detail's too small to be neglected, Bigswell. Mind you, he's probably read the papers by now and knows that he's wanted in connection with the murder. His photo will be in all the later editions of the evening papers to-night. Still, there's just a chance that he may take the risk and let the girl know where he is. He'll guess she's worried. Particularly as they didn't meet according to arrangement last night."

"And the Chief?" asked the Inspector anxiously.

"Oh, I'll square him," grinned the Superintendent affably. "After all, your theory does seem to hold water. He can't deny *that*. Looks to me as if it's a mere case of routine work now—a thorough comb-out of the metropolitan area by the London police—bless 'em! I think you can congratulate yourself, Bigswell, on a pretty slick bit of work."

The Inspector left the Superintendent's office with a somewhat lighter heart than when he had entered it. He had propounded his theory in the nick of time. If he had not evolved his line of enquiry on his way back from Boscawen that evening, by now the Chief would have, doubtless, been through to Scotland Yard, arranging for a couple of experts to be put on the case.

Outside the Police Station he dismissed Grimmet, who was waiting with the car, and turning left along Marston Street he made his way to Fenton's Quick Service Garage.

Fenton himself, in greasy dungarees, with a cigarette-stub behind his ear, hurried up as the Inspector entered the garage. Fenton and Bigswell were old friends, for since the car had entered more and more into criminal activities, police and garage-owners were in constant touch with each other. Over Fenton's desk in the little glass-windowed cubby-hole which served as his office, there was more often than not pinned a list, giving the numbers of "wanted" cars.

"Evening, Inspector. Come about the car in the Tregarthan murder case, eh?" asked Fenton in what he considered a voice of official secrecy. "Gave me a bit of a jolt, I can tell you, when I knew we'd had that chap in here. It's this way," he added in an undertone. "Nothing's been meddled with."

It was obvious that the garage-proprietor was considerably impressed and excited to be connected, even in a remote way, with a sensation which had flung black headlines across the evening Press.

He guided the Inspector through a maze of dismantled cars, engine parts, tools and empty petrol cans, to where a sliding door gave on to a smaller garage behind the general workshop. Only a few cars were in—a sleek, high-chassised

Daimler, a Trojan van, a couple of baby Austins and in the far corner a mud-spattered, rather sorry-looking Morris, with a dilapidated hood and a rust-spotted radiator.

"Hardly a beauty, is she?" said Fenton. "Seen better days, I should say. It's a marvel to me how these old cars stand up to it. You can't wear 'em out. Bad look-out for us, you know."

The Inspector agreed, but it was obvious that he was not paying any attention to Fenton's rigmarole. His practised eyes were straying over the car, above which burnt a single, naked bulb. The hood, torn in two places, was still raised and a little pool of water had gathered in a fold at the top. The mudguards and bonnet-sides were thick with splashes and the wheels themselves encrusted with dried mud. It was obvious that the car had been driven at a reckless speed along the Boscawen–Greystoke road.

With methodical precision the Inspector went through the pockets, looked under the seats, searched the tool-box, even probed the upholstery in the hope of unearthing some clue which would verify his lately expounded theory. But he drew a blank. All the usual clutter which succeeds in finding its way into the nooks and crannies of a car—maps, spare plugs, rags, old gloves, pocket-torch and a couple of A.A. books—but beyond that, nothing which might be of any use in elucidating his ideas. He then, with equal precision, examined the outside of the car. But there again he found nothing unusual—even the licence was in order. As he concluded his examination, during which Fenton had stood by in respectful silence, the Inspector pointed to the spare wheel.

"What d'you make of that, Fenton?" he asked. "Careless chap, eh?"

Fenton took a closer look at the worn tread of the tyre and whistled.

"Some burst! Bet that caused him a moment's panic! These old high-pressure tyres are the very devil when a front-wheel blows off. Can't quite see the point of him travelling with a wheel like that though, Inspector, it's not the slightest use to him if one of the other tyres goes. He ought to have had it replaced."

"Exactly," said the Inspector. "As I remarked—a careless chap." Adding as they walked toward the door of the main garage, "Can we go into your office a minute, Fenton? There are one or two questions I want to ask you. Nothing sensational. The usual formal stuff about identification. We can? Good! Then lead on."

And with the taking of Fenton's evidence the Inspector decided to bring his day's work to a close. He was well satisfied as to the progress of his investigations. The mists were slowly clearing. In a couple of days the arrests might be made. Yes—as the Superintendent had said—he had every reason to congratulate himself. Damn the experts!

CHAPTER X

THE SINGLE SHOT

ON Wednesday morning Inspector Bigswell looked out of his bedroom window to find a thick sea-mist enveloping the town. It was chill and damp and miserable, and this meteorological development threatened to be a hampering factor in the day's investigations.

Nevertheless, after an early breakfast, he set off briskly for headquarters, where Grimmet had been ordered to have the car in readiness. The chauffeur seemed a trifle dubious about the Boscawen journey, and put forward a tentative suggestion that they might wait for a time to see if the mist thinned. But the Inspector wouldn't hear of it. After the Superintendent's somewhat favourable reception of his theory he felt keen and eager to push his investigations to a definite conclusion. He was scheduled to meet Mrs. Mullion at half-past nine at Grouch's office, and he had an idea that she might possibly have seen or heard something on the Monday night. She must have passed Greylings within fifteen minutes either side of the estimated time of the murder. She might have heard the shots fired. It seemed almost certain that she *must* have heard them fired if she had left Towan Cove before the murder was committed. And as far as he could see, the woman would scarcely have passed by the bottom of the garden without noticing the figures in the uncurtained window. If she had passed after Grouch arrived on the scene, she must have guessed something was the matter. But so far she had not come forward. It was curious. The only explanation was that she knew nothing, so far, of Tregarthan's death.

The car crawled through the almost deserted streets of the town and nosed its cautious way onto the Boscawen road. At a higher level the bleak moorland was almost destitute of mist and Grimmet, taking advantage of a clear stretch, sent the speedometer up to fifty and held it there. Nearing the coast, however, the visibility grew gradually worse and it was at a snail's pace that the car ground down the final hill in second-gear.

Grouch, like a sensible man, had come out on foot to meet the Inspector and it was the flashing of his pocket-torch which first reassured Bigswell that they had arrived at the outskirts of the village. Guided by Grouch, who rode on the running-board, the car at length drew up outside the Constable's office.

Inside the office, a barely furnished room with a high desk and a stool, a cheerful fire was crackling in the grate. The Inspector threw off his cloak and got down to business without delay.

"Well, did you arrange with Mrs. Mullion last night, Grouch?"

"Yes, sir." The Constable glanced up at the plain-faced clock on the varnished wall. "She should be along at any minute now. She's got something to tell us, I think. Something pretty lively, sir. It was all I could do to prevent her from making a statement last night. But I pointed out that she may as well save her breath to cool her porridge because she'd have to repeat it all to you this morning."

"If it was important," said the Inspector testily, "then why the devil didn't she come forward before she set out for Porth yesterday morning?"

"She hadn't heard the news then. First she knew of the murder, sir, was when she came home last night. Seemed properly upset."

There was a scrunching on the gritty road outside, followed by a timid knock on the door.

The Inspector nodded toward the inner room.

"You and Grimmet had better slip in there and read up the case in the daily papers. You may learn something you didn't know!"

As his grinning subordinates went into the Constable's parlour the Inspector opened the outer door and admitted the midwife.

"Mrs. Mullion?" he enquired.

"That's right, sir. The Constable said that you wanted to see me about this dreadful happening up at poor Mr. Tregarthan's."

"Quite right, Mrs. Mullion. Come in and take a chair by the fire."

He hoisted himself onto the high stool.

"I thought perhaps you might be able to help us with our enquiries, Mrs. Mullion. I understand from Doctor Pendrill that you were attending a case on Monday night over at Towan Cove. You returned to Boscawen by the cliff-path, didn't you?"

"Yes, sir. It's a short cut between the two coves, and I started home rather later than I intended."

"Have you any idea what time it was when you left—let's see—" he consulted his note-book, "Mrs. Wither's cottage at Towan Cove?"

"About nine o'clock or thereabouts, sir."

"You're more or less certain about the time?"

"Within five minutes one way or the other I am. I remember looking at the clock at ten to nine and I left the cottage shortly after, sir."

"You came straight along the cliff-path, I suppose?"

"Yes, sir, as fast as I could. The storm was still hanging about and it was pitch-dark so I had to be careful. Besides, a heel had come off my shoe getting out of the Doctor's car earlier in the evening. It didn't make walking any the easier."

"You had a pocket-torch?"

"A lantern, sir. But when I was half-way along the cliff between Towan Cove and Mr. Tregarthan's house the wind blew the candle out. Mr. Withers had lit the lantern for me before I left his cottage and I hadn't any matches. Luckily, after I'd been walking for about ten minutes, the last of the storm blew over and the moon came out."

"How near were you to Greylings then, Mrs. Mullion? Could you see the house?"

"I could see a light coming from a lower window—but I couldn't see much else, sir."

"And you don't think anybody, say, standing in the garden of the house, could have seen you?"

"No, sir, I'm certain they couldn't. As a matter of fact it wasn't until I was within a stone's-throw of the garden myself that I noticed Miss Ruth."

"Miss Ruth Tregarthan!" exclaimed the Inspector. "You're quite certain about that?"

"Positive. She was standing on the cliff-path at the bottom of the garden and the light from the window was shining straight onto her face."

"Did she see you?"

"No, sir—she didn't. There's a clump of furze bushes just beside the path before you come to the garden wall, and when I saw what she had in her hand, I was so surprised that I stopped dead and sort of drew back into the shadow of the bushes."

"Something in her hand?" The Inspector had the greatest difficulty in concealing his excitement and elation. "What exactly do you mean by that, Mrs. Mullion?"

"A revolver, sir. She was turning it over in her hand and looking at it."

The Inspector's elation increased. Mrs. Mullion's evidence, if it was accurate—and there was little reason to doubt the truth of her statement—fitted in perfectly with his theory. This was exactly what he had expected. Ronald Hardy had dropped the revolver on the cliff-path and the girl had picked it up.

"She had it in her hand you say? You didn't by any chance see if she had picked it up off the path?"

"She might have done," acknowledged Mrs. Mullion. "But when I first noticed her she had it in her hand. I can tell you, Sergeant"—the Inspector smiled—"it gave me quite a turn when I saw what it was!"

"What happened then, Mrs. Mullion?"

"Well, Miss Ruth had a quick look round, sort of frightened like, and ran round the corner of the wall and let herself into the house by the side door."

The Inspector nodded. The little bits were dovetailing together with commendable neatness. He was growing more and more certain in his mind that Ronald Hardy had killed

Tregarthan, and that Ruth Tregarthan was his accomplice in the crime. Mrs. Mullion's evidence seemed to exclude, finally, the supposition that Ruth Tregarthan was innocent of any complicity. If she were innocent, then why hadn't she come forward at once with information about her discovery of the revolver on the cliff-path? She must have realised that it was the weapon which had discharged the fatal shots and yet she had said nothing about it. It was possible, of course, that she recognised it as Ronald Hardy's revolver and, without having anything to do with the crime herself, had decided to conceal the weapon to shield him from suspicion. Foolish, without a doubt. Dangerous, too. But there it was—a woman in love was always a foolhardy and unreasonable creature, though not devoid, as the Inspector realised, of a certain inspired cunning.

He felt that it was imperative, considering how much depended on the midwife's evidence, to make sure that she had not been mistaken.

"I must warn you, Mrs. Mullion, to be very, very careful on this point," he said with deliberate solemnity. "You were quite sure *at the time* that it was a revolver? What I am getting at is this—last night when you returned from Porth you learnt for the first time that Mr. Tregarthan, whilst standing in the sitting-room window, had been shot through the head. On Monday night you saw Miss Tregarthan standing on the cliff-path with something in her hand. Now I want your assurance that the suggestion that this object *might* be a revolver didn't occur to you *after* you knew Mr. Tregarthan had been murdered. The association of ideas, you see?"

Mrs. Mullion's reply was blunt and emphatic.

"No, sir. I knew it was a revolver at once, long before I knew anything about this awful tragedy up at Greylings. I'll swear to that."

"Well, Mrs. Mullion," went on the Inspector after a moment's silence, "what you've told me is of the utmost importance. I must ask you to keep this information to yourself. I'm afraid it means you'll receive an official summons to attend the inquest to-morrow. I'm very glad that you've seen fit to come forward and I don't think I need trouble you any further." As Mrs. Mullion rose from her seat at the fire, the Inspector added: "Oh, just one other point. When you were coming along the cliff from Towan Cove, did you hear any unusual sounds—any revolver shots, for example?"

"No, sir. I heard nothing—except the thunder. There were one or two very loud cracks right over my head just after I'd left the cove—but I didn't hear anything else."

The Inspector got down from the high stool and ushered Mrs. Mullion out of the Constable's office.

He was more than pleased with the result of the interview. It was going to be easier than he had first anticipated to back up his theory with the necessary circumstantial evidence. If only it were possible to ascertain the exact time Tregarthan had been shot, his confidence would have been even greater. But so far nobody seemed to have heard the shots fired. There was, he realised, a feasible explanation of this fact. If the revolver had been discharged—the three shots in rapid succession—at the same moment as a loud burst of thunder, it was more than probable that the reports had been covered by the major explosion. Mrs. Mullion had commented upon the fact that several loud thunder-cracks had greeted her ears when she first left

Towan Cove. According to his estimate one of these thunder-cracks might easily have muffled the revolver shots.

He summoned Grouch and gave him a brief account of Mrs. Mullion's evidence. He also ran over the points of his pet theory with the Constable, who manifested an undisguised admiration for his superior's astuteness.

"There's just one thing, sir. Them hurdles."

"What about them?"

"If they'd been laid flat on the mud, wouldn't they have left an impression on the ground? We didn't notice that on Monday night, did we, sir?"

"The same point occurred to me, Grouch. But remember—they were wattle hurdles and after their removal it rained pretty heavily. The impressions would be shallow in any case and the rain, in my opinion, would soon flatten out any indentations. When Hardy walked over them the weight would be spread, not concentrated as in a footprint. There is one thing, though," added the Inspector after a moment's thought, "there might be mud on the first three or four hurdles in the pile. It's worth satisfying ourselves upon that point. Of course, the rain may have diddled us again, but I think we'll slip up to Greylings now and make sure."

He called for Grimmet, and the three of them got into the car. The mist was still thicker and it was only by the exercise of extreme care and a great deal of patience that they climbed the twisting hill out of Boscawen and thus up on to the open road. Leaving the car on the roadside near the Greylings drive-gate, Grouch and the Inspector walked down the sloping common towards the cliff. The hurdles were still piled against the north wall of the garden.

"What about these?" asked the Inspector, pointing to the hurdles which Grouch had used as barriers to the cliff-path. "You took them off the top of the pile, I suppose?"

"Yes, sir. The first two."

The Inspector went over the wattled surfaces with the greatest care, then returned to the little stack and examined the hurdles one by one. He was disappointed in the result of his search. There was no trace of mud on the wattle-work, nor was there any suggestion of an imprint left on the muddy surface at the corner of the wall. In this particular instance there was, he realised, no direct evidence to back up his theory.

Walking along the cliff-path, however, he came to the point where Ruth Tregarthan had stopped and looked towards the sitting-room window. Crouching low, he made a minute examination of the spot where he estimated Ronald Hardy had dropped the revolver from the wall. This time he gave a grunt of satisfaction and drew the Constable's attention to a curious indent in the soft mud, which Ruth Tregarthan's footprints, by a stroke of luck, had not obliterated.

"Well, Grouch, what d'you make of that?"

"I can't rightly say, sir. It looks as if something heavy's been dropped there. There's a sort of outline."

The Inspector agreed.

"The outline of a revolver, if you ask me! See—there's the curve of the butt. No mistake about that. And this looks like the ribbing of the magazine. I doubt if the barrel would leave much of an impression because the magazine-wheel of a Webley projects a good bit beyond it."

He took out a small, pliable, steel rule and measured up the width and breadth of the impressions, entering the measurements in his note-book. It would be an easy matter to verify his suspicions as to the nature of these impressions later on. If his measurements coincided with those of a Webley, he would be justified in supposing that Ronald Hardy had accidentally let slip the revolver and that Ruth (later seen by Mrs. Mullion) had picked it up. He felt rather annoyed with himself for not having spotted this rather obvious clue before. On Monday night, of course, he had not expected to find an impression of the revolver on the path, because he had not then formed his theory. It was easy to find a clue when one expected it to be there, and easier still to overlook it when one did not! Still, it was a reprehensible oversight. He had wasted much valuable time in trailing after wrong explanations.

On their way back to the car, a tall, hulking figure with a dog at his heel loomed up unexpectedly out of the mist. On seeing the Constable he called out and cut across to meet him.

"I've been looking for you, Mr. Grouch," he said. "I reckon I may be able to tell you a thing or two about Monday night."

"That's good," said Grouch. "This is Inspector Bigswell from Greystoke. This is Mr. Bedruthen, sir. He runs the sheep on the common here."

The two men shook hands.

"You want to make a statement, is that it, Mr. Bedruthen?" asked the Inspector.

"Aye—that's about it, sir. What I have to tell you may not be worth your while listening to. On the other hand——"

"It may," cut in the Inspector quickly. "Well, if you can spare us a moment now we'll get down to the Constable's office. It's a bit chilly to hold a conference out here, eh?"

The three men climbed into the car and Grimmet drove them back to the village. Once more in the cheerful atmosphere of the little bare-faced office, the Inspector began to cross-question the new witness.

"I take it you're a shepherd, Mr. Bedruthen?"

"That's it, sir. I work all the sheep along this bit of cliff-edge."

"And you were somewhere near Mr. Tregarthan's house on the night of his death?"

"Aye—I was up in Church Meadows. It's the start of the lambing season now, and I often have to make a late round to see that everything's going along all right. And on Monday night I was attending a few of my ewes in a fold up beside the church. It was a wettish night as you know, sir, and I was surprised when a chap came on me sudden out of the dark and asked for a light. At first I didn't recognise the man, but when he held the match to his pipe I saw it was Ned Salter." The shepherd grinned broadly. "I daresay Mr. Grouch here has a thing or two to say about Ned, eh?"

"The Inspector's up to date, too," said Grouch. "We don't need to go into his life-history, eh, sir?"

Bigswell shook his head.

"What time was it when you first saw Salter?"

"Just after a quarter to nine. I was working just under the church clock. It's a fancy affair, sir—chimes the quarters. Presented to the parish by one of Lady Greenow's forebears."

"I see. Go on."

"Well, sir, one of the reasons for my coming forward like this was on account of a rumour which I heard down at the 'Ship' last night. A lot of folks have it that Ned is somehow mixed up in Mr. Tregarthan's death, him having been seen a few hours before the murder having a violent quarrel on the Greylings drive. Ned himself came into the pub later and a lot of 'em started in to question him about his doings a-Monday night. Well, Ned being what he is, there was a tidy rumpus afore we could calm him down. He swearing all the time that he knew nothing about the manner in which Mr. Tregarthan was murdered. Then it struck me, Inspector, that it might be as well for me to come forward and establish Ned's innocence. As I told 'em last night down at the 'Ship,' if Mr. Tregarthan was murdered afore quarter to nine, well and good—Ned might have had a hand in it. If he wasn't, then Ned was innocent, because he wasn't out of my sight from a quarter to nine to pretty near quarter to ten. What's more, sir, Ned Salter was at my elbow when we heard the shot fired."

"Shot!" exclaimed the Inspector. "You heard a shot fired?"

"Aye. A minute or so after Ned came up to me in Church Meadows we heard it. A single shot."

"You're sure it was only one shot?"

"Aye—sure of it."

"Curious," mused the Inspector. "I suppose you know that three shots were fired at Mr. Tregarthan?"

"That's what I've heard, sir. I couldn't understand it myself. But it was a single shot we heard. I'll swear to it. So will Ned."

"Where did the shot seem to come from—the direction of Greylings?"

"Well, there I won't be sure, Inspector. It was a windy night as you know and sounds play funny tricks in the wind. It was that way, but to my mind to the left of the house. A bit nearer the village that is."

"And the time?"

"Ten minutes to nine or thereabouts. Ned hadn't been more than a minute or two with me when we heard the shot."

"You didn't suspect anything at the time, I suppose?" The shepherd shook his head. "You say Ned Salter was with you until about quarter to ten. What did you do after you heard the shot?"

"Ned gave me a hand in setting up a few hurdles and getting a couple of ewes into shelter, then we walked down on to the road, reckoning to get to the 'Ship' afore closing-time. That was nine o'clock. The clock struck the hour just as we reached the road. We set off along the road at a tidy jog-trot, seeing it was pretty wettish. About a hundred yards afore we reached the Greylings entrance we heard a car coming towards us. We drew into the side of the road, seeing that the car was travelling at a tidy pace. But as it went by I just had time to see who it was driving." He turned to Grouch. "That writer chap here— Hardy. Exceeding the speed limit, I reckon, Constable."

"That's just where you're wrong," corrected Grouch. "There isn't any speed limit. It's been abolished. You don't read your newspaper."

The Inspector cut short any further banter with a curt question.

"You're sure it was Mr. Hardy?"

"Aye. I know his car, too. There's no other car like it in Boscawen. Besides, Ned recognised him. I held up my lantern as he shot by and the light fell on his face. As the hood was up he wasn't wearing a hat. Oh, it was Mr. Hardy sure enough!"

But Inspector Bigswell still looked dubious about Bedruthen's assertion. A dark night, a fast car with the hood up and blinding headlights—it was curious how certain the man was as to the identity of the driver.

"But what about the headlights?" he asked. "Surely you were pretty well blinded at the moment when the car passed you?"

"That's just it," said Willy Bedruthen impressively. "There weren't no lights! He was driving his car hell-for-leather without so much as a pin's head of light to guide him." He turned to the Constable. "You'll be telling me next that lights has been abolished, eh?"

"No lights!" exclaimed Bigswell. "That's curious. Dangerous, too. How the devil could he see the road?"

"There was a faint glimmer of moonlight just after nine, sir," put in Grouch. "Enough to distinguish the lighter surface of the road from the common on either side."

"But why no lights?"

"Looks as if he didn't want to be seen," suggested Grouch. "People a long way off might have noticed the lights without hearing his engine. Looks as if he wanted to avoid that, eh?"

"It's the only feasible explanation," acknowledged the Inspector. He turned to the shepherd. "Anything more you wish to tell us, Mr. Bedruthen?"

"No, sir. Only it struck me that you might like to know about Ned Salter being with me from a quarter to nine and that we saw Mr. Hardy on the road just after nine o'clock."

"Quite right. What you've told us is very important. I think we can safely say that Ned Salter is entirely cleared of suspicion. We know that Cowper saw Mr. Tregarthan alive at a quarter to nine. Ned Salter met you a minute or so after the quarter. Unless my calculations are all at sea, I imagine it would be impossible for anybody to get from the cliff-path to the church in less than five minutes. The murderer must have wasted at least a minute in luring Mr. Tregarthan to the window. It's uphill all the way. Even a trained athlete could scarcely have covered the distance in the time, let alone the fact that it was slippery underfoot and dark at that. No—I think Ned Salter, thanks to you, Mr. Bedruthen, has got his alibi all right. He didn't appear out of breath when he asked you for a light?"

"Not a bit of it, sir."

The Inspector held out his hand.

"Well, we needn't keep you longer. You did the sensible thing in coming forward, Mr. Bedruthen. Good morning."

The shepherd, after shaking hands with the Inspector, nodded to Grouch and went out into the mist followed by his dog. They heard his heavy boots scrunching over the gritty road and die away in the distance.

For a long time there was silence in the little room.

Then: "Well, I'll be damned!" exclaimed Inspector Bigswell. "Where the devil are we getting to now, Grouch? Why only one shot? And how the devil did Hardy, supposing of course that he *did* murder Tregarthan, manage to leave Cove Cottage at a quarter to nine, take his car from the garage, drive up on to the road somewhere above Greylings, run down to the cliff, cross the hurdles, climb the wall, get his man to the window, murder him, retrace his footsteps, start the car and pass Salter and Bedruthen a few minutes after nine? Is it possible, d'you think, Grouch?"

Grouch considered the question for a moment.

"It could be done," he said at length. "Just."

"There's only one way to make sure."

"And that, sir?"

"We must make a test and time ourselves, Grouch. The moment this mist lifts, I'll get Grimmet to run the car into Hardy's garage and I'll see what I can do over the same course. Mind you, we can only make fairly sure—not absolutely— and even then we can't explain away the mystery of that single shot!"

CHAPTER XI

THEFT FROM THE BODY

As luck would have it, whilst Grimmet and the Inspector were lunching in the deserted parlour of the "Ship," the mist lifted. A breeze sprang up and within an hour the air was clear and sunlit. Wasting no time for fear that the mist might descend again, the Inspector ordered Grimmet to drive him up to Cove Cottage. There he explained to Mrs. Peewit that he wished to make use of Mr. Hardy's garage for a moment, and finding the door open he got Grimmet to back in the car and shut off the engine. From Mrs. Peewit he ascertained that Hardy usually kept the doors of the garage locked. He kept the key, along with others, in a drawer of his writing-desk. The Inspector decided, therefore, to start from the sitting-room and allow himself the necessary time for unfastening the padlock on the garage door.

Grimmet took out his watch. It was exactly 2.10. The Inspector walked at a fairly brisk pace from the cottage to the adjacent woodshed, which had been converted into the garage. Then he went through the motions of unlocking the doors, opened them and climbed into the car. Grimmet, watch in hand, hopped in quickly beside him. The Inspector pressed the self-starter, and the engine, after a couple of false promises, broke into a hum. The car swung out on to the hill and began to mount up out of the cove. At the crest of the hill, where the main road forked, Bigswell got into top gear and accelerated. The car gathered speed, humming along the deserted road, between the hedgeless sweeps of the common.

The speedometer trembled over the forty mark. In less than a minute Greylings hove in sight.

The Inspector had previously reckoned that Hardy would have drawn up about a quarter of a mile from the Vicarage. He did not want his car to be seen and commented on. The chances were, considering the lateness of the hour and the state of the weather, that nobody would pass along the open road. On the other hand, if he approached too near to the Greylings entrance, the car might have been noticed from a window of the Vicarage. Besides, it might occur to somebody in the Vicarage, when questioned later on, that they had heard a car stop just outside the gate and later continue on its way along the road. It was the sort of thing people did notice in an isolated house.

About four hundred yards from the Greylings drive, therefore, the Inspector pulled into the side of the road, shut off his engine and jumped out of the car. As he raced off diagonally down the sloping moorland to the garden wall, Grimmet called after him: "Five and a quarter minutes, sir!" The Inspector, anxious to save his breath, waved a hand in acknowledgment. He covered the distance with creditable speed and, coming to a point where he imagined the last hurdle had been placed, he went through the motions of unlacing his boots. Then striding across the intervening patch of muddy ground he climbed up on to the wall and worked his way cautiously to the middle of it. Allowing a feasible amount of time to elapse, during which he supposed himself to have flung the gravel against the window-panes and attracted Tregarthan, he fired, in imagination, the three shots. The revolver, as he saw it, dropped to the ground. A moment's hesitation—then he was off on his return journey.

He reached the end of the hurdles, made pretence of putting on his boots and roughly lacing them. Then with pounding heart and clenched fists he jogged up the steep rise towards the anxiously waiting Grimmet. He crossed the road, tumbled, breathless, into the car and restarted the engine. The car leapt forward.

On Grouch's reckoning he had formed a fairly good idea as to where Ned Salter and Bedruthen had met the car. Bedruthen had mentioned that they were about a hundred yards from the Greylings entrance. At this point, according to Grouch, there was a heap of stones used for road-mending. As the car rushed by this landmark, therefore, the Inspector sang out: "Now!" and jammed on his brakes.

Grimmet noted the time. It was exactly 2.29.

"Which means," said the Inspector after a quick calculation, "that I've taken just nineteen minutes. So if Bedruthen saw the car, say at nine-four, it was just possible for Hardy to have covered the course in time. D'you think a 1928 four-cylinder Morris could equal our performance, Grimmet?"

Grimmet considered the question for a moment.

"It's possible, sir," he acknowledged. "A lot, of course, would depend on the actual condition of the engine. But provided she wasn't missing badly and the chap that was driving her knew how to get the best out of the car—I think his time wouldn't fall far short of ours."

The Inspector grunted, and when he had changed places with Grimmet and ordered him to drive back to the village, he began to analyse the reliability of his test. It was pretty rough and ready, of course—nothing could be timed with absolute certainty. For instance, there was no actual proof that Hardy had removed his boots before crossing the hurdles and climbing the wall. He might, considering his extremely hurried exit from the cottage, have been wearing slippers. Shoes, too, would take far less time to unlace and kick off than boots. Then, again—the garage door—it might not have been locked on that particular evening. Tregarthan might have come to the window with greater alacrity than the Inspector estimated. Factors like these would do much to shorten the time—whilst a cold engine, a missing plug, the darkness of the night and so on, would considerably lengthen it. What exactly had he gained by the test? Simply this. Provided no unanticipated misfortune overtook Hardy from the time he left Cove Cottage to the time when he passed Salter and Bedruthen on the road, it was well within the bounds of possibility that he could have committed the murder.

It was, in a way, a negative result. It got him no further along the road to the actual solution of the mystery. It merely upheld the possibility of the theory which he had advanced in the Superintendent's office.

But the single shot still puzzled him. Three shots had been fired. One shot had been heard and that, according to Bedruthen's statement, at about ten minutes to nine. But at ten minutes to nine on Monday night Hardy, according to the test, would have just been on the point of drawing up at the roadside, about a quarter of a mile from the Greylings drive-gate. Then what on earth had induced him to discharge the revolver before he got out of the car? Had it been an accident? Had he perhaps been examining the Webley with one hand and driving with the other, and the revolver had gone off unexpectedly? He recalled Bedruthen's remark about the sound of the shot appearing to come from the left of the house. That would fit in with the theory. The only possible explanation, otherwise, was that the single shoot had nothing at all to do with the murder of Tregarthan. Just a chance factor, though a confusing one, in the case. But both Bedruthen and Salter believed it to be a shot, and who the devil would take a gun out in the middle of a storm to shoot rabbits? If Salter had not been with the shepherd it might have been his effort with a sawn-off shot-gun—but poachers usually affect less noisy methods and, besides, Ned *was* with Bedruthen.

Could it have been a signal from Ruth Tregarthan to show that the stage was set and the coast clear? Mrs. Peewit, though not certain of the time, believed the girl had arrived at the cottage at ten minutes to nine. This was the exact time when the shot had been heard. This theory, therefore, did not seem to hold water. Moreover, a signal of that sort was hardly in keeping with the cool and deliberate scheme which Hardy and the girl had obviously hatched between them.

How, then, to explain the single shot? The Inspector couldn't. He gave up the attempt. It was left to float like an irritating speck in the back of his mind.

Reaching the Constable's office he put through a call to Greystoke. But the Superintendent had nothing to report. So far the Yard had failed to trace the whereabouts of the missing man. Nobody had come forward to offer any information.

Inspector Bigswell cursed under his breath. As far as he could see there was little he could do to further the progress of his investigations until Ronald Hardy had been run to earth. Once lay his hands on the missing man and subject him to a detailed cross-examination, and he believed the final bits of the puzzle would fall into place of their own accord. The fellow, confronted by the evidence collected, wouldn't have a leg to stand on. He might deny the girl's complicity in the crime. That was understandable—even commendable— but his own case, on the face of things, was hopeless. Better for him to make a clean breast of it and let the law take its own inevitable, inexorable course. He was sorry for the girl. She had been too much under the sway of the man's influence. But there it was. Murder was murder. It was not for him to dissect the queer and tortuous reasoning of his fellow-creatures. It was for him to deal in facts and facts alone.

Inspector Bigswell's ruminations were cut short by the ringing of the telephone bell. He crossed to the Constable's desk and took up the receiver. He recognised the quiet and affable voice of the Reverend Dodd. The Vicar had thought it possible that the Inspector would be at the Constable's office. He was speaking on behalf of Miss Tregarthan. Would the Inspector have any objection if he, the Vicar, paid a visit to Greylings? It was a financial matter. Miss Tregarthan had the Cowpers' wages to pay and other current expenses usu- ally paid by her uncle. Her uncle, in fact, had been over to Greystoke on the morning of the 24th and cashed a cheque for forty pounds. As she had not been through the effects found on her uncle's person after the murder, she had not as yet had the money. Would the Inspector object to the Vicar going down, at once, to Greylings and collecting it? Yes—it was in notes. Tregarthan always drew out his monthly cheque in notes.

"You're quite sure, Mr. Dodd, that Mr. Tregarthan had this money on him when he was shot?" asked the Inspector.

"According to Miss Tregarthan he had," affirmed the Vicar. "What makes you ask?"

"Only that I went through Tregarthan's pockets, personally, and found only a handful of loose change. That's all, Mr. Dodd."

The Vicar's voice grew a trifle agitated.

"But surely ... I mean according to Miss Tregarthan——" He broke off abruptly, adding in a sharper voice. "Look here, Inspector, you don't think——?"

"I don't know what to think, yet," snapped the Inspector. "I'll come up to Greylings straight away. Meet me there, if you will. We'll go through those personal effects again."

He rang off and, fastening his cape, strode to the door. Just as he was about to climb into the car, Grouch came up followed by a thin, meagre individual with a ferrety face and shifty, bloodshot eyes. The Constable saluted.

"Well?" asked the Inspector impatiently.

"Ned Salter, sir. He wishes to make a statement."

"To corroborate Bedruthen's evidence, I suppose? I can't see to it now, Grouch. Take down the statement yourself and get the witness to sign it. I'll be down here again later."

"Very good, sir."

The car thrummed up the hill, whilst Grouch, followed by the somewhat penitent and chastened figure of the poacher, disappeared into the little office.

The Inspector was worried. This matter of the money was puzzling. He felt quite certain that when he had gone through the pockets of the dead man on Monday night, save for a handful of silver and copper, Tregarthan had no other money on his person. Moreover, the Vicar had, on Tuesday morning, gone through the desk which stood in the sitting-room, and obviously had not come across the notes there. Where, then, had the money vanished? Was it possible that Tregarthan had spent the full forty pounds after leaving the bank at Greystoke? That seemed an unlikely hypothesis. According to the Vicar's explanation over the phone, this money was a sort of monthly allowance set aside by Tregarthan for the payment of wages and ordinary household expenses. It seemed improbable that he had spent the lot in a single day. The Inspector sighed. It looked as if a new complication was on the way. Robbery. But surely Tregarthan had not been murdered for the sake of the forty pounds in his pocket? There was no indication that the murderer had gained access to the sitting-room after the crime and taken the notes from the dead man's wallet. The wallet had been there. He remembered that. An ordinary soft leather wallet containing a few visiting cards—his own and other people's—a couple of tickets for a charity concert at Greystoke, a new gun licence—but no Bank or Treasury notes. Moreover, if, as he suspected, Ronald Hardy was the man they were looking for, what on earth would induce the fellow to risk his life for a measly forty pounds? No man of Hardy's calibre would murder for money—at least, not for such a paltry amount. Something was wrong somewhere. But what?

"Confound it!" thought the Inspector. "Is this going to knock my unassailable little theory on the head? We don't want the experts—bless 'em!—shoving in their noses at this stage of affairs."

It was in a mixed mood, therefore, of annoyance and bewilderment that Inspector Bigswell met the Vicar on the Greylings drive and preceded him into the sitting-room. The burly Constable in charge declared emphatically, when questioned, that nobody had entered the sitting-room since he had been on duty. Both the keys of the french windows and the door had not left his pocket. Nothing had been touched.

The Inspector, on Monday night, had collected the various articles found on the dead man and locked them away in a small attaché case bearing Tregarthan's initials. He himself had kept the key since Monday night.

This case he at once opened and, selecting the pocket-book and the wallet as the only possible hiding-places for the notes, he carefully searched them. There was no trace of the money!

"But this is incredible!" exclaimed the Vicar, who had anxiously watched the Inspector's proceedings. "Ruth swears that her uncle drew the money from the bank on Monday morning. He went over to Greystoke expressly for that purpose."

"Well, it's not here now," said the Inspector bluntly. "D'you know where Tregarthan banked?"

"The London and Provincial. I bank there myself. I've met Tregarthan there more than once."

"Then it will be an easy matter to find out if he *did* draw the cheque as Miss Tregarthan supposes. But it may prove a more ticklish matter to find out what happened to the money after he left the bank. Does Miss Tregarthan know if her uncle had the money on him, say, at dinner on Monday evening?"

"I really can't say," said the Vicar. "I didn't feel justified in asking her any questions on my own account. But if you care——"

The Inspector nodded.

"I think it advisable, Mr. Dodd. This may or may not have some connection with the major crime, but in any case the matter's got to be investigated."

Leaving word with the Constable to relock the door and pocket the key, the two men climbed back into the car and were driven to the Vicarage.

Ruth was in the drawing-room sitting over afternoon tea with Ethel Dodd. On learning that Inspector Bigswell wished to see her in the study, she hesitated, paled a little, apparently disconcerted by this sudden request. But realising that the interview was unavoidable she crossed the hall, followed by the Vicar, and went into the study.

The Inspector touched his hat.

"Sorry to trouble you again, Miss Tregarthan," he said, watching the girl closely. "But I've come about——"

He hesitated deliberately.

"Yes?" demanded Ruth with patent anxiety.

"I've come about this money which your uncle drew out of the bank on Monday morning."

Her relief was obvious—a fact which did not escape the Inspector's notice. Had she thought, perhaps, that he had other more disagreeable news to impart? The announcement, perhaps, that Ronald Hardy had been run to earth, and under the pressure of cross-examination made a full confession to the crime.

"Well, what about it, Inspector?"

"Simply, Miss Tregarthan, that we've been through the effects which were on your uncle's person and the notes are not there."

"Not there? But he had them on him at dinner on Monday night. I remember asking him for a couple of pounds for household purposes, and he took out his wallet and handed me the two notes."

"Putting the wallet back into his pocket?"

"Into his inside breast-pocket. Yes."

"And you imagine the full forty pounds was in his possession then, Miss Tregarthan?"

"Oh, I'm certain of it. Thirty pounds of it was in five-pound notes and the remaining ten in pound Treasury notes. He took out the whole amount and placed it on the table, counted roughly through the amount, and handed me the two pounds."

"Can you account for the fact that the money was not found on his person later that same evening?"

Ruth shook her head. She seemed genuinely puzzled by the mystery.

"I can't understand it at all, Inspector. The only other place where he might have hidden the notes was in his cash-box. But, Mr. Dodd, as you know, went through my uncle's desk yesterday morning. The cash-box was always unlocked since my uncle thought it sufficient safeguard to lock the desk itself. As a matter of fact the lock on the cash-box was broken."

"And you found nothing in that box, Mr. Dodd?" asked the Inspector, turning on the Vicar.

"Nothing."

Bigswell pondered for a moment, as if seeking for a new line of attack, then he said briskly: "You'll have no objection, Miss Tregarthan, if I verify your statement as to your uncle's action on Monday morning?"

Ruth looked surprised. A quick flush of resentment heightened the colour of her cheeks.

"You doubt my word?"

"No, it's not that. I would just like to make sure that there has been no mistake about the amount."

"Very well," said Ruth coldly. "I'll make the enquiry straight away if you wish. I happen to know Mr. Potter, the local manager of the bank. He lives over the premises. So if you're amenable, Inspector, I'll ring through to him now and find out what you want to know."

"I should be grateful," said the Inspector graciously, not in any way ruffled by the girl's unconcealed asperity.

He felt that he was within the bounds of possibility that Ruth had invented this story about the forty pounds, in order to put him off the scent. If Ruth guessed that he was suspicious of Hardy, she might have invented the story to confuse him as to the motive for the murder. He was taking no chances.

But ten minutes later he knew without any doubt that the girl had told the truth. Tregarthan had drawn a cheque for forty pounds. Mr. Potter himself had attended to the matter. He had handed Mr. Tregarthan six Bank of England notes for five pounds and ten one-pound Treasury notes. Had he the numbers of the Bank of England notes? But most certainly he had. If the Inspector would like——. The Inspector did like, and there and then he copied down the numbers in his notebook. Then, with renewed apologies for breaking in on Miss Tregarthan at tea-time, he returned to Greylings.

The next step in this additional mystery was to question the Cowpers. They alone had access to the sitting-room after the murder was committed and before Ruth Tregarthan had found her uncle's body. The idea that Ruth herself had taken the notes from her uncle's wallet he dismissed as absurd and fantastic. The girl was genuinely shocked by the tragedy and, in any case, there would have been little enough time for her to have slipped the wallet from Tregarthan's pocket, extracted the notes, replaced the wallet and hidden the notes on her person. According to the Cowpers' evidence, she called out to them the moment she had entered the room and found her uncle shot. This left him with the Cowpers.

Suppose the Cowpers had heard the shot fired. Suppose they had heard Tregarthan's body crash to the floor and thereafter no further sound. Suppose Cowper had gone into the sitting-room to investigate and, finding his master dead, stolen the money, closed the door, and thereafter acted as if he had no previous knowledge of the tragedy. This was a possible explanation. It would have given him time to plant the notes in a secret place. It was also within the bounds of feasibility that he did not know that Tregarthan had been shot when he entered the room. Any ordinary duty might have taken him in. The rest was a mere matter of seizing the opportunity, with the very likely chance that the theft of the notes would be connected with the murder.

It was on these lines, therefore, that the Inspector intended to work, when he once more entered the sombre, grey-stoned house and proceeded without delay to try to unravel yet one more tangled thread which was woven into the yet more tangled skein of the major crime.

CHAPTER XII

THE OPEN WINDOW

WHEN the Inspector re-entered Greylings he found Mrs. Cowper clearing away the tea-things in the kitchen. The Constable had his feet up before the range and, in his unbuttoned tunic, was enjoying a pipe. On seeing his superior in the doorway, he jumped to his feet and hastily started to rebutton his tunic. But the Inspector waved him back into the Windsor arm-chair.

"It's all right, Fenner. It's not you I'm after. You can finish your pipe." He turned to Mrs. Cowper. "Your husband is about, Mrs. Cowper?"

The housekeeper nodded toward a second door which led into a large scullery.

"He's through there, sir. Sawing logs in the woodhouse. He finds it good for his liver when there's not much to be done in the garden. Keeps him out of mischief, too."

The Inspector grinned affably.

"Mischief, eh?"

"Yes, sir. Horse-racing. Always slipping off to study what he calls 'form' and such. If I didn't keep a tight hand on his wages we'd be a good deal poorer than we are. And that's saying a lot!"

Bigswell appeared interested.

"You mean he likes to have his little bit on—is that it?"

"Yes—and it would be more than a little bit if he had his way. He's got it into his head, has Cowper, that horse-racing means easy money. And so it does, sir ... for the bookmakers."

The Inspector agreed heartily. He realised, at once, from Mrs. Cowper's manner that she was riding one of her favourite hobby-horses. It was obvious that her husband's predilection for gambling was a thorn in her side. This voluntary information about Cowper's hobby might prove a useful factor in building up a theory later on.

"I wonder if you could spare me a moment, Mrs. Cowper," he went on. "Perhaps we could go into the dining-room."

A little worried and disturbed by this sudden request, Mrs. Cowper followed the Inspector across the hall. She wondered, uneasily, if she had opened her mouth too wide about her husband's weakness. She was not certain how the law stood toward betting on race-horses. She was immensely relieved, therefore, when the Inspector, without further mention of her husband, returned to her own movements on the night of the murder.

"Now I want you to try to remember exactly what you did, Mrs. Cowper, when Mr. Tregarthan finished his dinner. According to your previous statement you took in his coffee at a quarter to nine. Now, previous to that, what did you do?"

Mrs. Cowper pondered for a moment, as if desirous of marshalling her recollections, before setting them out in front of the Inspector.

What had she done? Well she and Cowper had cleared the dinner-table and taken the dirty crockery into the butler's pantry. Yes—they always washed-up in the pantry. Whilst her husband was stacking logs into the trudge, she had made the coffee and taken it in to Mr. Tregarthan. Before retiring from the sitting-room she drew the curtains across the french windows. She then arranged with Cowper that he was to do the washing-up, after he had taken in the logs, as she wanted to sort out the soiled linen. The laundry van always called early on Tuesday morning. She then went upstairs and proceeded to do this, returning to the kitchen only a few minutes before Miss Tregarthan entered hurriedly through the side-door.

"You were upstairs for about twenty-five minutes then?"

"About that, sir."

"And during this time—where was your husband?"

"As far as I know in the butler's pantry. When Miss Tregarthan called out for us to come, Cowper hadn't quite finished with the washing-up. I remember seeing him come out of the pantry at the same moment as I rushed out of the kitchen."

"And the wood had by then been taken into the sitting-room?"

"Oh, he'd taken it in all right. Earlier, I suppose. The trudge was beside the fender where he always placed it. As a matter of fact, Inspector, seeing that nothing has been touched in the room, I expect it's still there now."

"It is," agreed the Inspector. "I noticed it myself. Well, that's all I wanted to ask you, Mrs. Cowper. You might send your husband in to me here now."

When Mrs. Cowper had gone the Inspector swiftly reviewed the housekeeper's evidence. More than ever was he inclined to think that Cowper had something to do with the disappearance of the forty pounds—or to be exact, the thirty-eight pounds left in Tregarthan's wallet. He had been alone for nearly half an hour in the butler's pantry, though there was no reason why he should not have walked where he liked on the ground-floor without being seen by his wife. Cowper in his statement to Grouch spoke of his entry into the sitting-room at a quarter to nine or thereabouts. That was to say, a few minutes after Mrs. Cowper had taken in the coffee. But had he really entered the room at that time? Had he perhaps made a false statement of the time in order to make it look as if he entered the room when Tregarthan was alive. Knowing that his wife had taken in the coffee round about 8.45, he realised that if he claimed to have seen Tregarthan a minute or so later, there would not have been time enough for the murderer to lure him to the window and commit the crime. Grouch would naturally assume, as Bigswell had assumed, that Cowper was the last person to see Tregarthan alive. But what if this were not the case? What if Mrs. Cowper was the last to set eyes on the living Tregarthan? What if Cowper had not taken in the logs straight away, but remembered them later as an afterthought? Then there would have been ample time for the murder to have been committed. Cowper might have gone in, found Tregarthan shot, stolen the money and returned to the butler's pantry. Nobody was in a position to dispute his account of his own movements. He was, apparently, an inveterate gambler. He might have fallen into the bookmaker's clutches. Found himself in a hole—frightened, perhaps, of losing his job if the business came to light—seen the opportunity to clear off his debts and, in a headstrong moment, seized it.

All further supposition was cut short by the entrance of the man in question. Bigswell was astonished by his appearance. There was no doubt that Cowper's self-respect had considerably deteriorated since the night of the murder. His clothes were untidy and unbrushed. He wore no collar and the rim of his shirt was greasy with dirt. His eyes, heavily underlined as if through sleeplessness, were bloodshot and shifty, and his face had assumed a yellowish pallor. About his person hung a strong aroma of whiskey.

"Letting himself go," thought the Inspector. "Something uncomfortable on his mind by the look of it. Turned to the whiskey bottle for Dutch courage!"

The man's manner toward the Inspector, too, was characterised by a sort of surly defensiveness and it was not until Bigswell adopted a peremptory tone that he showed any inclination to speak up. He repeated his story of Monday night, merely adding that after he had taken in the logs at 8.45 he had retired to the butler's pantry and proceeded to wash up the dinner things. He had remained there until Miss Tregarthan's cries had summoned him post-haste to the sitting-room.

"You took in the logs," asked the Inspector, "after your wife had gone upstairs to see to the laundry?"

"Just after," said Cowper shortly.

"And this butler's pantry—where is it?"

"Beyond the sitting-room—at the far end of the hall."

"Opposite the kitchen?"

"That's it."

"I should like to have a look at the room," said the Inspector tersely. "Now!"

Cowper clip-clopped along the hall in a disreputable pair of felt slippers and opened the door of the pantry. The Inspector realised, with a certain amount of surprise, that it was adjacent to the sitting-room. A single wall had divided Cowper from the room in which Tregarthan had met his death.

The pantry was not very large. A sink and a draining-board ran along one wall, whilst a large cupboard, with glass doors and shelves, occupied the wall next to the sitting-room. In the wall opposite the door was a smallish window set about four feet from the ground. Beneath this was a long, oak stool.

"That window," said Bigswell," what does it give on to?"

"The garden," replied Cowper, obviously resenting the Inspector's curiosity.

"Which means that it's in line with the french windows of the sitting-room, eh?" Cowper nodded. "Was the window open or closed when you were in here on Monday night?"

"Closed," said Cowper promptly. "There's enough draught in this ruddy place without leaving the windows open."

"I see that it does open."

"Oh, it opens all right," agreed Cowper in surly tones. "But it's not been opened this side of of Christmas. You can take my word for that."

The Inspector moved to the window and took a close look at it. He was about to place his hand on the latch, when he thought better of it and turned suddenly on Cowper, who had been furtively watching the Inspector's procedure.

"Look here, Cowper—there's one thing which puzzles me in this case. You say you were in this room from eight-forty-five until Miss Tregarthan found her uncle dead. Out there, through that window, is the garden and at the end of the garden, the cliff-path. On the other side of this wall is the sitting-room. Mr. Tregarthan was murdered by some unknown person who fired three shots at him from the path. One of those shots was fatal. On the other side of the wall, say twelve feet from where we are standing, Mr. Tregarthan—a heavily built man mind you—fell to the ground shot through the head. On Monday night you made a statement to the Constable. You were asked if you heard any unusual sounds between eight-forty-five and nine-seventeen. You replied that you didn't. D'you still stick to that statement, Cowper?"

"Why shouldn't I?" asked Cowper truculently. "It's the truth, isn't it? You know as well as I do that there was a storm right over the house. If the chap that killed Mr. Tregarthan chose his moment and fired at the same time as a thunder-clap, how the devil could I be expected to hear the sound of the shots?"

"It's curious—that's all," answered Bigswell meaningly. "The shots being so close and the window apparently open."

Cowper gave him a sudden, furtive look of enquiry.

"The window open? Didn't I tell you it was shut!"

"Then how do you account for this?" asked the Inspector in a quiet voice, pointing to the window-sill. "D'you see those marks, Cowper? D'you know what they are, eh? You don't? Then I'll tell you. They're rain spots—recent, too, by the look of them. It's curious how driving rain will dapple the surface of dark paint and remain spotted until the marks are cleaned off. What have you to say about that, eh? You realise, Cowper, that it hasn't rained since Monday night. The storm had gone over completely by nine-thirty. It rather looks as if somebody *did* open that window on Monday night. Your wife perhaps. If so I can easily put the question to her and make sure. The same applies to Miss Tregarthan. If neither of them opened the window, then it rather looks as if you've not been telling the truth, Cowper. Well?"

During this exposition of logic Cowper's face had assumed the look of a man who finds himself in a tight corner and can't see his way out of it. His features were ashen. His fingers worked nervously at the tapes of his green baize apron.

"Well, then," he mumbled uneasily, "let's say I made a mistake. With so much happening in the house, it's nothing but natural, isn't it? Daresay I did open the window earlier in the evening. A chap can't remember everything when he's upset."

"I see. So the window was opened on Monday night?"

"Come to think of it," said Cowper, with a kind of despairing heartiness, "you're right there, Inspector. Can't think how I came to forget it! I'd been filling the oil-lamp in here what I use in the wood-shed. Just afore dinner that would be. Paraffin hangs about, as you know. So I opened the window to clear the air a bit, not wanting Mrs. C. to fall on me for filling the lamp in the pantry. She's a stickler for having things just-so."

"A very commendable quality," Bigswell observed dryly. "Well, I won't keep you any longer, Cowper. You can get back to your job."

Without waiting to be told twice Cowper, with a faint smile of relief, slipped out of the pantry and returned to his sawing. He was pleased with his own smartness. He had not suspected that he was the possessor of a highly inventive mind. He had parried the Inspector's stroke, he felt, with extreme deftness.

But the Inspector was far less gullible than Cowper imagined. From the moment he had discovered the rain-spots on the window-sill he knew that Cowper had been lying. He had lied to Grouch. It would have been obvious to the least observant man that Cowper was hiding something from the police. He felt certain in his own mind now, that the man had stolen the notes. The next problem to be solved was where had he concealed the money? In the pantry itself? It was a very probable hiding-place.

Closing the door, Inspector Bigswell made a minute search of every nook and cranny of the little room. But there was no money. At the conclusion of his search, however, his gaze was attracted to the polished surface of the long, oak stool under the window. It had been scratched, recently it seemed, and on looking closer the broken outlines of a footprint were faintly discernible. Whoever had stood on the stool had worn nailed boots—boots such as a gardener might wear or a man whose duties carried him outside the house. A few pieces of gravel were dusted over the dark, shiny wood. It was identical with the gravel which the Inspector had found on the Greylings drive and on the cement outside the french windows.

But why had Cowper mounted the stool? The window was set fairly low down. There was no reason why Cowper should have climbed on to the stool to open the window. But he had climbed on to it. Why?

Leaving this question for the moment, Bigswell let himself out of the side door and, leaving the light on in the pantry, walked down to the cliff-path. It was now almost dark and the orange square of the frosted window shone out brightly from the grey bulk of the house. The Inspector realised at once that the pantry-window was set at the extreme right-hand corner of the house. But that was not all! Directly beneath the window, running at right angles to the house's façade, was the southern wall of the garden.

For a moment, unable to suppress a quick thrill of excitement, he pondered the full significance of this fact. Was his Ronald Hardy-Ruth Tregarthan theory at sixes and sevens? Was Cowper responsible, not only for the theft of the notes, but for the murder itself? How damnably easy for Cowper, knowing the coast to be clear, to climb out of the pantry window, creep along the wall, shoot Tregarthan and return, unnoticed, to the house. No tracks on the surrounding paths or the flower beds. Little chance of being surprised in the act, since he had a perfect knowledge of everybody's whereabouts. And following up the murder, the theft of the notes. Perhaps he had misjudged the man's true character. Perhaps, driven to desperation by his bookmaker's threat to divulge the secret of his debts to Tregarthan, he had decided in cold blood to murder his master, having full knowledge that he carried the monthly cash-allowance on his person. And the revolver? Well, the same theory would still hold water. It had slipped from his hand when he was on the wall. Ruth Tregarthan had come along and picked it up in the belief that it was Hardy's. She probably knew that he possessed a Webley. She knew of the quarrel between Ronald and her uncle. She knew Ronald was liable to sudden emotional storms and, putting two and two together, had jumped to a very possible conclusion. True it was that Hardy's revolver was missing from its holster. But that might have been an unfortunate coincidence. On the other hand the man had disappeared and the revolver with him. Was his disappearance to be dismissed also as an unfortunate coincidence?

Bigswell suddenly felt disheartened. Where was he really getting to? This affair of the stolen notes had opened up an entirely new line of reconstruction. In some way Cowper was implicated. He had climbed on to that stool. He had, in spite of his initial denial, opened the pantry window. Was it not a perfectly logical argument to say that the theft was connected with the murder and that Cowper was the "wanted man" on both counts?

CHAPTER XIII

CORONER'S INQUEST

BEFORE returning to Greystoke, Inspector Bigswell called in at the Constable's office to acquaint himself with Ned Salter's evidence. Cross-examined by Grouch, who had full knowledge of the Bedruthen interview, the poacher had given a perfectly satisfactory account of his movements on the night of the murder. His story fitted without flaw the account already given by the shepherd, and the Inspector realised that, as far as Ned Salter was concerned, he had absolutely no connection with Tregarthan's death. He had guessed that Salter's alibi was unassailable the moment Bedruthen had come forward, but it was with a great sense of relief that he found himself in a position to cross at least one suspect from his list.

He returned to Greystoke and went at once to the Superintendent's office, where he made a concise report of the day's investigations. On the whole Bigswell felt little progress had been made. The theft of the money was an annoying complication, which had considerably shaken his faith in the theory which he had advanced the night before. The Superintendent, too, was worried by the introduction of yet one more suspected person into the already overcrowded picture. In his opinion the Coroner's verdict was already a foregone conclusion. Confronted with such a mass of conflicting evidence he could do little more than to bring in a verdict of "murder by person or persons unknown." The Superintendent had no doubt that the Chief would get in touch with the Coroner and suggest that the inquest should run along these lines. Unsatisfactory, perhaps. But there it was. The Inspector had done his best in the limited time, but it looked as if the problem was of a more stubborn nature than they had first anticipated.

The next morning proved fine and Bigswell was early on the road to Boscawen. Although the police had subpœnaed a number of witnessess, he expected little to come of the inquest. Mrs. Mullion's evidence would probably cause a sensation. He was curious to see how Ruth Tregarthan would parry the unexpected blow. The fact that she was seen on the cliff-path with the revolver in her hand would certainly prejudice public opinion against her, but the police were by no means in a position to issue a warrant for the girl's arrest. Hardy was still missing and his statement was an essential factor in building up a foolproof case against the girl. On top of that there was this new complication arising from the theft of the notes and Cowper's lie about the open window. It seemed ridiculous to suppose that Cowper was hand-in-glove with Ronald Hardy and Ruth Tregarthan, but if he had acted on his own, why had Hardy disappeared directly after the murder?

Still turning these problems over in his mind the Inspector went to the Constable's office. Grouch was not alone. Seated on a bench under the clock was a tall, shambling fellow with a knitted balaclava helmet completely encasing his head and ears. A huge muffler encircled his scraggy neck. On seeing the Inspector this extraordinary figure rose from the bench and demanded in a penetrating voice to know the time. Bigswell, rather taken aback by the strange request, grinned and pointed at the clock. The man grinned back and started to count aloud on his fingers. The Inspector threw an enquiring look toward Grouch. The Constable beckoned him over.

"It's all right, sir," he said in a quick undertone. "It's only old Tom Prattle. Quite harmless as long as you don't pull his leg, but a bit——" He tapped his forehead. "You know, sir."

"What's he here for? Drunk and disorderly?"

"At this time of the day, sir?" Grouch chuckled and shook his head. "It's *that*, sir. That's the reason for his visit. Curious, eh?"

The Inspector moved over to the desk. Then he stopped short and whistled.

"Hullo! Hullo!" he said. "What the devil's this?"

Lying on a sheet of blotting paper was a Webley service-pattern revolver!

"That's just what I can't make out, sir. Tom here found it this morning. He's a hedger and ditcher for the Rural District. And he came across it lying at the bottom of a ditch up on the Vicarage road."

"Whereabouts on the road?"

"Well, as far as I can make out from Tom, about a quarter of a mile this side of the Greylings drive gate. Funny, eh? Looks rather as if——"

"Exactly," cut in the Inspector. "We'll get this fellow to show us the exact spot."

He took up the revolver gingerly in his gloved hand. It was speckled with rust and splotched with daubs of dried mud. Finding it loaded, the Inspector emptied the cartridges into his hand. He was surprised. Every chamber was filled. He looked at the butt of the revolver. Crudely scratched on the metal, obviously with some blunt instrument, were the perfectly defined initials—R.H. Hardy's revolver! Precisely. But why fully loaded? And how the devil had it found its way into the ditch by the roadside, when according to Mrs. Mullion's evidence, Ruth Tregarthan had handled this very revolver on the cliff-path some hundreds of yards away?

He turned to the grotesque figure, who was sitting with splayed knees on the extreme edge of the bench.

"Can you show us exactly where you picked this up?"

"Oh—oi. I can do that right enough."

"Good!"

The three men went outside and clambered into the car, but not before Tom Prattle had enquired the time of Grimmet and informed the Inspector in a lugubrious voice that Mr. Tregarthan had been murdered by a German spy.

Grouch winked.

"Got Germans on the brain, sir. It was the war that sent him rocky. He's always talking about the Jerries. Poor devil!"

On that short drive the Inspector did some pretty rapid thinking. He was at an entire loss to explain away the revolver's sudden appearance in the ditch. It would have been impossible for Ruth Tregarthan to have planted it there when she had crept out of Greylings on Monday night. She would not have had time; moreover her track round the outskirts of the wall had corroborated her explanation. No—if Ruth Tregarthan had picked up a revolver from the cliff-path and later thrown it into the sea, it was not Hardy's revolver. She may have thought it was Hardy's revolver. But she had been mistaken. Then whose revolver had she picked up? Cowper's? That seemed the only feasible supposition. Then it was Cowper and not Hardy who had lured Tregarthan to the window and shot him? Well! Well! So much for his pretty little theory about the Ruth-Ronald collaboration. Was it after all going to be a case for the experts?

At that moment the car drew up beside an ordinary road-man's barrow from which projected a red flag.

"Is this the spot," asked the Inspector over his shoulder.

"Oh—oi. This is it. Down in the trench, corporal—just here it was."

Tom clambered awkwardly out of the car and the men formed a little group about his swaying figure.

"You see that big stone, hay? Right aside that it was lying, Corporal. Left there in a hurry, I reckon, by some poor, ruddy German."

The Inspector examined the spot carefully. There was a deep indent in the almost liquid mud which lay in the trough of the ditch, but it was impossible to say if the impress had been made by the revolver. But Bigswell was less interested in the ditch than in the springy ribbon of turf which divided the ditch from the road. He worked along this ribbon of spongy turf for about five yards either side of where Tom Prattle had found the revolver. Suddenly he uttered a little exclamation of satisfaction. About six feet away from the parked car was the unmistakable tread of a tyre. It had left a series of diamond-shaped prints in the damp turf.

"When I made that test yesterday, Grimmet, where did we park? About here?"

Grimmet shook his head.

"Fifty yards further on, sir."

"And these marks?"

"Not the tyres on our own car, sir. We've got bramble-markings."

The Inspector nodded and with a word of thanks to Tom Prattle, climbed back into the car and ordered Grimmet to drive back to the Constable's cottage.

There he put through a call to Fenton's Quick Service Garage. Fenton himself answered the phone.

"Morning, Fenton. I want you to do something for me. Take a look at the markings of the tyres on Hardy's car for me, will you? I didn't notice myself when I was over on Tuesday."

"Right!" snapped Fenton. In a few moments he was back at the phone. "Criss-crosses," he said, "sort of diamond-shaped pattern."

"Thanks. That's all I wanted to know."

He hung up the receiver and turned to Grouch.

"No doubt about it, Grouch. Hardy parked his car up on the Vicarage road on Monday night."

"And the revolver, sir?"

"His without a shadow of doubt."

"But how——?"

"Don't ask me," said the Inspector testily. "This damned case is fairly bristling with snags. No sooner do we round one awkward corner when we come on another. Look here, Grouch, let's tabulate all those points which, at the moment, we can't explain."

At the end of ten minutes Bigswell had drawn up a pretty formidable list. It ran:

(1) *Why did Hardy leave his revolver in the ditch near the scene of the crime instead of ridding himself of it on his way to Greystoke station?*

(2) *Why, if he did not intend to murder Tregarthan, had he taken the revolver out of its holster that evening?*

(3) *Why did he park his car near Greylings on the night of, and at the estimated time of, the murder?*

(4) *Unless he was implicated in the murder, why had he disappeared?*

(5) Did he murder Tregarthan?

(6) *Whose revolver did Ruth Tregarthan have in her hand when seen by Mrs. Mullion?*

(7) *Did she believe it to be Hardy's?*

(8) *Was that the reason for her subsequent actions later in the evening? Had she thrown that particular revolver into the sea?*

(9) *Was it Cowper's revolver?*

(10) Did Cowper murder Tregarthan?

(11) *Why was it, since three shots were fired, that Salter and Bedruthen both swore that they had heard only a single shot?*

(12) *If those shots had been fired from Hardy's revolver, why had he ejected the empty cartridges, fully recharged the gun and cleaned the barrel?*

All these questions seemed, at the moment, unanswerable. Questions 5 and 10 combined to form a damning indication of the Inspector's state of indecision. After nearly three days of intensive investigation he was asking himself which of two men had committed the murder. Until yesterday evening he had not even suspected Cowper to be in any way connected with the crime. But now, since the discovery of that second revolver, he was already inclined to think that Cowper, and not Hardy, was the wanted man.

Grouch cut into his train of thoughts.

"This man—Tom Prattle—shall I serve a summons on him to appear at the inquest, sir?"

"No. I don't think there's any need to bring up the matter of this second revolver this afternoon. This case is quite complicated enough as it is. Besides the verdict's a foregone conclusion. Let's see, Grouch, whom have we called?"

"Miss Tregarthan, of course, sir—the Cowpers, Dr. Pendrill and Mrs. Mullion."

"I see. Well, we'll stick to that list. In the meantime I'd like to put my feet up in your parlour, Grouch, and run over my notes. I'll lunch at the 'Ship.' The inquest's at two sharp, remember."

The Inspector's remark was prophetic, for punctually at two o'clock, the Coroner, a Greystoke solicitor, opened the proceedings. The room, an erstwhile billiard saloon, was packed to the walls, and outside a small crowd, unable to gain admittance, waited with patience to hear the result of the inquest. A long trestle table, which the landlord of the "Ship" hired out for school-treats and the like, ran down the centre of the room. At the head of the table, in a wheel-back arm-chair, sat the Coroner. Ranged on his right hand were the jury; whilst opposite the jury, looking somewhat oddly assorted now they had been collected together, were the various witnesses subpœnaed by the police.

As the tinny ormulu clock on the mantelshelf chimed two, the Coroner struck the table with his gavel and the excited hum instantly died down.

The proceedings opened according to the usual formula. Ruth Tregarthan identified the body of the deceased as that of her uncle and went on to describe, in a quiet and rather tremulous voice, her discovery of the crime. Despite the ordeal to which she was being subjected she set out her evidence with commendable clarity, pausing every now and then to consider a quietly interposed question of the Coroner's, and then continuing with her story. Ruth sat down and Mrs. Cowper was called. She described how, in answer to Miss Tregarthan's call, she had rushed into the sitting-room and found Mr. Tregarthan lying shot on the floor. The housekeeper was obviously nervous and she delivered her evidence, for the most part, in a husky and quavering whisper. At a request from one of the older jurymen, who was a trifle hard of hearing, the Coroner asked her to speak up. But it was with an audible sigh of relief that Mrs. Cowper collapsed on her chair and surrendered her unenviable position to her husband.

Cowper, though more spruce in his attire than when the Inspector had last seen him, was by no means at his ease. His glance shifted from the Coroner to the jury, from the jury to the packed audience wedged tightly together on the benches at the far end of the room, and finally alighted with a stare of glassy anxiety on Inspector Bigswell. The Inspector did not move a muscle. Disconcerted, Cowper's gaze swung back on the Coroner, who was questioning him, and he began in a glib voice to corroborate his wife's story as to the discovery of the dead man. His relief was even greater than Mrs. Cowper's when the Coroner waved him into his chair and called on Doctor Pendrill.

The Doctor gave his evidence in a brisk, professional voice. Death, he said, had been due to gunshot wounds and was almost certainly instantaneous. As far as he could say the revolver had been discharged at fairly close quarters, for the bullet had entered the forehead, completely penetrating the skull. He further believed, on evidence since corroborated by the police, that the bullet was of a .45 calibre, such as was used in a Webley service-pattern revolver. Questioned by the Coroner, Bigswell endorsed this statement and the Doctor sat down.

Mrs. Mullion was then called and for the first time since the proceedings opened Inspector Bigswell's face was illuminated by a flicker of interest.

The Vicar, too, sitting on the front bench beside his sister, suddenly pushed his shooting-hat under the seat, leaned forward and clapped his hands over his splayed knees. He knew, of course, that Mrs Mullion had passed along the cliff-path on Monday night, but he was utterly surprised to see her subpœnaed as a witness. The Inspector had told him nothing about Mrs. Mullion's statement and he prayed fervently that the midwife's appearance in court had nothing to do with Ruth. The poor child had already suffered so much. He felt her distress so keenly. This was a ghastly enough ordeal for her, without her being badgered by a further cross-examination.

Once sworn in, Mrs. Mullion delivered her evidence at a breakneck speed, every now and then drawing in a huge gulp of air, which, like the momentary pause of a gear-change, only served to increase the speed of her narrative. Once again the deaf juryman lodged a complaint with the Coroner. The Coroner smiled in sympathy and asked the midwife to speak a little slower.

Then Mrs. Mullion came to the point in her story where she first saw the figure of Ruth Tregarthan on the cliff-path. She described how she had stayed in the shadow of the furze bushes and watched Miss Tregarthan's subsequent actions.

"You are certain that it was Miss Tregarthan whom you saw, Mrs. Mullion?" demanded the Coroner. "It was a darkish night, remember."

"Oh, it was her right enough, sir. The moon was out by then as I said before and the light from the house was shining on Miss Tregarthan's face."

Here the Inspector, amid the buzz of excitement which Mrs. Mullion's evidence had produced, quietly got to his feet and asked if he might put a question to the witness. The Coroner acceded to the request.

"You speak of a light coming from the house, Mrs. Mullion— what exactly do you mean by that?"

"From the sitting-room, sir. The curtains had been drawn back, as you may know, and the lights was full on."

"And this light came only from the sitting-room?"

Mrs. Mullion pondered this question for a moment. Now that her flow of evidence had been interrupted she was losing her confidence and growing self-conscious. She fiddled with her hair, reset her hat, and said at length:

"Now you come to ask me—there *was* another light. It was coming from a smaller window at the end of the house."

"I see," said the Inspector. "Thank you. That's all, Mrs. Mullion."

He turned to the Coroner, gave a half-salute and sat down.

"Now, Mrs. Mullion," resumed the Coroner. "You say that when you saw Miss Tregarthan you shrank back into the bushes. Surely that was not a natural thing to do? I take it that you know Miss Tregarthan?"

"Oh, yes, sir."

"And yet you didn't walk on and have a word with her?"

"No, sir. I didn't. Not when I saw what she had in her hand, I didn't. I was taken aback."

"Something in her hand?" queried the Coroner in a silken voice. "What was that, Mrs. Mullion?"

"A revolver!"

The effect of this statement, as the Inspector had anticipated, caused a sensation. An immediate murmur of excited voices rose and mounted to a veritable cross-fire of questions and exclamations. In the midst of this babel Ruth Tregarthan sprang up, pale and distraught, and faced Mrs. Mullion, who stood at the far end of the table. Doctor Pendrill placed next to the girl tugged at her sleeve. He whispered a few words into her ear and reluctantly, after a despairing look at the Coroner, Ruth sat down. The sharp hammering of the Coroner's gavel resounded above the general din. Abruptly a silence fell.

"Please! Please! Ladies and gentleman," said the Coroner in a disapproving voice. "You will kindly remember where you are and for what purpose this court is sitting." He turned to Mrs. Mullion, who, alarmed by the sensation which her evidence had evoked, was shrinking back from the united stare directed upon her. "Now, Mrs. Mullion, I want you to be absolutely certain on this point. You're on oath, remember. You still uphold that the object which you saw in Miss Tregarthan's hand was a revolver?"

"Yes, sir," replied Mrs. Mullion in faltering tones. "I'm sure of it!"

"Very well. Go on, Mrs. Mullion. Will you tell the jury what happened subsequently."

Mrs. Mullion described in a few, breathless words how Ruth Tregarthan had stared at the revolver, turned it over in her hand, and after a frightened look round, run to the side door and disappeared in the house.

This concluded Mrs. Mullion's evidence.

At once Ruth Tregarthan sprang up. The Coroner jerked his glasses a little down his nose and looked quizzically over the top of them.

"Do I take it, Miss Tregarthan," he said with a lugubrious air of perplexity, "that you wish to make a statement?"

"I do," replied Ruth with emphasis. "If it's in order. I should like to dispute the evidence of the last witness."

The Coroner considered the point for a moment, obtained the jury's feeling on the matter, and gave his consent.

Ruth swung round to where Mrs. Mullion, a pathetically shrinking bundle, was trying to hide herself behind the meagre frame of her husband. Both Inspector Bigswell and the Vicar were amazed by the change which had come over the girl. All her former timidity had vanished and it was with flushed cheeks and unnaturally bright eyes that she faced the unfortunate midwife.

"Now, Miss Tregarthan," said the Coroner, "what is it you want to say?"

"It's about the revolver. Mrs. Mullion is mistaken. That's all. I didn't have a revolver in my hand. What Mrs. Mullion saw may have looked like a revolver from the distance—but it wasn't. It was an ordinary electric pocket-torch."

"A pocket-lamp!" exclaimed the Coroner. "But surely it would be difficult to mistake a pocket-lamp for a revolver? Mrs. Mullion declares that you looked at it and turned it over in your hand. Do you deny having done that, Miss Tregarthan?"

"No."

"But if it was an ordinary pocket-lamp doesn't that strike you as rather an unusual thing to do? Your actions suggest that you were examining an object with which you were not familiar."

"I can easily explain that," said Ruth in a calm voice. "Just before I reached the wall of the garden, the torch flickered and went out. This rather surprised me since I had put in a new battery only the day before. When I came into the rays of light streaming from the window, I naturally stopped, looked at the torch, shook it and turned it over in my hand."

"I see. Well, Miss Tregarthan, I'm in no position to deny the truth of your statement. You're on oath. I have heard the evidence of Mrs. Mullion. She, too, is on oath. I can only, therefore, assume that owing to the indifferent light Mrs. Mullion was mistaken in what she saw. It's a case of your statement against hers. You realise that?" Ruth nodded. The Coroner turned to the jury. "I think, gentlemen, you will agree with me that we shall get no further by pursuing this particular matter. Out of fairness to Miss Tregarthan, however, I must ask you to dismiss the evidence of the previous witness. She, no doubt, was quite sincere in her belief that the object in Miss Tregarthan's hand was a revolver. But even the most cautious of us are liable, at times, to make mistakes, and, owing to a combination of various circumstances, Mrs. Mullion, in this case, was in fact … er … mistaken."

At the conclusion of this speech Ruth sat down and the Coroner, after glancing at the notes before him, addressed the jury.

"Now, gentlemen, you have heard the evidence of Miss Tregarthan and Mr. and Mrs. Cowper. You have further heard Doctor Pendrill's report as to how, in his opinion, the deceased met his death. You are concerned with three main points. Firstly—was the fatal shot discharged by accident? If you believe this to be the case, on the evidence given, you will bring in a verdict of accidental death. Secondly—was the shot fired by the deceased himself with the intention of putting an end to his own life—in which case you will bring in a verdict of suicide. Thirdly—was the fatal shot fired by a second person with the deliberate intention of killing the deceased, in which case, of course, you must bring in a verdict of murder. With regard to the first two suppositions—I need only remind you that three shots entered the room and that it has been proved, on the evidence of no less than three witnesses that the deceased himself must have drawn back the curtains of the sitting-room; which leads us to infer that the deceased was *deliberately* lured to the window by some person outside the house. Are you justified, therefore, in assuming that the shots were discharged by accident? Did the deceased commit suicide? Here I need only remind you that three shots entered the room from outside the house. This, I think you will agree, rules out the possibility of suicide. We are left, therefore, with the third assumption—that some person or persons wishing, for reasons not yet evident, to put an end to the deceased, deliberately, with malice aforethought, planned to kill him and on Monday last, the 23rd of March, succeeded in so doing. If you believe this to be the case you have no alternative but to bring in a verdict of wilful murder and—in lieu of further evidence as to the identity of the murderer—a verdict of murder by person or persons unknown. I therefore call upon you now, gentlemen, to consider your verdict."

After a brief discussion, without a retirement, the foreman of the jury rose and brought in the expected verdict. The Coroner got up, declared the proceedings at an end and, in a respectful silence, walked out of the room. The crowd, chattering excitedly, filed after him. The ormulu clock struck three.

CHAPTER XIV
THE NOTE

LATER, on Thursday evening, after an excellent dinner, Doctor Pendrill and the Vicar sat talking in the latter's study. It was the first real opportunity they had had to discuss in detail the mystery which surrounded Julius Tregarthan's death. Although the Doctor was sanguine as to the police's chance of making an early arrest, the Vicar was far less optimistic. If Inspector Bigswell was still following up his previous lines of investigation, with his suspicions centring on Ronald and Ruth, he felt that the police were barking up the wrong tree. Of Cowper's unspectacular entry into the arena he, of course, knew nothing. He knew the money had been stolen, but as the Inspector had not granted him another interview since Tuesday evening he had no idea that Bigswell had more or less driven home the theft of the notes to the gardener. He assumed, therefore, that Ronald Hardy was still the central figure in the Inspector's reconstructed picture of the crime. Pendrill, too, was under a similar impression.

"It's curious," said the Doctor, "that Hardy should draw attention to himself by disappearing. You'd think that any intelligent man would see the fallacy in an action of that sort. To my mind, Dodd, it's the strongest indication of his innocence. If he *had* murdered Tregarthan with malice aforethought, as the Inspector seems to suggest, then he would have carried on in a perfectly normal way. I'm sure of it. Hardy's got a first-class mind. He'd be incapable of such a piece of crass stupidity."

The Vicar in a mellifluous voice, born of perfect gastronomic harmony, agreed.

"Quite. Quite. I've never doubted his innocence for one moment. Whatever the cause of Ronald's sudden disappearance, I'm sure it's nothing to do with the murder of poor Tregarthan. Doubly sure, as a matter of fact, since the inquest this afternoon."

"On account of the failure of Mrs. Mullion's evidence? A ridiculous show, Dodd!"

"No, nothing to do with that. It was something I learnt *after* the inquest."

The Vicar, it appeared, had walked home from the "Ship" along the Vicarage road. There Tom Prattle had hailed him and asked him the time. They fell into conversation. Tom, bursting with pride at his discovery, had soon narrated the complete history of the rust-stained revolver; assuring the Vicar that, although the police chaps thought he wasn't listening, he had overheard one of them say that it belonged to Mr. Hardy. He spoke of the initials scratched on the butt. For himself, of course, he knew it wasn't Mr. Hardy's revolver. It was a German revolver hidden "in the trench" by a "ruddy German spy."

The Vicar guessed that for all Tom's idiosyncrasies he was telling the truth. A man of his mental calibre would be incapable of enlivening a barefaced lie with so many matter-of-fact details. Certainly he garnished his story with a strong Teutonic flavour, but the essence of the story was obviously based on facts.

"What I want to know," concluded the Vicar, "is why Ronald, who had ample time and opportunity to get rid of his revolver later on, threw it into a ditch a few hundred yards from the scene of the crime. You see, Pendrill—it's absurd! The more I look into the Inspector's theory the more flaws I see in it. What had Ronald to gain by murdering Ruth's uncle? Why didn't we find his footprints on the cliff-path? How was it that a man standing about twenty feet from the window put three shots into the room at such widely scattered points? Does that argue a man with war service? A man who knew how to use a revolver? Ronald, for example?"

"I know," said Pendrill, scratching his chin with the stem of his pipe, "that last point has puzzled me from the start. It might suggest a woman in the case. But somehow I don't think it does."

"Ruth? Mrs. Mullion?" enquired the Vicar "We can dismiss them completely. We *know* they didn't have a hand in the crime. Our intuitions tell us that. Then who, in the name of Heaven, Pendrill, *did* murder Tregarthan? I wondered last night, when I was turning things over in bed, if there had been a struggle on the cliff-path. That would account for the widely scattered shots. But did we see any sign of a struggle on the path? We didn't. In my opinion, the fact that the three shots entered the window at such diverse points is of far greater importance than we first supposed. I couldn't stop thinking about this curious factor in the case. Why, Pendrill, at twenty feet even I could put three successive shots through the door of a french window without hitting the side windows. I could almost do it with my eyes shut. Perhaps it would not be stretching the truth too far to say that a child could do it. But the fact remains, the three shots were scattered, and I believe than when we have found an explanation for this peculiarity we shall be a long way toward solving the problem of Tregarthan's death."

Pendrill's interest quickened.

"You've got a theory—is that it, Dodd?"

The Vicar hesitated before answering this question; then he said slowly:

"Let's say I have the glimmering of an idea which if followed up may put us on the road toward elucidating the identity of the criminal." Whereupon, diving into his waistcoat pocket, he produced a little square of paper. This he handed to the Doctor. "Read it," he suggested.

The Doctor did so.

> *I'm not wanting your money. I shall hold my*
> *tongue not for your sake but for his. I've no wish*
> *to hear further about this. M.L.*

"Well," asked the Vicar. "What do you make of it?"

"Nothing," said Pendrill, handing back the paper. "What the devil is it?"

The Vicar explained how he had come across the note in Tregarthan's desk and how he had handed the original to the Inspector.

"I kept a copy of the note," he explained. "It interested me. It rather looks as if poor Tregarthan was bribing somebody for the sake of their silence, doesn't it?"

Pendrill agreed.

"Probably a woman," he said, with the superior attitude of the confirmed bachelor toward the world feminine. "In a matter of this kind there's nearly always a woman at the bottom of it, Dodd."

"For once," said the Vicar with a twinkle, "I believe you're right."

"Of course I'm right," growled Pendrill. "I see it like this. Tregarthan had been having an affair with a married woman. Things had turned out awkwardly—the inevitable illegitimate, I suppose—and fearing the woman would let the cat out of the bag and tell her husband, our friend J. T. tried to square her with a good big wad of notes. How's that for a brilliant piece of deduction, eh, Dodd?"

"Oh, not bad. Not at all bad!" acknowledged the Vicar, leaning forward and patting Pendrill on the knee. "Have another drink?"

"Thanks," said Pendrill. "I'll mix it myself, Dodd, if you've no objection. I know your teetotal prejudices. I've always suspected that you've got a tidy packet of shares in a soda-water company!"

And with a look of stubborn severity he mixed a good stiff whiskey and soda, held it up to the light and blandly drew the Vicar's attention to it's deep, amber translucence.

"A layman's drink," he observed as he shovelled himself into the depths of his arm-chair. "Now, Dodd, to return to this note—who is M.L.?"

"Ah, there you've got me! I've been puzzling over those initials myself. It may or it may not be somebody in the parish. If, as you suggest, Tregarthan was having an affair with a married woman I'm inclined to think that it was outside the village. A scandal of that sort would scarcely pass unnoticed in a small place like Boscawen. Then, according to your theory, there was the child. What about the child, Pendrill? How was the woman to hush up the affair when the child was born?"

"Well that's simple enough," said Pendrill expansively. "Passed it off as her husband's child, of course! Heavens, man!

that sort of thing is done every day of the year and nobody a penny the wiser."

"But if the husband knew nothing about it, then this note has no connection whatsoever with the murder of Tregarthan."

"Who suggests that it has?"

"I do," said the Vicar promptly. "I have an idea that the note supplies us with a motive for the crime. Pure supposition, of course—but then, all theories spring at first from pure suppositions. Suppose the woman was unable to conceal the secret any longer. Suppose the thought of what she had done so preyed on her mind that she confessed to her husband. What then? Mightn't the husband, through motives of revenge, blinded by jealousy perhaps, decide to put an end to Tregarthan's life? It's a feasible supposition, isn't it?"

"Oh, quite," said Pendrill in sarcastic tones. "It explains away the scattered shots; the foot-prints, or rather the lack of them, on the cliff-path; the theft of the money from Tregarthan's person after he was killed. It explains everything, in fact!"

The Vicar, quite unruffled by the Doctor's criticism, went on in a quiet voice.

"No—wait a bit, my dear chap. Perhaps I've not been fair with you. I'm not hoping to explain away the mystery by solving the problem of the note alone. The note is just a little piece of the puzzle, that's all. But suppose we solve the problem of the note and the problem of the scattered shots and find that the answers to these two problems bear some relationship to each other. And further—suppose I have another little bit of the puzzle in my hand and I place this bit next to the other two bits, and then find that the three bits dovetail flawlessly, one into the other—what then? Aren't we perhaps on the way to seeing the identity of the murderer take shape?"

"And this third bit you speak of?"

"No! No! Don't ask me yet, Pendrill. Give me time to build up my theory a little more securely. At the moment it's shaky. It may fall to the ground at the first breath of criticism. I'm groping in the dark. But I do believe, Pendrill, that provided I can add a few more pieces to the three central bits of my puzzle—the picture of the murderer may, in the long run, emerge."

"And what exactly do you need now," asked Pendrill with sweet sarcasm, "to help you in your marvellous deductions?"

"A big ball of string," said the Vicar in a solemn voice.

Doctor Pendrill looked at his old friend with glum commiseration.

"You need a long holiday, Dodd. The shock of Tregarthan's murder has been too much for you."

"Drink up your whiskey!" retorted the Reverend Dodd, as he threw a couple of logs on to the already roaring fire and settled deeper into his chair. "It's time all good Christians were in bed!"

CHAPTER XV

COWPER MAKES A STATEMENT

INSPECTOR BIGSWELL was immensely puzzled. At every step the case was becoming infinitely more complicated. He was forced to confess to himself that for all his tireless investigation, he was little nearer the truth of Tregarthan's death than he had been when he first stepped into the Greylings sitting-room and found the man lying with his head in a spreading pool of blood. Two recent factors had entered in and upset the theory which he had expounded to the Superintendent—the theft of the notes, with the possibility that Cowper was the murderer, and the discovery of Hardy's revolver in the ditch. And now, after the Coroner's inquest, a third snag confronted him.

Had Mrs. Mullion really been mistaken about that revolver? That's what puzzled him. She had been so emphatic as to the absolute veracity of her evidence when she had first delivered it at the Constable's office. She had made an equally emphatic statement at the inquest It was quite obvious that the midwife really believed that Ruth Tregarthan had a revolver in her hand—and that, *before* she knew Tregarthan had been murdered. On the other hand, the girl was equally emphatic in her statement that it was not a revolver, but a pocket-torch.

Ruth Tregarthan's explanation was both simple and feasible. She had set out along the cliff at the height of the storm—what more natural than for her to be armed with an electric torch? The further fact that she had stopped, looked at the torch, turned it over in her hand, had also been satisfactorily accounted for. Which statement, therefore, was he to accept? As the Coroner had rightly said, it was a case of the midwife's word against the girl's. In the Coroner's case, he had justly decided against the acceptance of Mrs. Mullion's story, since the light was none too good and the woman was standing some little way off. But was he, the Inspector, justified in dismissing the woman's story without further thought? Surely not.

The girl's explanation of her escapade on Monday night was thin, extremely thin. He could not get away from the idea that her stealthy exit from the house that evening was connected with the revolver which she had picked up on the cliff-path. Of one thing he felt reasonably certain—the revolver which Tom Prattle had found in the ditch was not the weapon discharged by the murderer. A further minute examination of the Webley had revealed the fact that the inside of the barrel, although thinly speckled with rust, had not been fouled by a recent discharge. Why then had Hardy taken the revolver from its holster on the night of the murder and later, for no apparent reason, thrown it into the road-side ditch?

Was it possible that not one man, but two unconnected persons, each with an entirely different motive, had decided by some strange freak of chance to murder Tregarthan on the same night? And that one of them, Hardy, had failed, whilst the other had succeeded. And was the successful one Cowper? Cowper was a constantly recurring image in his mind. Guilt had been written all over the man's features at the inquest, but whether on account of the theft, the murder, or the theft and the murder combined, it was impossible to say. He decided, however, before returning to Greystoke to make further enquiries at Greylings.

When he arrived at the house, the Cowpers had just returned and Cowper, himself, was seated before the kitchen range removing his boots. Any doubts as to the identity of the broken foot-marks on the polished stool in the pantry no longer remained. The heel of the boot which Cowper was in the act of removing was studded with a horse-shoe of projecting nails.

"That's a good sensible pair of boots," Bigswell remarked casually. "Comfortable, too, by the look of them."

Cowper eyed the Inspector with unconcealed suspicion. Mrs. Cowper, however, was in a more amiable and talkative mood. Although nervous, she had been flattered by the publicity afforded her at the recent inquest.

"Oh, they're comfortable all right," she assured the Inspector. "But I wish he wouldn't wear the great, clumping things in the house. Laziness, that's what's the matter with him. Why only on Monday night, sir, just before——"

"A chap can't change 'is boots when 'e's always popping in and out of the place," cut in Cowper surlily. "I'm neither fish, fowl nor good red 'erring here. Odd-job man! That's what it amounts to. A 'ibrid—'alf gardener, 'alf butler. It's sickening."

"What happened on Monday night, Mrs. Cowper?" asked the Inspector, ignoring her husband's lament.

"Only that he clumped all over my nice clean kitchen in those very boots."

"And your nice clean sitting-room carpet as well, eh? By the way, Cowper, you were wearing those boots in the butler's pantry, weren't you?"

"Well—what of it?" asked Cowper, immediately on the defensive.

"Oh, nothing," replied the Inspector lightly. "Only I still can't see why you climbed on to the stool when you could easily have opened the pantry window from the ground. "That's all."

The result of this shot in the dark far exceeded, in the violence of its effect, the Inspector's most sanguine anticipations. Cowper, livid with anger, sprang to his feet and hurling his boot into the fender, swung round on Bigswell.

"What d'you mean by that, eh? What the 'ell are you after with me? You've done nothing but peer and pry into my doings ever since Monday night. What have you got on me? What if I did open the window? What if I did climb on to that stool? You can't prove nothing by that! If it's the money that's biting you——"

"The money!" exclaimed the Inspector.

"I said the money, didn't I? The money what was stolen from Mr. Tregarthan's wallet. Don't make out it's news to you."

"It isn't," said the Inspector in an icy voice. "But it's news to me that you knew anything about it. Surprising news! Who told you, eh? Come on—out with it! Where the devil did you get your information?"

For a moment Cowper stood with a stupefied look on his face, swaying on his stockinged feet, absolutely dumbfounded. His mouth hung open. His eyes were fixed in a fascinated stare on the Inspector's grim features. Then suddenly he crumpled up and collapsed in his chair.

"I ... I was——"

"Well?"

"It was Miss Tregarthan what told me," announced Cowper in a hoarse voice. Adding weakly: "Over the phone."

The Inspector smiled at the man's futile attempts to wriggle out of the predicament in which his own stupidity had placed him. He *knew* now that Cowper had stolen the notes.

"Well, that's easily verified," said the Inspector in brisk tones. He turned to Constable Fenner who stood in the doorway. "Get on to the Vicarage for me, will you, Fenner, and ask Miss Tregarthan if she will spare me a moment."

As the Constable turned to execute the order, a low groan broke from the man cowering before the fire. He buried his twitching face in his hands.

"All right," he whimpered. "All right."

With a wave of his hand the Inspector arrested Fenner's exit.

"Going to make a clean breast of it, Cowper?" he asked quietly. "Better in the long run, I assure you."

"What do you mean?" cried Mrs. Cowper, who now stood completely flummoxed by this sudden turn of events. "You're not trying to make out that Cowper has been stealing, Inspector? From Mr. Tregarthan? And him … dead!"

"That's exactly what I am trying to make out. I'm sorry. It's a shock for you—but facts are facts. Well, Cowper?"

Cowper scrambled, white-faced and shaky, to his feet.

"I've had a bad run of luck these last two months. 'Orses don't seem to——"

The Inspector cut in quickly.

"You can leave that now, Cowper. I must warn you, however, that anything you may say now will be taken down in writing and used in evidence. I'll take an official statement over at Greystoke." He motioned Fenner to take the man in charge. "You're under arrest, Cowper—understand? Take him out to the car, Constable."

When the sorry-faced man had lurched silently out of the kitchen, the Inspector turned to the housekeeper.

"I'm sorry for you, Mrs. Cowper, but duty's duty. I'll inform Miss Tregarthan about all this. She may want to make some new arrangement about looking after the house. You can't very well remain here by yourself."

Mrs. Cowper, on the verge of tears, nodded dumbly. She tried to speak but the words were choked by her rising emotions. Laying a kindly hand on her arm the Inspector murmured something about "I understand" and went out to the car.

Later, over at headquarters, Cowper was led before the Superintendent and formally charged with the theft of the notes. A statement, which ran as follows, was then taken.

"On Monday night, March 23rd, I was washing up the dinner things in the pantry. My wife was upstairs seeing to the soiled linen. Just after nine I realised I hadn't taken in the trudge of logs to Mr. Tregarthan. I got them from the kitchen and took them into the sitting-room. I found the master lying on the floor near the window. His head was in a pool of blood. I put down the trudge and took a look at him. I saw the bullet hole in his forehead and knew he was dead. There was a wallet sticking out of his inside breast-pocket. I could see a thickish wad of notes in the wallet. I was going to raise the alarm. Then my betting losses came into my mind. I thought I could see a chance of squaring my book-maker, who was pressing me for past debts. I took the wallet out of the master's pocket, using a handkerchief. I put the notes in my own pocket and stuck the wallet back in his. I noticed the trudge in the middle of the room where I'd left it. I put it by the fire-place, made a note of the time and went out of the room. I returned to the butler's pantry. Nobody had seen me, my wife still being upstairs and Miss Tregarthan out. I realised I'd got to get rid of the notes before the police came and made enquiries about the murder. I thought they'd connect the theft with the murder. After a bit of thinking, I remembered that one of the stones in the garden wall was loose. I opened the pantry window, got up onto the stool and climbed onto the wall. It was raining. I didn't want to leave any footmarks. I took out the stone and hid the notes behind it. I then returned to the pantry and closed the window. Later, when Miss Tregarthan found the master dead, I rushed out of the pantry and pretended I knew nothing of the murder."

When this statement had been taken, the Inspector, after a short conversation with the Superintendent, asked a few questions on his own account. He was not yet absolutely sure in his mind that Cowper was beyond suspicion with regard to the major crime. His story, of course, fitted in very accurately with the facts already known to the Inspector, but there were one or two points that he still wanted to clear up.

"With regard to the time, Cowper—you say you remembered about the logs just after nine o'clock. What exactly do you mean by that?"

"Well, just afore I came out of the sitting-room I took note of the time by the clock on the mantelshelf. It was then just on ten minutes past nine—so I must 'ave remembered those logs a bit before."

"You didn't move the body at all when you removed the notes?"

"No, sir."

"Nor move anything in the room?"

"No."

"And you didn't see anything unusual outside the uncurtained windows?" Cowper shook his head. "Had you been on the drive at all that evening?"

"Yes—I 'ad."

"Why?"

"To change the porch lamp. Just afore my missus went in to clear the dinner-table she noticed that the lamp outside the front door 'ad gone out. So I slipped out there and then and attended to the job."

This, as the Inspector realised, was obviously the truth. Cowper, in giving his explanation, must have realised that it would be easy to verify the truth of his assertion by questioning the housekeeper. Well and good. This accounted, then, for the gravel which had collected between the nails of his boots and which, later, the Inspector had found deposited on the oak stool.

"Ex-service man, Cowper?"

"Yes, sir," acknowledged Cowper with a pale grin. "Lance-Corporal in the——"

"Ever handled a revolver?" cut in the Inspector quickly.

"Never, sir."

"Never owned one, I suppose?"

"No, sir."

Inspector Bigswell turned to the Superintendent.

"That's all, sir. Thank you."

The Superintendent motioned to the Constable standing in the doorway and Cowper was led away to the cells, there to await his appearance before the local magistrates. It was pretty well certain, however, that his case would come up, eventually, at the quarterly sessions. Particularly as the theft bore some connection with Tregarthan's murder.

As soon as they were alone, the Superintendent turned to Bigswell, who was seated on the far side of the desk drumming his fingers on his open notebook.

"Well—what d'you make of it, Bigswell?"

"A blind-alley business," replied the Inspector with a dismal grin. "Waste of valuable time, I'm afraid. The man's telling the truth. You agree, Sir?"

The Superintendent did.

"A petty criminal type—not the major article," was his pertinent verdict. "Still it was snappy work, Bigswell. I'll see that the Chief gets an ungarbled account of your smartness."

"For those kind words ... many thanks!"

The two men laughed.

"No news of Hardy, I suppose?" asked the Inspector, obviously expecting a negative answer.

"None. The Yard are engaged in the usual routine combout of all the likely places—but so far without result.

The Inspector sighed, and shutting his note-book got slowly to his feet.

"A trifle depressed, eh, Bigswell?"

"Well, sir, things aren't turning out any too well. Until I can get hold of Hardy and put him through a bit of third degree I'm, more or less, at a standstill."

He explained briefly the results of the day's investigations— the collapse of Mrs. Mullion's evidence and the discovery of the initialled revolver.

"So you can see what I'm up against, sir. With Cowper and that poacher fellow struck off the list, I'm left with Ronald Hardy. But since Hardy's revolver has been found in the ditch, fully loaded and with the barrel unfouled, I'm damned if I quite see how *he* enters into the business now!"

"You don't think it was a plant?"

"The revolver, sir? But why?"

"Misleading clue. He might have initialled the revolver specially for the occasion, removed the spent cartridges after the murder, reloaded it and cleaned the barrel."

"Umph! Seems a trifle unlikely somehow. There may be something in it, but I'm still inclined to believe that the Tregarthan girl *did* have a revolver in her hand when Mrs. Mullion saw her."

"And perjured herself at the inquest?"

"Exactly."

"But why?"

"Because she wanted to shield Hardy."

"Then he must have had two revolvers."

"That's just the conclusion I've come to, sir. With one revolver he commits the murder. The second, the initialled one, he previously drops in the ditch, perhaps realising that it would be found by Tom Prattle."

"It certainly seems the only explanation," agreed the Superintendent without much enthusiasm. "By the way—anybody on duty at Greylings to-night? I see Fenner came back with you."

"Yes—the local Constable. I saw him before coming over. I've also let Miss Tregarthan know about Cowper. The housekeeper is moving up to the Vicarage this evening, which leaves Grouch in sole charge of Greylings."

"Then you'll get in touch with him and corroborate Cowper's statement about the hiding-place of those notes."

"I was going to, sir."

"Good."

"Nothing more, is there, sir?"

"Nothing."

"Right, sir—then I think I'll get home and run over my notes. I may have missed something. You never know."

"In my opinion," said the Superintendent slowly, "an armchair review of a case is often far more profitable than any number of enquiries and cross-examinations. You get a better perspective. More wood. Fewer trees. You agree, Bigswell? Good night!"

CHAPTER XVI

THE VICAR MAKES AN EXPERIMENT

IT was a long time before the Vicar got to sleep after Pendrill's departure that Thursday night. Little scraps of their conversation floated into his mind and started him off on all manner of speculations. He was troubled as to the identity of the person who had written the note. That it was a woman, he did not doubt. The handwriting alone was characteristic enough of the female sex to leave little doubt in his mind on that score. But the initials puzzled him. Although he racked his brains in an effort to recall some woman in the locality whose name would fit the initials M.L. he failed entirely. There were many L.'s in the village and, to his knowledge, three M.L.'s, but not one of them could possibly be identified with the sender of the note.

With regard to the scattered shots, he now felt reasonably certain that he had found an explanation and it was his intention to put his theory to the test the very next morning. It would mean an interview with the Inspector because the experiment which he was desirous of making necessitated his entry into Greylings.

Next morning, therefore, he rose early and breakfasted alone before the womenfolk showed up. Then donning his inevitable shooting-hat and selecting a stout ash stick from the luxuriant spray in the umbrella-stand, he set out for the village. There he made his way to the Boscawen General Stores, which purveyed everything from hams to hair-pins, and bought a large ball of string. With this purchase under

his arm he returned along the cliff-path to Greylings. There
he found the Inspector in conversation with Grouch. Bigswell
greeted him cheerily.

"Good morning, sir. You're the very man I was coming to
see." He slapped a wad of notes on to the table. "Firstly about
those. Cowper made a full confession when we got him over
at Greystoke last night. He'd hidden the stuff in the garden
wall. It's all there, Mr. Dodd. Thirty-eight pounds."

The Vicar beamed genially.

"I must congratulate you, Inspector, on your astuteness. Do
you wish me to hand over the money to Miss Tregarthan?"

"If you will. And there's another point. With Miss Tregarthan's
permission, now that the Cowpers are no longer here, I should
like to lock up the house for the time being. I don't want things
touched and it's a waste of the Constable's valuable time for him
to remain on duty. Do you think she'll raise any objection to the
idea, sir?"

"Oh, dear, no —none whatever. I'm quite sure of it. In fact
I'll take the full responsibility for giving you her permission,
here and now, if you wish."

"Well, Mr. Dodd, it would save time."

"Then perhaps I could lock up the house for you and return
the keys to Miss Tregarthan?"

The Inspector readily agreed to this plan and, after he and
Grouch had made a tour of the windows to see that all was
secure, they climbed into the police car and drove off in the
direction of the village.

The Vicar was elated. So far so good. He was now in a
position to carry on with his experiment without fear of

censure or further interruption. If the Inspector should return he could always put forward the excuse that he was making a final examination of Tregarthan's papers. Humming a little tune he unwrapped his parcel and without delay proceeded to work.

He first reascertained the exact spots where the two bullets, which had missed Tregarthan, had buried themselves in the wall opposite the french windows. The picture of the windjammer had now been taken down, so that the first of the bullet holes was clearly visible about two feet below the ceiling. Taking a large drawing-pin from a box in his pocket, the Vicar pinned the loose end of the twine exactly into the hole. He then unwound about forty feet of the string from the ball and cut it off with a penknife. A second and equal length he then securely drawing-pinned to the second hole in the wall—in this case only an inch or so below the ceiling. Testing his handiwork by pulling lightly on the two strings, he reinforced the single drawing-pin with one or two more and then, satisfied that they would hold, he led the two strings across to the french window. There he threaded the loose ends through the two starred holes in the glass, corresponding to the two holes in the wall.

His next action was to place a chair opposite the glass-paned door at the approximate spot where Tregarthan must have been standing when the fatal bullet entered his brain. To the back of this chair he lashed his walking-stick, so that it projected considerably above the top of it. Tregarthan's height he calculated at a little under six feet and, seeing that he was possessed of a high forehead, he drew out a tape-measure from his pocket and marked out a spot on the walking-stick about five feet nine inches from the ground. Round this point he tied a third length of string and threaded it through the bullet-hole in the glass door.

All this the Vicar did with extreme deftness, completely absorbed in his curious task. He realised, not without a thrill of expectation, that the results of his experiment might lead him on to a new and definite conclusion about the murder. Should this line of investigation meet with success, he felt certain that the fresh evidence accruing from it would be sufficient to convince the Inspector that both Ruth and Ronald were innocent of the crime.

Leaving the sitting-room, he crossed through the kitchen into the scullery, where in one corner he found a tall bundle of faggots. From this he selected three fairly thick stakes, which he pointed with his penknife. A further search revealed a serviceable coal-hammer. Armed with this and the three sharpened poles he returned to the sitting-room, unlocked the door of the french windows and went out into the garden.

Placing the poles and the hammer on the cliff-path, he returned to the window and one by one led the strings across the lawn and over the seaward wall. Then, with surprising alacrity for one so tubby, he vaulted the wall and with trembling hands, immensely keyed-up and excited, he took up the middle string and pulled it taut.

Over this part of the business the Vicar exercised abnormal care. He had to make quite certain that the tautened string was at no point touching the splintered rim of the bullet-hole in the window. The slightest deviation and the true line of the bullet's flight would be falsely estimated. Satisfied, at length, that he had hit upon the exact point from which the bullet was fired, he drove in the first of the stakes. It was no easy matter, since the stake was a good seven feet high, but by balancing himself on the wall he eventually succeeded in driving the pole into the ground. Then, once more making an exact and delicate adjustment of the middle string, he tied it to the stick.

Fifteen minutes later, the three stakes with their corresponding strings were in position.

Instantly the Vicar realised that his experiment had succeeded far beyond his most sanguine hopes. He was elated beyond measure. There was no atom of doubt left in his mind, then, that the theory which he had evolved to explain away the scattered shots was the right one. The only one in fact. The Inspector was wrong. Neither Ruth nor Ronald could have shot Tregarthan. It was out of the question.

Suppose that Tregarthan *had* been murdered from the cliff-path. It seemed reasonable to affirm that the murderer had fired the three shots in quick succession, whilst standing at one particular spot. This being so, the three strings, corresponding to the line of flight of the three bullets, should converge, more or less, at one point. One stake, in fact, should have been sufficient to accommodate all three strings. But this was by no means the case. A good six feet separated the outer poles from the centre one. In other words, the three bullets had been fired from three entirely different spots. But why? Surely, when speed of execution was all-important, once the criminal had lifted his revolver and taken aim, he would discharge the three shots in rapid succession? He would not fire his first shot, walk six feet or so along the path, fire again, walk on and fire a third time. The idea was illogical.

This was the first factor in the Vicar's startling discovery.

The second factor was even more startling and even less explicable, if the murderer had shot Tregarthan from the cliff-path. The strings terminated, not at eye-level as one would expect, but at a point nearly seven feet from the ground. This meant, then, that the criminal had not only walked along the path discharging the three shots at intervals, but, at the same time, he had held the revolver in an impossible position high above his head and fired accordingly. Even if one accepted the possibility of the first factor it was inconceivable that one could accept the second. No man, however excited, however nervous and fearful, would attempt to murder a man by shooting him, without taking some sort of aim.

What, then, was the conclusion the Vicar arrived at by result of his experiment? Simply that Tregarthan had *not* been shot from the cliff path.

But the Vicar was prepared to go further than this. He was prepared to accept the fact, with absolute certainty, that Tregarthan had not been shot by any man on land at all. He knew, then, that his suspicions were correct. His theory held water.

Tregarthan had been shot from the sea!

In his moment of triumph the Vicar had no doubts about this. A small boat fairly close in under the cliff—what simpler explanation for the scattered shots? A man in a rocking boat would have the greatest difficulty in taking accurate aim.

There was, at all times of the day, a strong current sweeping round the head of the ness. The boat would not only rock, but drift. Wasn't that drift indicated by the fact that the three shots had been fired from three different points? It was a more than feasible theory.

The Vicar triumphed.

If the shots were fired from the sea, according to the evidence collected by the Inspector, neither Ruth nor Ronald Hardy could now be incriminated. Their alibis were perfect. Ruth was seen on the cliff-path by Mrs. Mullion. Ronald was seen by Bedruthen in his car up on the Vicarage road. The only possible landing-places along that line of coast were Towan Cove and the cove at Boscawen itself. It would have been impossible for Ronald to have left Cove Cottage at 8.40 (on evidence supplied by Mrs. Peewit), driven his car down to the cove, boarded a boat, pulled out to the ness, shot Tregarthan, pulled back to the cove and be seen on the Vicarage road at nine o'clock. No—if his theory was correct—the reason for Ronald's sudden disappearance had nothing to do with the murder.

Other facts emerged. The strange lack of footprints on the cliff-path, for example. Now it was obvious. The murderer had evolved a foresighted scheme in which footprints were non-existent.

What to do then?—the Vicar wondered. Might it not be a good scheme to walk along to Towan Cove and borrow Joe Burdon's boat. He could then row along under the cliff and put his new-found theory to the acid test. If, at a short distance from the land, the low cliff did not intervene between the boat and the french windows, it was pretty well certain that this was the method of approach adopted by the murderer.

Leaving his strings in position, since they would aid him in his immediate project, he returned with a brisk step to fetch his hat from the sitting-room. Entering the hall, however, much to his confusion and annoyance, the front door was flung open and Inspector Bigswell entered.

"Still here, Mr. Dodd?"

"Yes ... yes," stammered the Vicar. "Still here. A little matter I had to clear up, Inspector. A ... private matter."

The Inspector crossed into the sitting-room. His voice rang out sharply.

"In the name of heaven, Mr. Dodd, what the thunder's all this?"

Realising that the cat was hopelessly out of the bag, feeling rather like a small boy caught in some nefarious act, the Vicar offered a hasty explanation. The Inspector listened in profound silence. At first he was sceptical, but when the Vicar came to the point of elucidating the discrepancies between the supposed and actual flight of the three bullets, the Inspector sprang to his feet and whistled.

"I believe you've hit on a valuable clue, sir! Can't think why the idea didn't occur to me. Here, let's go down to the cliff-path. This is going to mean something, if I'm not mistaken! Something pretty conclusive, Mr. Dodd."

With long, eager strides the Inspector crossed the little lawn and vaulted the wall. The Vicar, secretly enjoying the Inspector's amazement, continued with his explanation.

"You see how I mean, Inspector? Those poles are over six feet apart."

"Oh, I get it all right!" growled the Inspector. "No doubt about the shots having come from three different points. It beats me! What's your explanation, sir?"

The Vicar pointed with a solemn look at the glittering spread of the Atlantic.

"The sea!" exclaimed the Inspector. "A boat!"

"Exactly."

With a diffident air, as if excusing himself for propounding a theory in the face of a professional detective, the Vicar ran over the reasons for his assumption.

"Well, it seems reasonable enough, Mr. Dodd," acknowledged the Inspector grudgingly. "If you're right then, of course, it knocks my idea of the Ruth Tregarthan-Ronald Hardy collaboration on the head. But wait a minute. Not too fast! You said just now that no man in his senses would fire a revolver, holding it at an arm's length above his head. Quite right, sir! He wouldn't. But suppose our man was not on the cliff-path but on the wall—what then, eh?"

"On the wall?"

The Inspector rapidly unfolded his idea about the hurdles, the possibility that Hardy had climbed along the wall and dropped his revolver by accident on to the cliff-path.

"What then? The eye-level is about right if a man was kneeling up on the wall, isn't it? And besides, what about the revolver? Oh, I know Mrs. Mullion's evidence was turned down by the Coroner—but I have an idea that Miss Tregarthan was not telling the truth."

"But that would be perjury, Inspector!"

The Inspector grinned.

"It's not unknown. Young ladies wishing to shield their young men commit perjury—I was going to say—as a matter of course. There's another point which makes me believe that the girl wasn't telling the truth. The broken impression of a revolver. I found it midway along the path here." The Inspector crouched down and examined the drying mud. "You've just about hammered your darned stick right through the centre of it! But it was there right enough. You can take my word for it. I verified the measurements after the inquest and they tallied. A Webley .45. How are you going to account for that, Mr. Dodd?"

"Simply," replied the Vicar in a genial voice. "Dear me, Inspector, the more I look into my assumption, the more clearly I see the whole truth of the matter. Suppose after murdering poor Tregarthan, the man rowed in close to the cliff. He had only to toss his revolver up on to the path to add an extremely confusing factor to the case. Because you believed the revolver to have been on the cliff-path you naturally assumed that it had been dropped by somebody on land. As it happens, you suspect it was dropped by accident from the wall. But surely, Inspector, if Hardy was on the wall when he shot Tregarthan—as you suppose—isn't it highly improbable that he'd fire the shots from three widely different points? The hurdles, I see, are over there, to the left. That means he mounted the wall at that corner. Now what on earth possessed him to crawl, not only to the middle of the wall, but very nearly to the far end of the wall, when we can see quite clearly that Tregarthan would have been visible from any point on the wall? Peculiar, isn't it, Inspector?"

Bigswell nodded dolefully. Already he could see his carefully erected case collapsing like a house of cards.

"It certainly looks as if you're right," he admitted.

"I've been barking up the wrong tree. What do you propose now, Mr. Dodd? I can tell you—your lines of investigation," he pointed with a wry smile at the three strings emerging from the house, "have properly upset mine!"

The Vicar apologised.

"I fear I've been a trifle presumptuous. But as things stood—I feel sure you understand, Inspector?"

"And now?"

"Well, my idea was to borrow a boat and have a look at things from the murderer's point of view."

"A good scheme," agreed the Inspector. "I'll come with you, if you've no objection, sir."

The Vicar laughed.

"It's rather fantastic, isn't it? But I want you to realise, Inspector, that as far as my very amateur attempts at deduction are concerned—well, shall we say, I hand them over to you? It's Ruth I've been thinking of all along. The rest doesn't matter a farthing to me. It's your job, Inspector— not mine. Shall we say no more about it? You can rely on my discretion."

Later, as they were walking along the cliff-path to Towan Cove, the Vicar said:

"There's just one person I'd like to take into my confidence over this—Doctor Pendrill. It's not often I get the chance of astonishing him. It will give me a certain ascendancy, I feel, over his confirmed agnosticism. He's inclined to poke fun at us clergy as impractical visionaries. I should like to disillusion him, Inspector. Who knows? A man's first step along the road to salvation is often brought about by the absurdest and most irrelevant events!"

CHAPTER XVII

ENTER RONALD HARDY

Leaving the Inspector to look round Towan Cove, the Vicar climbed up out of the gully on the far side and made his way along the cliff-top to the slate quarries. He found Joe Burdon, his eyes protected by a pair of monstrous goggles, trimming up the raw edge of a thick, green-grey slab of Cornish slate. The man touched his hat.

"Morning, Burdon," said the Vicar affably. "I've come to ask a favour of you."

"Aye?"

"I want the loan of your boat for about half an hour. Can it be done?"

"Aye, sir. You're welcome, such as she is. Not much of a tub to look at, I reckon—rather too broad in the beam for speed. Still, she's just had a fresh lick o' paint and she's seaworthy enough." He pushed up his goggles on to his forehead and peered inquiringly at the Vicar. "Going fishing, sir?"

The Vicar shook his head.

"Not exactly, Burdon. I want to have a look at something along under the cliff."

"Maybe it's something to do with the murder, eh? I heard as there's an Inspector on the job." He pointed down into the cove, where a little blue figure was strolling along the rocky quayside.

"That's him, maybe?"

"Quite right. It is something to do with the murder. I'm not in a position to tell you more than that, I'm afraid, but it's a matter of some importance to the police."

"Well, you know the boat, don't you, sir? Black with a white line. You can't mistake her."

And, touching his hat once more, Joe Burdon lowered his goggles and returned to his slate-trimming.

"There are six boats here," said the Inspector when the Vicar had joined him on the diminutive quayside. "Six boats—six possibles. That's from Towan Cove alone, and Lord knows how many there are over at Boscawen."

"A fair sprinkling," said the Vicar. "I don't think it's going to be easy."

The Inspector grunted his agreement and they climbed into the boat. She was a tubby little craft of a dinghy type, broad in the beam, yet astonishingly easy to handle. The Inspector took the oars and the Vicar sat in the stern, attending to the rudder-lines. In a short time the boat shot clear of the sheltering cove and responded to the long, slow swell of the open sea. Keeping well in under the cliff, they nosed along at a fair speed until the roof of Greylings hove in sight just above them.

"Now," said the Inspector, "we'll manipulate the boat so that we can find the nearest point to land from which Tregarthan would have been visible. This will give us some idea of the distance from which the shots were fired."

After one or two false starts, where, due to strong currents, they overshot the mark before being able to check up, the Vicar suddenly cried: "Now!" The Inspector brought the boat up short. A hasty look satisfied them that their assumption was not only feasible, but in view of their proximity to the cliff, a highly probable one. The distance, in all, could have been little over fifty feet. Given the fact that Tregarthan was silhouetted against the bright light of the room, it would not have been difficult shooting. Although the marksman was moving, the target was static, and with six bullets at his disposal the murderer had more than a fair chance of success.

"What about the gravel?" asked the Vicar. "You told me that you found gravel under the window. Is the distance too great, do you think, for our man to have flung a handful against the glass?"

"Oh, he'd reach the house easy enough. The wind was behind him, remember, blowing off the sea. Besides, he may have moved in a bit closer and flung it."

"Which means," said the Vicar, "that we're probably on the right track?"

"Almost certainly," agreed the Inspector. "Take a look at those lines of yours. If they were projected they would just about meet the sea at this spot. That's what we should expect. You see, Mr. Dodd, how it's all fitting in?" The Inspector dug a single oar into the water and smartly pivoted the boat. "Now I want to get hold of a complete list of all boats and their owners. Then, with your help, Mr. Dodd, I'd like to eliminate the probables from the possibles and the possibles from the impossibles." Adding dismally, "If there are any impossibles!"

Later, when they parted at Greylings, the Inspector held out his hand.

"I'll see you later, Mr. Dodd, if there are any developments. Mind you, I still hold to the theory that Tregarthan *could* have been shot from the wall. Hardy's disappearance hasn't been accounted for. Can't overlook that fact. Then there was that revolver of his found in the ditch. He *had* a revolver with him on the night of the murder. If he is innocent then why doesn't he come forward? And what about Miss Tregarthan's curious behaviour on Monday night and her behaviour at the inquest? Can't overlook that either. She, for one, thinks Hardy did it. That's why she perjured herself. And if she *thinks* he did, then we have every reason to suppose that he did do it. I'm sorry, Mr. Dodd. I know all this goes against your—what did you call it?—intuition theory, eh? But facts are facts and until I can find an explanation for every single one of 'em, then I'm bound to keep Hardy and Miss Tregarthan on my list of suspects," adding with a smile, "unless, of course, you can decorate this new road of inquiry with a few more signposts. It's a possibility anyway, and I'm going to follow up your supposition even if it does end in a blank wall. I promise you that, Mr. Dodd."

The men parted. The Vicar returned at once to the Vicarage, whilst Bigswell returned by car to the Constable's office. From there he and Grouch proceeded to the cove, where a number of boats were lying, like a catch of fish, on a concrete slipway. These the Inspector examined carefully, one by one, but no clue was forthcoming. He felt, therefore, that the only thing left for him to do was to draw up a list, with Grouch's help, of all those men who owned boats either in Boscawen itself or at Towan Cove. There was a chance, of course, that the boat had set out from a harbourage further up or down the coast, but, for the time being, Inspector Bigswell dismissed this idea as improbable. The storm had come up quickly and, accepting the fact that the murderer had reckoned on a thunder-clap to cover the sound of the shots, it seemed fairly conclusive that he had set out along the coast from a nearby point.

One thing puzzled him. If the Vicar's assumption was correct, how was it that the gravel under the window corresponded with the gravel on the Greylings drive? If the stuff had been thrown against the window by the man in the boat, then he must have collected a sample of this particular gravel beforehand. Was this another cunning attempt on the part of the criminal to shift suspicion from the sea on to the land? It was possible. On the other hand mightn't it argue an accomplice? Hardy, perhaps? Ruth Tregarthan? Even Cowper? If the man in the boat had flung the gravel, then it was quite possible that the remnants of the heap would still be lying in the bottom of the boat. He hadn't thought of that!

He returned, therefore, and made a further examination of the Boscawen boats, but again he drew a blank. He made a mental note, however, to re-examine the six boats over at Towan Cove. A single grain of that particular gravel in any one of the boats would, he realised, be sufficient evidence to drive home the crime to a particular individual.

As fate would have it, the Inspector was not destined to return to Towan Cove that morning. As he and the Constable breasted the short rise from the shore level, Grimmet appeared running smartly towards them.

"What is it?"

"You're wanted on the phone, sir. Greystoke headquarters. Urgent, sir."

Hurrying to the Constable's office, Bigswell took up the receiver.

"Hullo? Yes, sir. Bigswell speaking. You've what? Good heavens!—when, sir? Five minutes ago? Walked in, you say? No. No. I'll come over right away." He hung up and swung

round on Grimmet. "We're going over to Greystoke at once."
He noticed Grouch's ill-concealed look of enquiry. "Good
news, Grouch. Hardy's given himself up. He's just walked
into H.Q."

"A confession, sir?"

"Can't say yet. He's made no statement. I may be over later
to-day. In the meantime get that list of boat-owners ready.
I may want it."

The car shot off up the hill and disappeared over the rise of
the naked common, heading swiftly for Greystoke.

The Superintendent, obviously excited, was waiting for
Bigswell in his office.

"I've taken no statement as yet, Inspector. He's your pigeon.
Looks as if things are going to move at last, eh?"

"I hope so, sir," replied Bigswell fervently. "Can we have
him in right away?" The Superintendent nodded and gave an
order to an attendant Constable. "You say he walked in, sir.
What about the Yard?"

"They must have missed him. As far as I can make out,
Hardy came down by train in the normal way and reported
here without delay. Said he'd seen his photo in the papers in
connection with the Greylings murder and wished to make a
statement. Further than that I don't know."

"What I can't make out——" began the Inspector, but
a warning hiss from the Superintendent cut him short, as
the door opened and Ronald Hardy was ushered into the
room.

Bigswell was struck at once by the man's appearance. He
looked pale and haggard. His overcoat seemed to hang loosely
from his slim and rather boney frame. His movements were

those of a man in the throes of a violent nervous strain. In one hand he crushed a soft felt hat, in the other he grasped a pair of driving-gauntlets which he tapped incessantly against his thigh.

The Superintendent motioned the young man to a chair. With a faint smile of thanks he sat down, placing his hat and gloves beside him, and plunged his hands deeply into his over-coat pockets.

"This is Inspector Bigswell, Mr. Hardy," explained the Superintendent. "He's investigating the case you've come to see us about."

The Inspector saluted and Hardy acknowledged the introduction with a curt nod.

"Well, it's like this," he said without further preliminary. "I haven't opened a single newspaper since Monday until this morning. You can imagine the shock I received when I saw my own face staring at me from the front page. When I read of Mr. Tregarthan's murder I was more than shocked—I was horrified. You see, I'd known the Tregarthans for some time. In fact, I'd seen Mr. Tregarthan only an hour or so before he was murdered. Naturally, when I saw that I was wanted in connection with the crime, I dashed off to the station and caught the first train down. And here I am."

"It's a great pity, Mr. Hardy, that you didn't show up sooner," said the Inspector. "You realise that a lot of valuable time has been wasted in efforts to trace your whereabouts."

"No—I hadn't realised that," replied Hardy with complete frankness. "Why should I have done? I knew nothing about Tregarthan's death until this morning. I've told you that already."

"But a murder of this sort—it's on every newspaper plac-
ard. Everybody talks about it. You disappeared on Monday
night, Mr. Hardy—to-day's Friday. That's a lapse of nearly
four days. Do you mean to tell me that you have been out and
about in London for nearly four days without hearing a word
about the murder?"

"But I haven't been out and about. That's just it. I arrived in
London late on Monday night. I had made no arrangements
as to where I was going to stay, so I took a taxi out to Hampstead. Some years ago I had rooms there in Fellows Road
and I knew the landlady was an obliging sort—so I knocked
her up and got her to take me in. From that moment until
this morning I have not left the house. Mrs. Wittels, that's
the landlady, served all my meals in my room. I ordered no
newspaper. Mrs. Wittels apparently doesn't read a newspaper, else otherwise she must have seen my photo and drawn
my attention to it." Adding wryly: "Or at any rate ... Scotland Yard's!"

"Is it a custom of yours, Mr. Hardy, to keep to your room
for days on end?"

"Quite often I do—yes. Perhaps, as you know, I'm a novelist. Well sometimes, due to the actuation of a peculiar influence, I'm blessed, in common with others of the species, with
what is called inspiration. As it happened, when I arrived in
London, I was working on the final chapters of a novel and
I settled down there and then, after a night's sleep, to finish
it. This morning I did finish it. But it meant three days of
continuous writing. In the circumstances it was quite natural
that I should know nothing of Tregarthan's death. You see,
Inspector?"

"You realise," said Bigswell weightily, "that your sudden disappearance had placed you in a somewhat precarious position. You may be able to offer a satisfactory explanation, Mr. Hardy—but until you do I'm bound to view your movements with suspicion. You see why?"

"Of course. I quite understand that from the official point of view I may be a suspect. That's why I wish to make a full statement."

"Before you do that," put in the Inspector quickly, "let's divide the statement into three parts. Firstly, I would like to know exactly what you did after you reached London on Monday night until you arrived down here to-day. Secondly I want to know exactly what transpired at Cove Cottage between the hours of seven-thirty and eight-forty-five on Monday evening. And thirdly——what were your exact movements, Mr. Hardy, from eight-forty-five until you boarded the train here that same night. Now let's deal with them in order."

"Well, the first point I have already more or less cleared up. I took a taxi out to Hampstead and knocked up Mrs. Wittels. As luck would have it, she had a large bed-sitting-room vacant and I moved in there and then."

"And the address?" queried the Inspector.

"Plane House, Fellows Road, Hampstead, N.W."

The Inspector made a note of this so that he could easily verify the truth of Hardy's statements, if necessary, later on.

"For reasons which I will explain later," went on Hardy, "I slept badly that night, but the next morning, despite my lack of sleep, I got out the MS. of my novel and started to work on it. I explained to Mrs. Wittels that I wanted all my meals served in my bedroom and that I did not wish to be interrupted."

"You had packed the manuscript, I take it? You intended to work on it when you left Boscawen on Monday night, Mr. Hardy?"

"No, as a matter of fact, I didn't. I hadn't packed anything. When I left Cove Cottage I had no intention then of going to London at all." He smiled a trifle grimly. "My actual intentions were a little less commonplace, Inspector. But that again I must explain in due course. When I say I had the manuscript—it's not quite accurate. I had *part* of the manuscript in my pocket—the last few chapters that I had been working on the day before. I'd been out for a walk, you see, on Monday morning, and, as I like to read my work aloud, I'd gone down on to the shore by the cove and later stuffed the papers into my coat pocket. It was pure chance that they should be with me in London. A lucky chance, I admit. I explained, of course, to Mrs. Wittels that I'd left in a hurry and got her to run out on Tuesday morning with a list of the few articles that I wanted. All Tuesday I wrote. That night I slept soundly, and the next day, finding the mood was still on me, I continued writing. The same thing happened on Wednesday and Thursday. I had all my meals in my room. Save for the exchange of a few trite remarks with my landlady, I neither saw nor spoke to anybody. Late Thursday night I finished the novel and, utterly exhausted, fell asleep in an arm-chair. Early this morning, before breakfast, I went out for a constitutional on Primrose Hill. On my way back I called at a newsagent's to replenish my stock of tobacco. I also bought a couple of newspapers. The first thing I noticed when I opened the paper was a photo of myself, in uniform, below which was a caption demanding information as to my whereabouts. In an adjacent column was an account of the police's progress in the unravelling of what was called 'The Cornish Coast Murder.' That was the first I knew about Tregarthan's death. I was shocked and horrified. I had good reason to be." Again Hardy smiled—a wry and rather tortured smile. "You see, Inspector, I may as well be quite frank with you—Miss Tregarthan and I had been friends for some time. Intimate friends in fact. I realised what a terrible shock it must have been for her. I realised, too, from the newspaper reports that, on account of a series of unfortunate coincidences, I was suspected of having a hand in the crime. I repeat—Miss Tregarthan and I had been great friends. It was natural that I should wish to clear myself in her eyes. I rushed off to the station and caught the first train down to Greystoke. Fearing I might be recognised on the way, I muffled my face in my overcoat and pulled down my hat well over my eyes. That's all, Inspector. I think that explains all you want to know about that part of my doings."

"One thing, Mr. Hardy. You say you and Miss Tregarthan *had* been great friends. Why the past tense?"

"Simply that on Monday evening I learnt that she no longer wished to have anything further to do with me. As a proof of this I received a bundle of letters which I had written to her at various times. I burnt them and destroyed at the same time, Inspector, the finest memories of the last two years of my life."

CHAPTER XVIII

PERFECT ALIBI

"AND now," said Ronald Hardy, taking a deep breath, "let me deal with the second division of this statement—what transpired in Cove Cottage between seven-thirty and eight-forty-five on Monday night. I see, Inspector, that you've already found out that something *did* transpire. I'll be as brief and as clear as I can. I was sitting at my desk when Mrs. Peewit—I don't doubt that you've already made her acquaintance—came in and told me that Mr. Tregarthan wished to speak to me. I was tremendously surprised. He had never gone out of his way to speak to me or visit me—the opposite, in fact! For some strange reason he had always resented my friendship with his niece. I had never been invited to Greylings, though I had occasionally seen Ruth there when her uncle was safely out of the way. This unexpected visit was, therefore, a bit of a surprise. He hadn't been two minutes in the room, however, before I realised what had brought him to Cove Cottage. He came as an emissary from Miss Tregarthan. She had sent him, apparently not having the courage to come herself, to say that she no longer wished to see me. No reason given—understand? Just that. I was on no account to speak to her again. I was, of course, unable to conceal my emotions for I had been deeply in love with Ruth Tregarthan for some months. Tregarthan was quick to notice my dismay and for him it was doubtless a moment of triumph. I argued. I demanded an explanation of this sudden change in his niece's attitude towards me. He refused to speak further. I regret to say that I lost my temper then. I swore that it was his doing.

He had influenced his niece and engineered the whole business. Tregarthan responded with an equal show of anger and we had a regular set-to. The result was that he banged down the bundle of letters on my desk and, still raving, stamped out of the room.

"I was left staring at the letters, trembling and bewildered. It had all been so sudden. I was plunged into the darkness of absolute despair. What was left of the future? What was there left to live for? All that I had been striving for seemed to have been shattered in the wink of an eye. My work, my ambition—what did I care about my career? A curious mood assailed me. I fell into a sort of trance—mind you, my brain was working with absolute clearness—but my sense of reasoning seemed to be paralysed.

"I got to work quite mechanically. First I burnt the letters, one by one, in the fire. Then I tidied up my desk, sorted out all Ruth's letters from my correspondence and, in turn, destroyed them. This done, for a long time I sat at my window staring with blank eyes at the storm, which was approaching slowly across the sea. I knew exactly what I had to do. There were no doubts in my mind as to the sanity of my scheme. It was like an inevitable duty, an army order that had to be carried out.

"I opened the drawer in my desk where I kept my old service revolver. I slipped it out of its holster and put it in my pocket. Very vaguely I realised that Mrs. Peewit had previously come into the room and set my supper on the table. I left it untouched.

"What time I left the cottage I can't rightly say."

"Section three," put in the Inspector.

Hardy nodded absently, as if he did not fully realise the meaning of the Inspector's interpolation.

"I put on my hat and overcoat, went to the garage," he continued, "and took out my car. It was my idea, you see, to drive to a lonely spot somewhere along the coast road and there to put an end to my life. A wild and illogical idea, I confess. But there it was.

"Then something unforeseen happened—a trivial and rather ridiculous thing considering my highly coloured mood. Just before I reached the Vicarage, there was a deafening report and my front tyre burst. I skidded a bit and pulled in automatically to the side of the road and stopped my engine."

"A burst!" exclaimed the Inspector. "Why the devil didn't I think of that before? The single shot! I'm cracking up, sir, no mistake about it."

The Superintendent grinned.

"Go on, Mr. Hardy."

"Well that little accident had a peculiar effect on my outlook. Slowly I realised that what I was intending to do was a coward's way out. After all, I argued, if I had the courage to put a bullet through my brain, why shouldn't I summon up enough courage to face the facts of my adversity and turn my back on the idea of suicide? Did it mean that I was too great a coward to face the future? Was there no hope? Wasn't it possible that Ruth might suffer a change of heart? The more I thought about it, the more clearly I saw that I had acted hastily and without proper regard for the circumstances which had brought about my dismay. Wasn't it, perhaps, a trick on Tregarthan's part? Had Ruth really sent her uncle with those letters? Was it possible that he had stolen them from her desk to lend colour to his story?

"All the time I was turning these things over in my mind I was mechanically removing the damaged wheel and replacing it with the spare. It did not take me long. When I had completed the job my mind was made up. This trivial accident had sobered me completely. It had given me time to reflect.

"I snatched the revolver out of my inside pocket and flung it into the ditch by the roadside. I felt that in doing so I was flinging temptation behind me. I took a huge breath of mingled relief and determination and climbed back into the car.

"When I drove off I had no idea where I was going to. I intended to drive on through the night and evolve some plan as I went along. London never entered my mind then. I stamped on the accelerator, anxious to place as much distance as possible between myself and the revolver lying in the ditch. It was not until I was some way past the Vicarage that I realised that I had been driving without lights. Somebody shouted at me just before I reached the church and waved a lantern. I suppose that made me aware that something was amiss. Later I switched on the lights and, passing Towan Cove, went as fast as I dared along the coast road.

"Then, somehow, the idea of a complete change of environment came to me. I knew it was the only way—to get right away for a bit and get things straight in my mind. At Barrock Corner I swung off the coast road and drove back over the moors to Greystoke. I reckoned I should just have time to catch the late London express. I reached Greystoke with a few minutes to spare. I garaged the car at Fenton's in Marston Street and was on the platform just as the train came in.

"That's my statement, Inspector—the whole of it. It's the truth—every word of it. I can't do more now than hope that you'll accept my story, corroborate it, perhaps, by further evidence, and dismiss the idea from your mind that I had anything to do with the murder of poor Tregarthan."

At the conclusion of his statement, Ronald Hardy lay back in his chair with his eyes half-closed. The strain of telling his story, on top of all that he had suffered since Julius Tregarthan walked into Cove Cottage on Monday night, had obviously exhausted him. He was a man who had been through hell and at that moment, he looked like it.

The Inspector's words, however, brought a faint smile to his lips and a gleam of satisfaction animated his drawn and pallid features.

"What you have told me, Mr. Hardy, is extremely interesting. I needn't prolong your suspense. Your story fits in faultlessly with the evidence which I have already collected from various witnesses. You are cleared of all suspicion and I only regret that on top of your personal troubles you should have suffered any further inconvenience. But you see how we were placed? If only you had come forward at once, we should both have been spared a *hell* of a lot of trouble." He leaned toward the desk. "By the way—that's your property, I believe?"

He held out the Webley.

"Or shall I keep it for you?" he added meaningly.

Hardy shook his head.

"No—it's all right, Inspector. You can trust me with it now. One doesn't make the same mistake twice. At least, I won't, I promise you!"

He took the revolver, looked at it casually and dropped it into his overcoat pocket. Little did he realise that the revolver had been the cause of a major sensation and the devil's own amount of confusion in the unsolved mystery surrounding Julius Tregarthan's death.

"Is there anything further you wish to ask me, Inspector? Or am I free to go?"

"Perfectly free, Mr. Hardy. I should like to have some idea of your whereabouts in case I should need you later on. Your idea is to return to Cove Cottage, I take it?"

"Yes—that was my intention as soon as I had cleared myself of suspicion. There's my novel to be revised finally for the publishers. When that is done ... well I can't say. I shall probably return to London for an indefinite stay."

The Inspector cleared his throat, made as if to speak, hesitated and finally said:

"I shouldn't place too much reliance on Mr. Tregarthan's statements on Monday night if I were you, Mr. Hardy." He was thinking that if Mrs. Mullion was right about the revolver, Ruth Tregarthan could not be quite indifferent to the fate of Ronald Hardy. "I can't say more than that at present."

"And Ruth—Miss Tregarthan?" asked Hardy with great eagerness. "You'll tell her about all this, Inspector?"

The Inspector gave his promise and, after shaking hands with the Superintendent and thanking Bigswell for his reassurance, he was escorted from the room by the attendant Constable—a free man cleared of all suspicion, and a man greatly enlivened by the Inspector's veiled hint about Ruth Tregarthan's attitude.

"Well?" demanded the Superintendent when he and Bigswell were alone. "Where are we now?"

The Inspector shrugged his shoulders.

"Hardy's got a perfect alibi, at any rate. Every incident in his story checks up with the collected evidence. Tregarthan's visit, the quarrel, the tyre burst, the revolver in the ditch, the man with the lantern, even the fact that he was driving without lights,—not a single point was omitted from his statement. I'm the only man in complete possession of all the facts, so nobody could have put him wise before he walked in here this morning. That's certain."

"And the girl?"

"Well, sir, I have an idea that when she learns that Hardy's innocent, she'll come forward with the truth. I'm going back to Boscawen at once. To the Vicarage. I want a word with that girl, right away. She's been hiding something and I want to know what it is."

Five minutes later the Inspector was speeding along the familiar moorland road which linked Greystoke with the coast.

Hardy's statement had knocked the bottom out of his previous theory. He realised, with a sigh of dissatisfaction, that it meant starting all over again. Since Hardy was innocent, there was every probability that Ruth Tregarthan was a victim of a mistaken belief rather than an accomplice in the murder of her uncle. What then was there left to work on? The Vicar's theory? It certainly looked like it. More than ever did the result of the Reverend Dodd's experiment seem to bear on the case. The hurdle theory had gone west with the establishment of Hardy's innocence. This being the case, it was almost certain that Tregarthan had *not* been shot from the wall. How then to account for the fact that the line of flight of the three bullets was so impossibly high? It only left one supposition. The Vicar was right. Tregarthan *had* been shot from the sea.

Still hard at work trying to plan out his new line of investigation, the Inspector suddenly realised that the car had swung off the coast road. A second later it was at a standstill outside the door of the Vicarage.

CHAPTER XIX

REUNION

RUTH TREGARTHAN had not been present at her uncle's funeral that afternoon. Tregarthan's sole relation, and elder brother, had motored down from London and picked up Ramsey, the solicitor, in Greystoke. The Vicar had officiated at the brief and simple ceremony, which was attended by a good sprinkling of curious villagers. The three men had returned, at once, to the Vicarage, where Ramsey was to read the will.

It was a perfectly straightforward affair. Tregarthan had left everything unconditionally to his brother, including all his property and various monies invested in industrial and government concerns. He was not, as the Vicar had previously suspected, a wealthy man. His income accruing from property and investments was, in fact, far smaller than seemed compatible with his mode of living. The will read, Tregarthan's brother, John, pointed out that no mention had been made of Greylings. Ramsey's eyebrows lifted and his obvious surprise was doubled when Ruth, too, questioned him as to the future ownership of the house.

"But surely, Miss Tregarthan, you were aware that Greylings was held in trust by your uncle until such times as you should marry—or in the event of your not marrying, until you reached the age of thirty? Your father arranged this matter with me a year or so before his death. Eight hundred a year was settled on you; and your uncle, Julius Tregarthan, was left with full powers to administer your income as he saw fit until such times as I have stated. If you married or when you reached the age of thirty your uncle's trusteeship automatically ceased. Your father had great faith, apparently, in your uncle's financial abilities and, I need scarcely add, integrity. Surely you were aware of this arrangement, Miss Tregarthan?"

Ruth shook her head in amazement.

"Uncle always gave me to understand that he alone benefited from my father's will. I knew he was my legal guardian until I reached my majority, but I had absolutely no knowledge of this settlement!"

"But when you reached the age of twenty-one, surely your uncle spoke to you about your father's arrangement?"

"Never!" contested Ruth. "He told me that since I was of age and capable of managing my own affairs, he was prepared to settle an allowance on me—but he made no mention of the fact that it was my father's money!"

"And the amount of this allowance?"

"A hundred and fifty a year."

"A hundred and fifty!"

Ramsey looked incredulous.

"And the house?"

"I always understood it was my uncle's property and that, in the event of his death, it was to come to me. I had no reason to doubt this statement."

"Well! Well! Well!" said Ramsey with the air of a man who is asked to swallow more than it was humanly possible to credit. "So your uncle has been keeping back some six hundred and fifty pounds per annum, which was, by reason of your father's arrangement, legally due to you. Have you any idea what has happened to this money?"

"I really can't say, Mr. Ramsey. I've never really troubled about money. I've been quite content to go along as I have been doing down here. It never struck me that my uncle was concealing anything from me."

Ramsey turned to John Tregarthan.

"We shall have to go into this, of course. With your permission, Miss Tregarthan, I'll get in touch with the manager at the bank and make a few inquiries. Much as I dislike speaking ill of the dead—*de mortuis nil nisi bonum*, you know—I can't help suspecting that your uncle has been misappropriating the money which he held in trust. I haven't looked into the trust account naturally—but we must do so without delay."

And after certain formalities had been concluded, a very puzzled solicitor left the Vicarage for Greystoke. John Tregarthan accompanied him.

Only a few minutes after Ramsey's departure, the Inspector's car drew up at the door.

He was admitted to the study, where presently he was joined by Ruth.

"Once again I've got to trouble you, Miss Tregarthan," said the Inspector. "But it's good news this time."

"Thank heaven for that," sighed Ruth. "Does it mean you've at last found the murderer?"

"I'm afraid not." It was Bigswell's turn to sigh. "But I'm glad to say I've eliminated a possible suspect from my list."

"And who is that?"

"Ronald Hardy," said the Inspector.

"Ronald!" exclaimed Ruth. "You've found him? You know where he is?"

"Well, if I'm not mistaken," smiled Inspector Bigswell, "he's probably having his tea, at this minute, down at Cove Cottage."

"He's here!" In a flash the girl's whole appearance seemed to undergo a transformation. Anxiety seemed to slip from her. The worried look in her eyes gave place to one of relief and thankfulness. "Why didn't I know before? Why didn't he tell me? Didn't he know I was at the Vicarage?"

"Aren't you being a little illogical, Miss Tregarthan? I understand from Mr. Hardy that on Monday last you sent a message to say that you never wished to see or speak with him again. He also mentioned a packet of letters which you returned."

Ruth stared at the Inspector with blank astonishment.

"But it's ridiculous! Absurd! Ronald's letters, as far as I know, are still in my desk down at Greylings!"

"Then it was a trick," mused Bigswell with evident satisfaction. "Just as I thought."

"Indeed it was a trick!" agreed Ruth with spirit. "I learnt that night at dinner what my uncle had done, but I knew nothing about the letters. Oh, it was mean of him! Despicable! He must have deliberately stolen them from my desk for this purpose. But tell me about Ronald, Inspector. What happened that night? Where did he go? What did he do?"

Bigswell re-edited, as succinctly as possible, the essence of Hardy's recently given statement. Ruth grew more and more astonished as the Inspector proceeded. She could scarcely curb her impatience and wait for the end of the Inspector's story, before setting out to straighten things up with Ronald. She realised how deeply he must have suffered during the last few days. Anger at her uncle's duplicity was mingled with a tender compassion for the man who had been so bitterly deceived by his cruel and heartless trick.

"It's strange that your uncle should have been so antagonistic toward your friendship with Mr. Hardy," concluded the Inspector. "Have you any idea as to why he took such a strong attitude in the matter, Miss Tregarthan?"

"An hour ago I hadn't, Inspector. But I think I see it all now." She explained what had just transpired with the solicitor. "He must have been using this money of mine for his own purpose. Perhaps got into a difficult corner, Inspector. Naturally, if I married, the whole business would come out, since I should then be legally entitled to handle the settlement myself."

"Speculation," put in Bigswell. "Stock Exchange. Curious how people get bitten with the gambling spirit when it's other people's money they're risking!"

"And now," said Ruth, rising quickly. "If you'll excuse me——"

"A moment," cut in the Inspector. "I want to ask you just two questions before you go, Miss Tregarthan." Ruth looked up and nervously scrutinised the Inspector's unsmiling countenance. "Firstly, why did you lie to me about your actions on Monday night? Why didn't you give me the real reason for leaving the house when you had been asked not to do so? And secondly—why did you perjure yourself at the Coroner's inquest?"

"So you know!"

The cry was involuntary. The Inspector smiled.

"I know everything," he said. "Well?"

"I can tell you now. I can tell everything, Inspector. It was Ronald. I thought Ronald—may God forgive me for my suspicions—was responsible for my uncle's death. I knew he hated the sight of my uncle because of his unreasonable attitude toward our friendship. I knew, too, that he had a revolver. About a year ago he showed it to me as part of his varied collection of war mementoes. I found that revolver was missing on Monday night!"

"Let's start from the beginning," suggested the Inspector. "Let's start at the moment when your uncle returned from his interview with Mr. Hardy at Cove Cottage."

Ruth subsided into a chair and, after a moment's thought, plunged into her story.

"The whole trouble started at dinner that evening. My uncle told me what he had done. He tried to make me believe that there was some secret reason why I should have nothing more to do with Ronald. He led me to think that there was something disreputable about his past life. Needless to say I did not believe the implication. We quarrelled violently. I told him that he had no right to interfere with our friendship and that I was perfectly capable of managing my personal affairs myself. The result of the quarrel was that I left the dinner table in a towering rage. I intended to go at once to Cove Cottage and explain to Ronald exactly what my uncle had said. I went as you know along the cliff-path.

"When I reached Cove Cottage I found that Ronald had just left, apparently in a hurry. I was disturbed. I knew that Ronald was liable to fits of extreme melancholy when in trouble of any sort. It was the outcome of shell-shock in the war. At those moments he seemed to have little control over his emotions. He acted unreasonably and violently. Twice already I have had to pit my persuasive powers against his moodiness and, in each case, I was successful in winning him over to a more sensible frame of mind. Of late, however, these moods have been less frequent.

"I don't want you to think, Inspector, that when I first entered the cottage the idea of murder entered my head. It didn't. I was troubled, not on my uncle's account, but on Ronald's. I knew how he would react to my supposed message of dismissal. I knew he possessed a revolver. I was mad with anxiety that he had acted on the spur of the moment and rushed from the house, with the fixed idea of taking his own life.

"When Mrs. Peewit was out of the room, I opened the drawer where I knew he kept his revolver. It was gone. You can imagine my state of mind! Making a hurried excuse, I left the cottage and returned as quickly as possible along the cliff-path to Greylings. I had an idea of enlisting my uncle's help in finding Ronald. I thought perhaps he might be frightened by the result of his abominable trick.

"I reached the garden wall. Suddenly my toe came in contact with something hard that was lying on the cliff-path. I stooped down and picked it up. In the light that was coming from the sitting-room windows I saw that it was a revolver. A service revolver. Ronald's! Quickly I hid it in my mackintosh pocket and rushed into the house.

"What I found there you, of course, know. But coupled with the shock of finding my uncle murdered was the even more distressing thought that Ronald was the murderer. Had I been in a more normal frame of mind I daresay I should have questioned my first suspicions. I only know that, ever since Monday night, I have been in a storm of indecision. I have hated myself for my disloyalty, only to be plunged, the next minute, into the depths of hopelessness and despair because I could not completely allay that suspicion.

"I managed to take the revolver from my mackintosh pocket and hide it upstairs in a drawer of my dressing-table before the Constable arrived. I realised that if I wanted to shield Ronald from the police, it was essential for me to get rid of the revolver. You know now, of course, how I did it. I crept downstairs when you were talking to the Constable in the sitting-room and let myself out of the side-door. I went down to the cliff-path and threw the revolver into the sea. When later you questioned me as to the reason for my leaving the house, I had to invent an excuse on the spur of the moment. I'm afraid, Inspector, it was not a very plausible or convincing excuse! I could see then that you doubted my story. But what else could I do? I was so certain then that Ronald, in a fit of violent anger, had shot my uncle from the cliff-path. I had to shield him.

"At the inquest it was the same. Mrs. Mullion's evidence, I don't mind admitting, flung me off my balance for the moment. I got up to deny her story. Luckily Doctor Pendrill pulled me down until Mrs. Mullion had finished making her statement. This gave me time to think and when, later, I asked the Coroner if I might speak, I was ready with a simple but very reasonable explanation. I committed perjury. I admit it. I am quite ready to face the consequences of my action. I'm ready to face any charge the police may bring against me now that I know Ronald is innocent and safely back in Boscawen.

These last days I have been living a nightmare existence. Nothing has seemed real. I thought I should never learn again what it meant to be happy and free of care. Always there was the thought of Ronald's safety in the background of my mind. That terrible, unworthy suspicion, too, that he had killed my uncle.

"Thank heaven that cloud has passed over! You will never begin to realise, Inspector, what your words meant to me, when you told me of Ronald's innocence. You know my story now. I'm prepared to face the charge of perjury. You needn't fear that I shall try and escape from the consequences of my actions. Only don't keep me now—please, Inspector! I must go to Ronald! I must comfort and reassure him. The thought of the misapprehension under which he is labouring nearly drives me mad when I think of it. He must think me heartless and callous, without any claim on his sympathy and understanding. I want to set everything right—now. At once!"

Ruth's voice had taken on a deeper, impassioned note. She was no longer setting out facts, she was giving the Inspector a glimpse of her inmost thoughts and feelings. She was no longer a witness under cross-examination. She was a woman moved by the stress of strong and genuine emotions.

"You've answered my two questions," said the Inspector quietly. "That's all I wanted, Miss Tregarthan. If any further action is to be taken with regard to your behaviour at the inquest, I needn't bother you with that now. You are free to do as you wish. I've no further claim on your time." He rose and held out his hand. "Goodbye, Miss Tregarthan."

"You've got your car outside?" The Inspector nodded. "You are going in the direction of the village?"

"Yes—to the Constable's office. You want a lift?"

"If I may."

"Of course."

Thus it was that Ronald Hardy, sitting at his desk, was suddenly aware that a police car had come to a standstill outside the gate. He sighed. More officialdom, he supposed.

Then with a little cry he sprang to his feet, amazed beyond measure to see Ruth Tregarthan, hatless, coatless, running up the path toward him. They reached the door at the same moment. For an instant they stood staring at each other, puzzled, bewildered, an enquiring, wondering look—then Ruth stepped forward murmuring something unintelligible about a mistake and the door closed.

"Step on it, Grimmet," said the Inspector in a terse voice. "What the devil are you staring at?"

"I'm thinking somebody's glad to see somebody else, sir," replied Grimmet with a broad grin.

"Then you shouldn't think," growled the Inspector. "Thinking's ruined many a man … and woman, before to-day. Particularly *wrong*-thinking, Grimmet!"

The car slid off down the hill through the deepening twilight, to where an orange square of light glowed from the dark face of the Constable's cottage.

So much for Inspector Bigswell's pet theory!

CHAPTER XX

THE LITTLE GREYSTOKE TAILOR

IT was striking six when Inspector Bigswell climbed out of the car and entered the Constable's office. Grouch was perched on the high stool, writing at his desk. On seeing his superior, he pushed aside his work and took up a slip of paper which was lying under a paper-weight.

"Any luck, Grouch?"

"Fairly full list, I think, sir. I got one of the local fishermen here to identify the boats lying in Boscawen Cove and Jack Withers helped me with the Towan Cove lot. In those cases where the boats aren't named, I've taken down a bit of description so we can sort out which is which, sir."

"Good," said the Inspector. "Then you'd better stick that list in your pocket and come over to Towan Cove with me straight away. I want to follow up that idea we had of looking for the gravel. By the way, are *all* the boats accounted for?"

"I think so, sir. There's nothing but local-owned boats in the two coves at the moment. In the summer it's different. Chaps on holiday sometimes hire boats then and keep 'em on the slipway here. But there's nothing of this sort lying about now. I've got the names and addresses of every one of the local owners."

"Right! Then let's get going."

They climbed into the car and sped along the Vicarage road toward Towan Cove. On the way over the Inspector gave Grouch a rough idea of what had transpired in the Superintendent's office that afternoon. He did not believe in keeping his subordinates ignorant of what was happening outside the circle of their own particular vision.

Leaving Grimmet to turn the car at the top of the rough road which slid down precipitously into the cove, Bigswell and the Constable proceeded on foot. At some little distance from the milky line of breakers which marked the shore, the Inspector drew up short and pointed down into the hollow.

"What d'you make of that, Grouch?"

"Looks like somebody with a pocket-torch, sir."

"Wonder who the devil he is and what he's up to?" said the Inspector in puzzled tones. "Must have dropped something during the day and come back to look for it. Quietly does it, Grouch. We'd better take a closer look."

Keeping to the turf at the side of the slatey track, the two men descended into the cove. The figure was apparently unaware that it was being watched, for the bright circle of light travelled slowly over the line of boats, which lay side by side on the long slab of rock.

"Searching the boats for something, sir," said Grouch in an undertone.

"Suspicious, eh?" demanded the Inspector.

Grouch agreed. On careful feet they moved nearer, when the Inspector suddenly stepped forward from the shadows and flung the light of his own pocket-torch directly on to the figure. The man swung round, startled. The Inspector laughed. It was the Reverend Dodd!

"Who's that?" demanded the Vicar sharply, for the dazzling light had temporarily blinded him.

"Inspector Bigswell."

It was the Vicar's turn to chuckle.

"Dear me, Inspector, we seem destined to run into each other to-day. I thought you'd gone back to Greystoke."

"What's the idea, Mr. Dodd? Stealing a march on me?"

"Gracious, no! Not intentionally that is. I was suddenly blessed with a minor inspiration over tea and I wanted to reassure myself that it was a genuine inspiration. As you see, I'm making a careful examination of the boats here. I wasn't satisfied with the cursory way we looked over them this morning. As a matter of fact, Inspector, I'm searching for gravel."

"The deuce you are!" exclaimed Bigswell. "Then we may as well join forces because I came over here for exactly the same reason. Great minds think alike, eh, sir?"

"Or conversely, Inspector—fools seldom differ. It's curious how these old proverbs cancel each other out with such charming inconsequence. Since we've decided to join forces, I might add that many hands make light work—to which you might aptly reply: 'Too many cooks spoil the broth.' You see how beautifully it all works out?"

"I suppose we're both after the same clue?" asked the Inspector.

"Oh, no doubt about it. You said to yourself, if Tregarthan was shot from the sea then the man who shot him was the man who flung the gravel against the window. That being so, he must have had a small pile of gravel in the boat, which in turn leads us to suppose——"

"Exactly," cut in the Inspector. "Well, Mr. Dodd—what luck have you had?"

"None … so far. I've examined these three boats at this end of the row. Not a trace of gravel in any of them."

"Well, let's examine this one," suggested the Inspector, directing the rays of his torch on the boat which lay nearest to them. "If I'm not mistaken this is the tub we took out this morning, isn't it?"

"That's right—Joe Burdon's. Freshly painted with a white line running round it. Quite distinctive."

They made an exhaustive search, even removing the loose boards which rested on the curved ribs at the bottom of the boat. But there was no trace of the gravel. They turned their attention, therefore, to the next in the line, a nondescript, rather clumsy-looking dinghy, with tarred sides and rusty rowlocks. Crudely painted on either side of the blunt bows was the name—*Nancy*. The bilgeboards were rotting at the edges and nearly awash in a pool of viscid water which had obviously seeped in through the keel of the boat.

Suddenly the Vicar, who was craning over the blunt prow, uttered a sharp and excited exclamation.

"Well?" queried the Inspector.

The Vicar pointed to the painter which lay in a small coil on the boat's bottom. In the hollow centre of that coil was a little scattering of gravel. Not much. Just a few grains, but sufficient to justify the assumption that if the murderer had used a boat, then this dinghy was the boat in question.

The Inspector collected a few tiny stones in the palm of his hand and examined them closely under the light of his electric-torch.

"No mistake about it, Mr. Dodd. It's gravel right enough. Seems that we've found exactly what we were looking for."

He turned to Grouch. "Got that list of owners on you, Grouch?"

"Yes, sir."

"Then look up the name and address of the chap who owns the *Nancy*. Strikes me that when we've had an interview with that gentleman we'll be well on our way to solving this infernal problem. Well, Grouch?"

"Belongs to a Mr. Jeremy Crook, sir."

"Umph—Crook sounds promising! And the address?"

"Not a local one exactly, sir. A Greystoke address."

"Good heavens! Not Crooks the outfitters in Castle Street?"

"That's it, sir. Now I come to think of it, Jack Withers mentioned he was a tailor or something of the sort. Appears that he's a keen fisherman and comes over week-ends to try his luck, sir. I've seen him about myself, sir, once or twice— little chap with a big moustache and glasses. Mild-mannered I should call him—chatty sort of chap, too."

"Maybe, Grouch. But that doesn't alter the facts. As far as I can see it, Tregarthan was shot by a man in this boat, and as the boat belongs to Jeremy Crook we've every right to suppose that the man in the boat *was* Jeremy Crook. Unless he's got an alibi for Monday night of course."

"Which means?" inquired the Vicar, mildly.

"That I'm going back to Greystoke without delay, Mr. Dodd. It looks to me as if your—that is *our* theory is the right one. The more so since Mr. Hardy has been cleared of all suspicion."

"Ronald cleared?"

"Oh, I was forgetting. Of course you don't know. Yes—he walked into Greystoke headquarters this morning and made a statement."

Very briefly the Inspector explained what had taken place in the Superintendent's office and, later, in the study at the Vicarage.

"I'm delighted! Delighted!" exclaimed the Vicar. "I wondered why Ruth didn't show up at tea-time. I thought she was resting. This is splendid news, Inspector. Splendid!"

"And a triumph for your intuition principle of deduction, eh, Mr. Dodd?" The Inspector saluted and after a hearty "Good night!" walked off briskly up the hill to where Grimmet was waiting with the car.

He did not know quite what to make of Jeremy Crook's entry into the arena. He knew the man by sight and reputation—an undeveloped, rather wizened little man, with an inoffensive, though somewhat servile manner; a teetotaller and the secretary of the Greystoke Bowls Club. The Inspector had never heard anything against him. But, for that matter, he had never heard anything *for* him. He was just one of those mild, moderately efficient, middling sort of men who never get talked about. Against his knowledge of the tailor's character was set the clue of the gravel in the boat. Whether or not Crook had used the *Nancy* on Monday night, it was essential that he should be questioned. If he had an alibi, well and good. If not—then it would be necessary to investigate further and unearth, if possible, a motive for Crook's assumed murder of Julius Tregarthan.

When the Inspector reached Greystoke, he ordered Grimmet to drop him at the top of Castle Street and take the car back to the police garage. He did not want to advertise his arrival at the outfitters. Although a few of the shop windows still displayed a blaze of light, the majority, and among them

Crooks, were closed. The shutters were up and only the glimmer of a by-pass showed through the fanlight of the shop-door. Adjoining the shop, however, was the tailor's private entrance, which gave by means of a narrow staircase on to the rooms above the emporium. The Inspector rang and, after a few minutes the door was opened by a young, fresh-looking girl, who was a trifle taken aback on seeing the Inspector's uniform.

"Good evening, miss. Is Mr. Jeremy Crook in?"

"No—I'm afraid he's not at the moment. He's just gone out to a meeting of some sort, I believe. Can I give him a message?"

"I'd rather wait and see him later. D'you know what time he'll be back, miss?"

The girl thought about nine, but she was not certain.

"You're his daughter, I take it?"

"Yes—that's right."

"Then before I see your father, perhaps I might have a few words with you?"

The girl offered no objection and the Inspector followed her up a dingy, ill-lit stairway into a cramped, over-furnished little sitting-room where a pale fire was flickering. After they were seated and the Inspector had whipped out his note-book, he began a guarded cross-examination. He was anxious not to alarm the girl in any way, seeing that she was already very nervous, and made no mention, therefore, of the murder.

"Now, Miss Crook, I understand from the Constable at Boscawen that your father owns a boat over at Towan Cove."

"That's right—the *Nancy*."

"And he's in the habit, I believe, of running over during the week-end for a bit of fishing?"

"Yes."

"Does he ever do any night fishing?"

"Not as far as I know—though he sometimes gets back here fairly late at night."

"I ask this, Miss Crook, because we believe that there is some smuggling going on along that bit of coast. I wondered if your father might be able to supply us with any information. On Monday night, for example—was your father over at Towan Cove that night?"

"Oh, I'm sure he wasn't. He left the house about seven. He told me he was going down to the billiard-hall. It's his great hobby in the winter."

"I see. And what time did he return?"

"Latish, I know, because I was in bed when he came in. After eleven I should think."

"Did you see him when he returned?"

"No."

"Does he usually return as late as that from the billiard-hall?"

"No. He's usually home by ten or even earlier."

"And he gave you no explanation the next morning?"

"None."

"I see. And this billiard-hall—where is it?"

"In Queen Street."

"I know. Charlie Hawkin's place." The Inspector closed his note-book. "Well, that's all I wanted to find out, Miss Crook. It's pretty obvious your father can't help us with regard to

Monday night, but I'll call back later on the off-chance that he may have noticed something some other time."

Leaving Castle Street, Bigswell made his way quickly to Charlie Hawkin's place in Queen Street. It was a respectable, well-run place, mainly patronised by elderly tradesmen, who looked upon it as a sort of home from home. The Inspector found the proprietor polishing glasses behind the bar, an annex to the billiard-hall.

"Evening, Mr. Bigswell. Anything I can do?"

"Just a little matter," said the Inspector in an undertone, glancing meaningly at the little group chatting at the bar.

Hawkins jerked his thumb toward a tiny glass-fronted cubby-hole behind the bar, the chief decoration of which was racing almanacs and various local tradesmen's calendars. When the proprietor had closed the door, Bigswell asked:

"Know a chap called Jeremy Crook, Charlie?" The proprietor nodded. "Come here often?"

"Yes—regular customer in the winter. Outfitter, y'know, in Castle Street. Little monkey of a chap. Deacon of his chapel. Teetotaller. Nothing against '*im*, surely?"

"Oh, just a little routine matter," said the Inspector lightly. "Was he in here on Monday evening?"

"Monday? Monday? Let's see?" Charlie Hawkins scratched his chin with a toothpick and expectorated into the fire-place. "That was the night of the murder, wasn't it? No—'e wasn't in 'ere that night. Sure of it. Couldn't have missed 'im if 'e was. I always make a good dozen rounds of the billard-room of an evening, just to keep an eye on things. But Jeremy Crook didn't show up on Monday night. Surprising, too, since it's 'is regular night."

"Thanks. That's all I was after, Charlie."

"Drink before you go, Mr. Bigswell?"

Hawkins beamed expansively. He believed in keeping on the right side of the police. The Inspector refused.

"No time now, Charlie. Some of us have to work for a living. 'Night."

He went out into the street profoundly puzzled. He realised that he was once more up against a problem. The girl said her father had gone to the billiard-hall on Monday night. Charlie was certain he had not turned up. Where, then, had Mr. Jeremy Crook spent the evening? And why had he deliberately lied to his daughter?

Still pondering these questions, Bigswell returned home, where his wife, always uncertain of her husband's erratic comings and goings, hastily prepared his dinner. Punctually at nine, however, relinquishing the comfort of a fireside pipe and a little light music on the wireless, the Inspector buttoned up his cape and returned to Castle Street.

Mr. Jeremy Crook was in. He was seated in an arm-chair by the fire, sipping a glass of hot milk. When the Inspector entered he rose jerkily and motioned his daughter out of the room. He bowed the Inspector into a second chair with the obsequiousness of a born shop-walker and politely inquired the reason for his visit.

"Surely your daughter has mentioned my previous visit here?" said the Inspector sagaciously.

"Yes—she did tell me something," acknowledged the tailor. "You wondered if I could give you any information about some smuggling down at Towan Cove on Monday, she said. Well, I'm sorry—I can't. I didn't go over to the Cove on Monday."

"Where exactly did you go, Mr. Crook?"

"As my daughter told you—to Hawkin's billiard-hall in Queen Street."

"Arriving there?"

"Oh, soon after seven, I imagine. I really can't say." The little man seemed anxious to avoid any further reference to his doings on Monday night. He kept on glancing at the closed door as if suspecting that his daughter was listening in to the conversation. He seemed, in fact, watchful and ill-at-ease. "You see, Inspector, I really can't help you much. In fact, I haven't been out in the *Nancy* for some months."

"Look here, Mr. Crook," said the Inspector, leaning forward and looking searchingly into the man's uneasy eyes, "you're not telling me the truth! You may as well confess to it. I know, as well as you do, that you did *not* visit the billiard-hall on Monday evening. You told your daughter that you were going to Queen Street. But you didn't. Why did you lie to her?"

"I can't see why I should answer all these questions," protested Mr. Crook in a squeaky, petulant voice. "I've told you all you want to know. I wasn't over at the Cove on Monday."

"But this matter's more serious than you realise," said Bigswell. "I haven't been quite frank with you, I admit. When I interviewed your daughter, I had no wish to alarm her. Understand? I'm not investigating a case of smuggling, but a case of murder. The Tregarthan murder. Certain facts lead me to believe that you may know something about the matter. It's essential that I should know exactly where you were on Monday evening between the hours of seven and eleven. If you can give me a satisfactory explanation ... well and good. I shan't trouble you further, Mr. Crook. I'm asking you these questions for your own good. Well, Mr. Crook, *where were you on Monday night?*"

The little man glanced curiously at the Inspector, jerked suddenly to his feet and walked across to the door. He flung it open. The dimly lit landing was empty. Having satisfied himself that his daughter was not eavesdropping, the tailor carefully closed the door, returned to his chair and sat down.

"All right," he said in an undertone. "I'll tell you the exact truth, Inspector. You're quite right—I didn't go along to Hawkin's on Monday. I had an appointment with a lady. As you may know, my wife died some ten years ago. Well, the fact of the matter is, I sometimes feel very lonely here now. My daughter is a good enough girl, but she's young and likes to get out and about. I don't blame her. It's only natural. But I'm a family man by nature. I miss the companionship of an older woman in the house. Lately I've struck up an intimacy with a lady whom I have known for a considerable number of years. She's still, I'm glad to say, unmarried. I'm telling you this in strict confidence, Inspector—even my daughter is unaware of my relationship with this lady. I've been in the habit of visiting her of an evening. She's lonely, too, and somehow we have found a great deal of happiness in being together. Unfortunately, I know my daughter would be opposed to this friendship. She's loyal to her mother's memory. So I've had to keep this intimacy secret. That's why I lied to her about Monday. I was not intending to go to the billiard-hall, but to see this lady. You understand?"

"Perfectly," said the Inspector. "But you realise that it's necessary for me to have this lady's address so that I can corroborate your story? All in the strictest confidence, of course."

The little tailor, after a moment's hesitation, gave the required name and address, adding:

"I'm happy to say, Inspector, that on Monday night I—er—proposed to the lady in question and she accepted me. I'm only waiting a favourable opportunity to tell my daughter, before making our engagement public."

The Inspector offered his congratulations and the wizened little tailor pulled heavily at his long moustaches, beamed with pleasure and took a long sip at his hot milk.

"One other thing," said the Inspector. "You say you have not been out in the *Nancy* for some months. When did you last take a look at the boat?"

"Last Wednesday. It's early-closing day, and I cycled over to see how the boat was standing up to the weather. Between ourselves, Inspector, I wasn't satisfied with her condition. It's my idea that somebody has been using the boat ... *recently*."

"What makes you think that?"

"For one thing, I always leave the boat keel upward in the winter. She was right side up. What's more, she was full of water—salt water, mind you. There was a rime of salt on her bows. I didn't have time to set matters right then as it was getting dark and I had no lamp with me. But she's been tampered with, right enough. Somebody's been out in her. No mistake about it!"

"Any idea as to who it is?'

"None. All the chaps in Towan Cove own their own boats.'

"I see. Well, I'll look into the matter and let you know if I find out anything. In the meantime, I'll slip along to this address." The Inspector rose. "By the way, have you a telephone here?"

"Yes—in the shop."

"And this lady—is she on the phone?"

"No."

The Inspector, satisfied that Jeremy Crook would be unable to put the woman wise before his cross-examination, shook hands with the tailor at the bottom of the dingy stairs and went off up the street.

He had no difficulty in finding No. 8 Laburnam Grove. The lady was in and quite ready to do all she could to help the Inspector. Yes, Mr. Crook had arrived there about seven-fifteen on Monday night and left shortly after eleven. He had not been out between those hours. Yes, it was true that they were now engaged, though the engagement had not yet been publicly announced. It was kind of the Inspector to offer his congratulations—the first she had received. At this, the brief interview terminated.

"So," thought Bigswell, as he trudged back to headquarters, dispirited, "it's a blind-alley line of investigation after all! Somebody else used the boat. That's obvious. But who?"

He realised that when he had found the answer to that question he would have answered the even more vital question—who murdered Julius Tregarthan? The search, at any rate, was narrowing down. The sign-posts were all converging on one point. Good!

But the vital question remained—who?

CHAPTER XXI

THE MYSTERY SOLVED

ON Saturday morning Inspector Bigswell proceeded, at once, to the Boscawen Vicarage. He had two reasons for this visit. He had good news for Ruth Tregarthan and bad news for the Vicar. Overnight he had put in his report at Greystoke headquarters, with the result that he was called in to interview the Chief Constable. The Chief, in view of the circumstances which had prompted Ruth to conceal information at the inquest, was inclined toward leniency. She was prompted to commit perjury from a motive which, although it formed no excuse in itself, was quite understandable. She wished to shield the man she loved from suspicion. As luck would have it, twenty-four hours after she had committed perjury, the young man had cleared himself of suspicion, thus enabling the girl to make a true statement of the facts. The Chief's attitude was that Ruth Tregarthan had not maliciously withheld information from the police. She had acted wrongly and, according to the letter of the law, criminally. But taking all the circumstances into consideration he decided that the police need take no further action in the matter. No charge would be brought against her.

Ruth was naturally delighted when Bigswell informed her of the Chief's decision. Not that she had really given much thought to the matter. It was quite obvious that she was far too absorbed in her reconciliation with Ronald, to worry her head about extraneous affairs. No sooner had she had a few words with Inspector Bigswell than she left the

Vicarage post-haste for Cove Cottage. Every minute spent away from Ronald was, to her way of thinking, a minute wasted!

The Inspector then settled down to have a chat with the Reverend Dodd, whose intellect and deductive abilities he was beginning to admire. The Vicar, he realised, had imagination coupled with a fine sense of the practical.

"Well," said the Vicar as they settled into their respective arm-chairs. "Were you barking up the wrong tree?"

"We were!" acknowledged the Inspector. "Nothing doing, sir. A blind-alley line of investigation. Mr. Jeremy Crook has established his alibi all right. Cast-iron. No doubt about it. But the fact remains that his boat was used on Monday night. Crook hadn't taken it out for months. So the question we've got to answer is, who *did* borrow the *Nancy* on the twenty-third, and why did he borrow it?"

"As I see it," said the Vicar, "there are three reasons why the boat was borrowed. Any one of these three reasons may be the correct one. Firstly, it may have been borrowed because the murderer had no boat of his own. Secondly, because the murderer's boat was under repair. Thirdly, because the *Nancy* was a less cumbersome boat to manage than the boat which we are justified in supposing was owned by the murderer. I say justified, advisedly, because it seems to me, Inspector, that whoever handled the *Nancy* on Monday must have been an extraordinarily good seaman. He must have owned his own boat or at least had the use of a boat lying over at Towan Cove. According to the Constable's list all the boat-owners are accounted for. As far as we know, nobody at Towan Cove

relies on another man's boat when he wants to fish or anything of the sort. There are six boats in the cove. These boats
are owned, as I happen to know, by Jack Withers, Parkins,
Staunton, Burdon, Haskell and our friend Jeremy Crook. To
my knowledge there is nobody else living in the cove who
can handle a boat. Haskell's son, I believe, is a fairly profi-
cient oarsman, but scarcely capable of undertaking the sort
of trip which the *Nancy* took on Monday night. To my mind
then, Inspector, we can dismiss the first reason as to why the
murderer needed the *Nancy*. And we can go further—we can
safely say that the man we are looking for is on our list of the
Towan Cove boat-owners. Jeremy Crook we can dismiss. That
leaves us with Jack Withers, Parkins, Staunton, Burdon and
Haskell. Withers, I think, has an alibi. You may remember
that Mrs. Mullion was returning on Monday night from the
Withers' cottage. Jack Withers was present when the midwife
left the cove."

"Quite right," put in the Inspector. "Mrs. Mullion mentioned the fact that Withers lit her lantern before she set off
along the cliff-path."

"Exactly! Which means that he would not have had time
to put off in the boat and murder Tregarthan before Mrs.
Mullion saw Ruth on the cliff-path at Greylings. That leaves us,
therefore, with Parkins, Staunton, Burdon and Haskell. Now
we come to the other reasons for the murderer's need to borrow the Nancy. Was his own boat under repair? Was his own
boat too cumbersome for the job? Now I dare say, Inspector,
that among the six boats which we examined last night one of
them was considerably larger than the others. That's the *Towan
Belle*—Haskell's boat. Is Haskell the man we want? That's one

question we've got to answer. On the other hand you may also remember that the boat we used was freshly painted. That was Joe Burdon's boat. Is Burdon the man we want? That's another question we've got to answer. Assuming that we've exhausted all the plausible reasons why the murderer borrowed the *Nancy*, you see how we have narrowed down our search? Haskell or Burdon. Which?"

"With the possibility," grinned the Inspector, "that we're once more barking up the wrong tree!"

"Dear me—yes. I'm not suggesting that my assumption is unassailable. It's full of theories which may or may not hold water. But with your permission those are the lines of inquiry along which I should like to work. Whether you want to work side by side with me is another matter. You may have formed an entirely new set of theories. Inspector—knowing my own intolerable weakness for making mistakes, I sincerely hope you have!"

"And what exactly do you propose to do, Mr. Dodd? Question these two men?"

"Gracious me—no! At any rate, not yet. My idea was to sit in this arm-chair for a couple of hours with a cigar—a policy of splendid inaction. At the end of that time I hope I shall have solved another little problem which has been worrying me for some time. I want you to understand, Inspector, that I'm not asking you to stand aside while I carry on. Far from it. But I'm going to ask you to give me a couple of hours in which to turn things over in my mind. If, at the end of that time, I'm no nearer a solution of the mystery, then I see no reason why you shouldn't cross-examine Haskell and Burdon. But until then, as a special favour, I'm going to ask you to adopt a similar policy to mine. Splendid inaction, Inspector! Will you grant me this?"

The Inspector considered the Vicar's strange request for a moment and then gave his promise. He would pursue no further enquiries that morning—at any rate where the two men were concerned. He decided to spend the time making a further examination of the six boats.

The moment Inspector Bigswell had left the Vicarage, with a promise to return for lunch, the Vicar took out his copy of that mysterious note which had caused him so much speculation.

> *I'm not wanting your money. I shall hold my tongue not for your sake but for his. I've no wish to hear further about this. M. L.*

Again and again the Vicar's thoughts had hovered over the exact meaning of this note. Again and again he had puzzled over the initials. M. L. suggested neither Haskell nor Burdon. Neither did the L fit in with the other two suspects on the list—Staunton and Parkins. Yet it was reasonable to suppose that the note had been written by a married woman or, at any rate, by a woman who was about to be married. The four possibles among the boat-owners at Towan Cove were all married. Burdon's wife had died some two years back but, since the note had obviously been sent to Tregarthan some time ago, it might just as well be his wife as Staunton's, Parkins' or Haskell's. He tried to visualise these four women—their looks, their characters, their past behaviour, and gradually things began to clarify. A memory stirred, like a germinating seed, grew and grew, budded and flowered. Other past incidents came to his mind once this initial train of thought had been started. From doubt he passed to a partial acceptance of his theory, from partial acceptance to a curious feeling of certainty. The little bits began to fit together.

He rose and crossed to his desk. He took out a parish register. With fierce anxiety he turned the pages, running his finger down the list of names. Then he started. Remained quite still for a moment. Why hadn't he thought of that before? Considering the nature of the note, it was quite natural that the woman should have initialled it with her Christian names. Mary Louise! That was it, of course. She had omitted the third initial, perhaps with the subconscious fear that at some future date this note might be used as evidence against her. Not that *she* had acted criminally, of course. Tregarthan was the criminal. But it would have been an awkward situation to explain away to her husband if he had found out. But hadn't she offered an explanation? Obviously. And the reason for this sudden revelation of her unfortunate secret was obvious, too. The Vicar saw it all then, but he was not elated. He was stricken with a feeling of sorrow and compassion, wavering between a desire to throw the note into the fire and confess himself beaten, and his sense of duty which cried to him that justice had to be done. To destroy evidence, to withhold evidence from the police was, in itself, a criminal act. A murder had been committed. Murder was a terrible and dastardly thing. He could not condone it, however extenuating the circumstances.

He sat by the fire and, with an unsteady hand, poured himself out a glass of sherry. He shrank wholeheartedly from the task which lay before him.

Punctually at one the Inspector returned, but it was not until lunch had concluded, that the Vicar made any mention of his discovery.

"Time's up!" said the Inspector when they were alone. "Well, Mr. Dodd?"

The Vicar sighed. He knew there was no escaping the demands of duty, however unpleasant that duty might be.

"There's no question about it now, Inspector. I can see the whole thing clearly. I only wish it could have turned out otherwise. *But I know now who murdered poor Tregarthan!*"

"You know?"

Inspector Bigswell was astounded.

"As far as any man can know by deducing his facts from circumstantial evidence."

"Then who is it?"

The Vicar shook his head.

"May I be allowed to work this in my own way and in my own time? Legally, of course, I have no right to keep back any information from you, Inspector. But somehow I should feel easier in my conscience if I could confront this man myself. You can be nearby—the Constable, too—concealed somewhere. But let me, I beg you, be the first to acquaint this poor man with the facts of the case. He's suffered already—God knows! Now it means more suffering … perhaps, his life. Most certainly imprisonment."

"Very well," said the Inspector shortly. "I'll get hold of Grouch and we'll go straight away."

The Vicar nodded.

"It would be best," he said quietly.

An hour later Inspector Bigswell and P.C. Grouch were ensconced behind a couple of thick furze bushes on the clifftop. Their eyes were fixed on a thin ribbon which serpentined up the rising slope of the common and, breasting the rise, disappeared beyond. Up that pathway, some fifteen minutes earlier, the Vicar had climbed. He held a police-whistle in one hand. In the other was the strange note.

The two men waited. The minutes dragged with intolerable slowness. Had the man made a dash for it? Had the Vicar been overpowered before he had time to blow his whistle? The Inspector was already beginning to kick himself for having let the Vicar have his way in the matter. It was a risk and a foolish one at that. Better to have made the arrest in the ordinary way—got out a proper warrant and made a workmanlike job of it. All this concession to a murderer's feelings was ridiculous. It was only out of respect for the Vicar's intelligence ... but a pretty fool he'd look at headquarters if the bird escaped from the net just when a capture seemed certain. Better, far better. ...

Grouch jerked his arm.

"It's all O.K., sir! He's coming back! Not alone either!"

A tall, gaunt figure, was walking with long strides beside the rotund little person of the Reverend Dodd. The two men seemed to be engaged in eager conversation. They approached with rapidity.

Suddenly the Inspector, followed by Grouch stepped clear of the bushes. The tall man halted at the sight of them, and turned to the Vicar. The little man threw out his hands.

The tall man hesitated a moment, then with a shrug of his powerful shoulders, walked forward toward the police.

Grouch turned with amazement on the Inspector.

"Good heavens, sir!"

"Well?"

"*It's Joe Burdon!*"

"Burdon?"

"That's right," said the man in question, who had overheard the Inspector's exclamation. "It's Joe Burdon—the chap whose boat you borrowed t'other day. Funny, eh? Loaning my own dinghy so as ye could collect evidence against me!"

Grouch and Bigswell closed in on either side of the gaunt quarryman.

"It's all right," he growled. "I'll go quiet enough. It's a fair deal. I've lost. You've won. I wouldn't have it otherwise, I reckon. Mr. Dodd here knows all about it. He advises me to make a full statement."

"I must warn you——" began the Inspector.

Joe Burdon waved his hand.

"Aye—I know. Everything I say will be used in evidence against me. That's as maybe. But all you'll hear from me now or later will be the naked truth. I promise ye that!"

"Then let's get going," said the Inspector. "I've a car waiting down in the cove. If you've got anything to say then you'd better save it until we see the Chief over at Greystoke." The Inspector turned on the Reverend Dodd. "And you, sir—coming our way? We can drop you at the Vicarage."

"No, really—I don't think so, thank you, Inspector. I'll just take a quiet walk home along the cliff." The Vicar held out his hand to the unemotional Burdon. "I'm sorry about this, Burdon, but I know you agree with me that it couldn't be otherwise."

Burdon gripped the Vicar's extended hand and shook it vigorously.

"Don't you be worrying, Mr. Dodd. Sooner or later I should have given myself up. Chap can stand so much and then his nerve cracks. Aye, sir, a man's conscience is a powerful thing and not to be overcome, I reckon. I'm ready for what's coming."

"Well ... good luck, Burdon," said the Vicar in husky tones. "I'll see that you're represented. Good luck and good-bye."

"Thank ye, Mr. Dodd." He turned to the Inspector. "I'm ready."

The trio set off down toward the cove, the tall, angular frame of the quarryman, swinging with an easy stride between the dark, uniformed figures of the law. For a long time the Vicar stood, immobile, staring after them, then with a deep sigh he followed slowly after, pondering on the curious ways of an almost childlike mankind. He had done his duty. By a lucky series of circumstances he had been guided to the solution of the mystery—but he felt no elation, no triumph, no satisfaction. Murder was all right in books and plays, but in real life it was a sorrowful, suffering business.

Never again did he want to find himself caught up in the sordid realities of a murder case. He felt utterly dispirited.

CHAPTER XXII

CONFESSION

THIS was the confession made by Joseph Alfred Burdon in the presence of the Chief Constable, the Superintendent and Inspector Bigswell at the divisional headquarters of the County Constabulary at Greystoke on Saturday, March 28th, 193–. It was in the form of a signed and written statement.

"I confess to the murder of Julius Tregarthan on Monday evening, March 23rd. I had deliberately planned his death. I had been turning over the idea of killing him for nearly two years. It was a job, to my way of thinking, that had to be done. He had ruined my domestic happiness. And, as I see it, was responsible for my wife's death. I had better start my story with events that happened three years ago, before the death of my wife Mary Louise Burdon. I am a quarryman employed by the Boscawen Slate Quarrying Co., which is about a quarter of a mile from my cottage in Towan Cove.

"As, at that time, we had no children, my wife was left alone for the most part of the day in the cottage. We were both happy in our marriage. She was a quiet, contented woman without a care in the world. I had a pretty good job and we had money enough to rub along without much worry. Our cottage was the property of Julius Tregarthan. We always paid the rent regularly every Friday, when Tregarthan himself made a round of his cottages in the cove and collected the money. As he used to call in the afternoon, I always gave my wife the rent-money and she paid Tregarthan herself.

"One Friday when I returned about six o'clock I found my wife upset. I could see she had been crying. I asked her what was the matter but she wouldn't tell me anything. I thought that she might have been feeling unwell and let the matter drop. I didn't think anything about it until a fortnight later. On that particular Friday when I got home I found my wife out. She did not come in until an hour later. She seemed strange and a bit wild in her manner. I again asked her if she was worrying about anything. She denied that anything was wrong.

"From that day, however, there seemed to be something between us. We couldn't get on in the old way at all. My wife seemed restless and uneasy and often sat for a long time without speaking, not even answering when I spoke to her. Things seemed to be going wrong in the cottage. I tried a hundred ways to find out if my wife had anything on her mind or if she was faced with trouble of any sort. But she never dropped a hint as to what was the matter.

"This went on for about three months. Then one day she suddenly told me that she was going to have a baby. I was naturally pleased and excited on hearing the good news. We had always wanted a child. I knew my wife would make a perfect mother and we had both looked forward to the birth of our firstborn. At once I saw the reason for her past moodiness and restlessness and I did my best to cheer her up by talking about the happiness which was coming to us in the near future. But my wife remained strangely depressed. Instead of looking forward to the day when her baby would be born, she seemed to shrink from the approaching event. I got it into my mind after a bit, that she didn't want the child to be born. I couldn't get rid of the idea.

"A black cloud seemed to hang over us. Then one day, on my way home from the quarries, I was met by Jack Withers, a man who lives in the cove. He brought me news that my wife had given birth to a son. I ran down as fast as I could to the cottage. My wife was suffering terribly. She was deathly white and fighting for breath. I knew somehow, as soon as I saw her, that she would not live. The child, too, was sickly, and lay at her side without a sound and making little movement. The Doctor told me there was small chance for either of them. I was almost off my head with grief. I had looked forward to this day for so long.

"At nine o'clock that night, the child died. My wife did not seem to understand what had happened and protested when they took the dead baby from her side. She realised that she was dying. I don't know how. A sort of instinct, I reckon. She called me to sit at her side. I did so. She told me that she had a confession to make. It was then that I first learnt to hate the very name of Julius Tregarthan. That child was not mine. It was Tregarthan's. The man had been making up to my wife when he called for the rent-money on Friday afternoons. He was cunning and in no hurry. He pretended, at first, to have a fatherly interest in my wife's affairs. She was taken in by his talk and began to look upon him as a friend. She never drew him on—that I'll swear! She was never that sort. Tregarthan played his hand with the devil's own cunning. My wife was quite taken in by his charming ways and his easy talk.

"One Friday there was a bit of a scene when he tried to kiss her. After that my wife began to dread his weekly visits. And then, one afternoon, he behaved like a brute beast, like the swine he was, and took advantage of her. A child was the result. Tregarthan got at her and forced her to make out that I was the father of the child. He even tried to bribe her with money, which my wife refused to accept. She was terrified that her secret would leak out. She knew that Tregarthan, with his smooth tongue, was capable of making out that she was in love with him, that the deception was mutual. If only she had not doubted my faith in her! It was the only wrong she ever did me!

"Late that terrible night, my wife died ... in agony. From that moment I had but one idea in my head, and that was to kill Tregarthan. I think he realised that I knew of his beastliness. After the death of my wife he never again called at the cottage for the rent. He arranged for me to leave the money with Mrs. Withers. I reckon he was afraid of meeting me alone. I was in no hurry. My idea was to plan out a perfect scheme so that when Tregarthan was murdered suspicion could never fall on me. Soon the plan began to take shape. I had an old service revolver, which I had scrounged in France, before being demobbed in '19, and several rounds of ammunition.

"By careful watching I got to know Tregarthan's habits of an evening. He was, I realised, a man of routine. I knew that when he had finished his dinner he always went into his sitting-room. My first idea was to lure him to the window and shoot him from the cliff-path. I turned over this plan for a couple of months, but I knew that it was by no means perfect. For one thing the sound of the shooting might bring people to the spot. I might have trouble in making myself scarce after the murder. Then, one night, there was a storm over the coast and I saw at once that, if I chose the right moment, I could fire under cover of the thunder-claps. But a thunderstorm usually means rain and rain means mud and mud means footprints. I gave up the idea of shooting Tregarthan from the footpath.

"My next step toward making my plan perfect was the idea of shooting Tregarthan from the sea. I owned a boat. I often did a bit of night fishing. Even if I was seen the chances were that nobody would think it unusual for me to be out in a boat after dark. I made several tests along under the cliff. I found out how near I could get to the cliff and still keep the window in view. I realised that it would not be very difficult shooting. The next thing was to divert suspicion from myself and make it look as if somebody on land had committed the murder.

"So, one night, I filled a flour-bag with gravel off the Greylings drive. I hid it away in the cottage. When I had fired my first scheme was to throw my revolver into the sea. But suddenly I realised that if I threw my revolver up on to the cliff-path, it would look more than ever as if somebody on land had killed Tregarthan. Then, with my plan all set, I waited for the right moment to carry out the job. For months I waited for a storm to come up at the time when I knew Tregarthan would be in his sitting-room. Time and again there were day storms and storms late at night. But I was in no hurry. I felt certain that one night my chance would come. And then on Monday, March 23rd, my chance did come.

"As ill-luck would have it, I had painted my own boat only the day before. I dared not risk getting paint all over my clothes. It would look suspicious if the police found out. So I borrowed Mr. Crook's boat, the *Nancy*. I dumped the flour-bag full of gravel in the boat. I put on gloves, polished my revolver and loaded it. Then I put out to sea. I kept a course close along under the cliffs until I came to Greylings. There was a light in the sitting-room window. I had to risk the fact that Miss Tregarthan might have been in the room. If I threw the gravel against the window and she came to it instead of her uncle, then I knew it was a matter of waiting for my next chance.

"I got in as close as I dared and flung the gravel against the glass. I waited until there was a very bright flash of lightning before I did this. I reckoned that Tregarthan would then just have time to get to the window before the thunder began. This happened. He pulled aside the curtains and stared out. There was a crash of thunder overhead and I fired quickly three times. I saw him drop to the ground. I steered the boat in closer to the cliff and tossed my revolver up on to the path. The bag of gravel I flung into the sea. There must have been a small hole in the bag. Mr. Dodd told me that some gravel was found in the *Nancy*. I rowed back as fast as I could to Towan Cove, drew up the boat on to the slip-way and, making sure that nobody saw me, returned to the cottage. I had left a light burning there all the time so that my neighbours should think I had been indoors all the evening.

"That's my story. The truth, the whole truth and nothing but the truth. Whatever happens I am prepared to face the consequences. I reckoned to keep my secret, but I have been found out. I am glad about that. A chap fights a losing battle with his conscience. It has been hell for the last five days. When Mr. Dodd came to me this afternoon and showed me a note which he had found from my wife to Tregarthan, I couldn't keep back the truth any longer. Truth will out, is an old saying. The truth is out and thank God for it!"

CHAPTER XXIII

THE VICAR EXPLAINS

"WELL, Mr. Dodd," said the Inspector as the men crossed from the study into the hall, "I can't do more than to congratulate you on your astuteness. I don't mind confessing that at one time I had pretty well abandoned all hope of solving the mystery. By the way—just one other point—the money? Miss Tregarthan's money? Have you heard anything about it?"

"Yes. Ramsey, the solicitor, was over this morning. Just as you thought. Tregarthan had been gambling on the Stock Exchange. Luckily he had been unable to touch the capital. Most of the interest which should have been accruing from the trust investments has been lost. I must say, Inspector, that Ruth takes the matter very calmly."

"Other things to think about, eh?" asked the Inspector with a quick grin.

The Vicar's eyes twinkled with delight.

"Dear me—yes. Most satisfactory. It will be publicly announced soon. The engagement, I mean. They talk of marrying in the summer. I'm delighted! Delighted!"

Inspector Bigswell held out his hand.

"Well, good-bye, Mr. Dodd. It's been a great pleasure to be associated with you in this case. I'm glad that something good has come out of the unfortunate business."

They shook hands.

"Good-bye, Inspector. May I add that watching your methods has been a great education for me. Your thoughtfulness and humaneness have been considerable. Your patience … amazing! Good-bye."

The Vicar saw Inspector Bigswell into his car and, a minute or so later, it swung out on to the Vicarage road and headed for Greystoke. With a small, conclusive sigh the Vicar returned to his study. The case was at an end. The mystery was solved. That was that.

He dropped with a beatific smile into his deep arm-chair, thrust out his slippered feet towards the blazing fire and lovingly filled his pipe. For a long time, meditating on the crowded events of the past week, he stretched there, puffing little clouds of smoke towards the ceiling. After all the worry and strenuousness of the last few days, he felt at peace. His mind was beset with no harrowing problems. He was free to browse among the pleasant pasturage of minor, commonplace affairs. Ideas for his new sermon drifted into his brain. He thought of new schemes for an approaching sale of work, drew courage from necessity and decided to tackle Lady Greenow about the redecoration of the church. His eye alighted on the calendar on his desk. Monday, March 30th. He started. Monday! Gracious! It was Pendrill's evening. For the first time in years he had nearly overlooked the little ceremony which was always enacted in his study on Monday night. From the calendar his glance shifted to the clock. Seven-thirty, exactly. The chimes of the Greenow clock in the St. Michael's tower came faintly to him through the closed window. The sound had scarcely died away when a gong clamoured in the hall and the wheels of a car crackled and swished up the drive.

The next moment Pendrill was announced.

"Just in time!" said the Vicar heartily. "I was just thinking of giving you up as a bad job, my dear fellow. Come on—hustle out of your coat. Dinner's served."

Later they returned to the sanctuary of the Vicar's study, comfortable in mind and body, and dropped into their customary arm-chairs. The box of cigars was produced. Pendrill, with a wry look, refused his host's offer and took out his pipe. The Vicar selected, pierced and lighted a Henry Clay. There was a deep silence for a space.

Then: "Let's hear about it, Dodd," said Pendrill. "No good sitting there and pretending you are disinterested. You're bursting to tell me how you managed it. Come on—out with it! How did you guess?"

"Guess is an inopportune word," contested the Vicar. "Guess-work is no good in criminal investigation. Proven facts are essential. Shall we say the collecting of unalterable data coupled with a vivid imagination?"

"Oh, say what you like! I don't give a damn for your methods. I want your story, Dodd, not a treatise—and an amateur effort at that!—on Deduction and Detection."

"Very well, I'll tell you."

"And you needn't look so smug about it," put in the Doctor. "I've no doubt providence or luck—call it what you will—was hand-in-glove with you from the start."

"In a way, my dear fellow, you're right. I did have luck. For one thing I've been blessed or cursed with a tenacious memory, and it was the recollection of past happenings which finally forced me to believe that Burdon had committed the murder. First of all, you know how puzzled I was about those scattered shots and the lack of footprints on the cliff-path— well those two factors led me to believe that Tregarthan had been shot from the sea. You know about the experiment I carried out and the results we obtained. We then narrowed down our search to those men owning boats over at Towan Cove. In one of the six boats there we found a few bits of gravel. Bigswell, as you may know, interviewed Crook, who owned the boat, and found that he had a perfect alibi on the night of the murder. It was obvious then that somebody had borrowed Crook's boat on Monday night. At that stage I had no idea as to the murderer's identity. I believed by a process of elimination that it could be one of four people—Parkins, Staunton, Burdon or Haskell. I had to find a reason why one of these four, who were all boat-owners, should find it necessary to borrow Crook's dinghy. And then, suddenly, I remembered a conversation I had had with Burdon up at the quarries. The Inspector wanted the loan of Burdon's boat to investigate Greylings from under the cliff. Burdon pointed out that I could easily distinguish his boat from the others on the slip-way because it was freshly painted. That remark proved illuminating. If Burdon's dinghy was coated with wet paint on the night of the crime, he would be forced to borrow another boat. I assumed, at once, that Burdon was the murderer. I then had to find a motive for the murder. You remember the note which I found in Tregarthan's desk?"

"Signed, M. L. Yes—go on."

"Well, I was convinced that this note was in some way connected with the crime. M. L. was obviously a woman and probably a wife. Burdon's wife was dead. I knew that. It occurred to me then that the woman's full initials were M. L. B. and that she had initialled the note with her Christian names. I looked in the Parish Register and there, sure enough, I found that my assumption was correct. Burdon's wife was Mary Louise. Why then had Mrs. Burdon written that curious note to Julius Tregarthan? There was some secret which they shared and of which Burdon, himself, was ignorant. I thought of your worldly suggestion, Pendrill—a liaison of some sort. And then my memory put a fresh spoke into the wheel. About two years ago I had called, one Friday afternoon, on Mrs. Burdon. My visit, I'm afraid, was a trifle inopportune. Tregarthan was just leaving the cottage with a scowl on his face and indoors I found Mrs. Burdon crying. I did my best to comfort her, but she offered no explanation as to why she was so upset. I thought perhaps there was trouble about the rent. Well this recollection suddenly took on a new significance when coupled with the note. It looked as if your suggestion was right, Pendrill. And then I recalled the night that Mary Burdon died. I called over at Towan Cove shortly after the child was born. Burdon had not yet come in, though I believe somebody had been sent post-haste to fetch him. Hearing from Mrs. Mullion that I was in the cottage, much to my astonishment, the woman sent word that she wished to speak to me. It was about the child."

"The child?"

"Yes. Mary Burdon seemed certain in her own mind that she would not live. I had the idea that she did not want to live. At the time I didn't understand, Pendrill. Now I do. Poor woman! Even in the midst of her suffering she had a thought for the child. She wanted it to be baptised and christened Joseph Alfred after her husband. I assured her that this would be done. But she seemed dissatisfied. She made me promise, *no matter what might be said*, that I would do as she wished. I solemnly gave my word. But that phrase puzzled me. 'No matter what might be said.' I couldn't understand her anxiety at the time. You see, Pendrill, I didn't realise then that the child was illegitimate.

"It was not until two days ago that I recognised the real reason for her anxiety. Tregarthan was the father of the child. That was the secret between them. After his wife and the child had died, Burdon, himself, came to me and made arrangements for the funeral. I was struck by the change in the man. Grief-stricken I expected him to be, but it was more than that. How shall I put it? He radiated a sort of bitter malice. When I mentioned the loss of the child and sympathised with him, he asked me fiercely never to mention the child again. He seemed to disown it.

"At the time I naturally accepted his strangeness as the result of his sudden bereavement. But two days ago I saw it all. I realised that his wife's secret was no longer a secret. She had confessed to him just before she died and mentioned Tregarthan as the father of the child. Here, then, was the motive for the murder. A crime of revenge. A motive, alas, all too common in the annals of crime. I got Bigswell's permission to confront Burdon myself. If I had made a mistake, you see, I didn't want him to know that the police were in possession of the facts of his private troubles. I simply went up to him and handed him the note which his wife had written to Tregarthan. He went deathly white. I asked him why he had borrowed Crook's boat on Monday night. I told him about the gravel found on the bilge-boards.

"He broke down then, Pendrill—he broke down completely! It was as much as I could stand. Murder is a terrible, inhuman thing—but somehow … well, what can one think? Is murder *ever* justifiable? In the eyes of the law—never!

I suppose that is as it should be. But in the eyes of God? Think of the provocation? Terrible! To Burdon it must have seemed that Tregarthan had killed his wife. An eye for an eye—a tooth for a tooth. It is curious how the latent savage in mankind still reveres that ancient, Hebraic principle. At any rate, Pendrill, you know the facts of the case now. I hope——"

There was a knock on the door. The maid entered, carrying a small crate which she deposited on the rug between the two men.

"The carrier's just brought it, sir. He's sorry he's late."

The maid retired.

The two men eyed the crate and then, simultaneously, glanced up and queried each other.

"Well," said Pendrill, "what about it? It was your turn to send in the list, you know. But I thought you might forget, so I did it myself. Shall we divide the spoils, Dodd?"

The Vicar hesitated and then slowly shook his head.

"I don't think so. Really, Pendrill. Somehow … dear me … I feel that I never want to read another crime story as long as I live. I seem to have lost my zest for a good mystery. It's strange how contact with reality kills one's appreciation of the imaginary. No, my dear fellow, I'll never get back my enthusiasm for thrillers. I've decided to devote my energies to worthier problems."

"Such as?"

"The problem of your disbelief, Pendrill. Your obstinate refusal to accept the Faith."

Doctor Pendrill grinned sheepishly.

"D'you know, Dodd, I've made up my mind. You seem to be a man of great practical common sense. You have an excellent analytical mind. I hadn't realised before. I'm going to give you a chance to talk to me without my contesting your arguments."

"When?" asked the Vicar.

"Next Sunday," replied the Doctor. "At church!"

The Reverend Dodd beamed.

THE END